HERITAGE

BOOK THREE OF THE GRIMOIRE SAGA

A NOVEL BY S.M. BOYCE

Acorn Valley
Press

THE GRIMOIRE SAGA

DEDICATION

For Geoff, my muse. I'll be by your side even when we're nothing but souls. You make my world beautiful.

TABLE OF CONTENTS

❧CHAPTER ONE

A FRESH START

A hand reached around Kara's waist and tugged her closer. Her body shifted over cotton sheets. The hem of her nightshirt caught and inched upward along her back. Hot breath sailed down her neck, setting her nerves on fire. She snuggled into a bare shoulder, her nose brushing against bumps of muscle as she itched to get ever closer to whomever held her.

Warm skin burned her cheek. A second, thick hand brushed hair from her face. Her blond locks fell over her shoulder like a sheet of silk.

Kara opened her eyes. A haze clouded the corners of her vision—the edges of a dream. She frowned. There was no fun in knowing none of this was real. It just meant she wouldn't be able to enjoy it as much.

Braeden smiled down at her. A few dark hairs fell across his olive face, blocking her view of those black eyes that glittered with mischief. He pulled her a little closer with his rough hands, even though no space remained between them. Her frown dissolved. Every bit of her crackled with energy. He ran his fingers along the hem of her shirt, pulling it higher.

She poked his side. "I miss you."

He ran a hand through her hair. "Come see me, then."

"You know I can't. Not yet."

He grinned. "Liar."

She faltered and glanced down at the mattress. Of course she couldn't leave. Not even a month ago, she discovered she was an isen—a creature that could steal souls. Though she hadn't even known what an isen was before she discovered the crazy world of Ourea, she had apparently always belonged to the hidden realm of monsters and magic. Her mother passed the isen gene to her, and their bloodline had a terrible curse: power and magic came easily to them. It sounded great at first, sure, but the power came too easily. Kara couldn't control herself. She could kill with barely any effort.

Every day, her control dwindled a little more. If she used the air to turn a page in a book, she ripped out the sheet instead. If she tried to hit a target with her favorite attack—red sparks that danced through her fingers like lightning—she blasted the target to bits. She refused to spar with anyone for fear of what she might accidentally do to her opponent.

After she discovered she was an isen, she'd spent every second of free time with her mentor, Stone. They traveled to a safe place to train: her village, the one she inherited from the ancient ghost who had given her the Grimoire.

Kara hadn't left the village yet only because she couldn't do anything without destroying something.

As if Braeden read her thoughts, he wrapped her in a hug. "It'll be all right."

"I'm just so lost, Braeden. I don't want to hurt anyone, but I don't know how to stop."

He pulled away and held her face in his hands. "You don't have to do it alone, you know."

"You're right, I guess." She smiled and slipped her arms around him in return, burrowing her face into his torso. Her fingers tightened around his waist.

Something shifted in her palms. A sharp *crack* cut through the dream. The crash of breaking glass rocked her. Braeden tensed in her arms.

Kara pulled away, trying to figure out what was going on. Braeden studied her, his smile gone. A fissure inched along his face as if he were porcelain and she'd dropped him. It splintered, dividing his handsome features into pieces. His eyebrows shifted upward, likely to question what was going on—or worse, what she was doing to him.

Kara gasped. Oh, Bloods! Did she hurt him, too?

She reached for him, unable to form words. Fragments of his shirt broke away like ice in her hands. The cracks in his face widened.

His voice shook. "You're not alone."

"Braeden!" she screamed.

Kara bolted upright in bed, her scream lingering in her chest.

White light swam in her vision, blinding her. Something crashed again, as if on replay from her nightmare. Glass tinkled. The wall vibrated with the thump of a heavy object ramming it with great force.

A breeze ruffled her hair. Chills raced down her back. She shivered. Salt stung her nose, as did the sweet tang of honeysuckle. Her fingers tensed, grabbing handfuls of the cotton bedspread as her vision blurred.

She rubbed her eyes.

Bit by bit, her familiar bedroom in the Vagabond's village shifted into focus. White walls. Wooden bed posts. Silk blue canopy over her bed. White comforter. Cotton sheets. Two mahogany bedside tables. A stack of paper on a desk in the corner. The pages shifted in the breeze, and a couple drifted to the floor.

Sunlight streamed through the windows on her left, catching on the jagged edges of a broken window. Wind rattled the drapes, shuffling them aside as it whipped through the room. Shards of glass littered the floor, glinting.

A red brick lay on the carpet in the middle of the pool of broken glass, a white piece of parchment tied around it with a string.

Kara jumped out of bed and tiptoed across the remnants of her broken window, though it didn't matter if she cut herself. She knew plenty of charms to heal a cut well enough to leave no scars.

She picked up the brick and yanked the note from the baked

clay. A few words covered the other side of the small square of paper, written in tight handwriting.

We're done with the basics. Your real training starts today. Meet me in the clearing in the forest behind the kitchens. You have much to learn.

—Stone

Kara cursed under her breath. Her mentor threw a brick through her window to wake her up. That dramatic son of a—

"Couldn't he just knock?" she muttered.

Her pulse settled. Adrenaline dissolved in her veins. She took a deep breath to clear her head, and the cold air swirled in her chest. Her worry hadn't been anything more than the panic of being woken from a dream.

She sighed. And until the interruption, it had been a wonderful dream.

Something squeaked by her bed. Her tiny pet Flick stretched from his place on the pillow beside hers, his bushy tail straight up in the air. His ears—still too big for his head, even though he was mostly grown—twitched as he shook himself awake. No bigger than a squirrel, the furry red creature hopped along the folds in the blanket, battling the valleys of fabric on his way to her.

"Morning, munchkin," she said.

He burped in answer. Charming thing.

Kara focused her attention on the broken window. She hadn't fixed a window before, but she could manipulate the air and start a fire with the magic coursing through her. Since the glass just needed to be fused back into place, fixing a window couldn't be too terribly difficult.

She reached her fingers toward the shards. With a deep breath, she borrowed the breeze sweeping through her room. Tension pulled on her hands, dragging her knuckles downward. She resisted, pulling back to lift the fragments of glass. The pieces hovered. Her palms warmed.

The shards slid through the air, and Kara directed traffic as best she could. When bits of the glass pushed into their neighbors, she focused the full weight of her gaze on the seam, fusing the pieces on contact.

In a matter of seconds, her window was once more whole. A little worse for wear, perhaps—she hadn't quite gotten rid of some of the cracks in the pane—but solid nonetheless. She smirked with satisfaction.

A dull pain throbbed in her wrist. She scratched at it, her nails catching on leather. She sighed and resisted the impulse to rip off the wrist guard on her right arm. The ornate leather band on her right wrist covered spikes that dug into her skin, helping keep her uncontrollable magic at bay. Her arm ached when she wore the thing, but even her grandfather, Agneon, had worn the band at one point to restrain his magic.

After Stone awoke her isen nature, he told her to never take off the wrist band for fear she would lose her last ounce of self-restraint. So far, she had obeyed.

She headed to her closet to change. However good Stone's intentions may have been, he'd forced her into the life of an isen. She hadn't wanted any of this. Since he turned her, Stone was her master and could control her. He could make her hit herself in the face if he wanted, but she listened to him out of respect. He'd lived for centuries.

Still, despite his vast knowledge and experience, she would give him a piece of her mind when she found him.

※

Twenty minutes later, Kara stormed out of the neighboring forest and into the empty clearing Stone mentioned in his note. Flick purred from his place on her shoulder. His fur tickled her neck, but she tuned out the sensation.

She had one mission: find Stone and rip him a new one.

Kara narrowed her eyes and glanced around the forest clearing where he'd said her training would begin. Dirt filled the unimpressive circle, the ground void of grass as though someone had tilled the soil. A breeze tumbled by, stinging her nose with the hint of raw carrots and rust. Trees surrounded her on all sides, their trunks blocking out everything beyond the mini arena in which she stood. Wind tussled with the canopy, interrupting the forest's silence with an eruption of clapping leaves.

A six-foot stack of bricks sat in the middle of the clearing. She tightened her hands into fists and walked over to it, not altogether convinced she actually wanted to know what Stone had up his sleeve this time.

Light poured through a three-inch hole in the bricks at shoulder level. She bent down and peered through to the forest line on the other side. One tree stood out from its brothers, perfectly centered through the circle. Dapples of sunlight broke through its leaves and glinted off a red "X" painted on its trunk.

"You have to hit that target," a voice said from behind her.

She spun. There hadn't been footsteps or even a breath, and yet Stone stood inches behind her. His tall frame blocked out a fair bit of the forest behind him. He frowned, his salt and pepper hair and beard framing his face.

Kara's fists tightened. "You broke my window."

He shrugged. "You fixed it, didn't you?"

"Why would you wake me like that?"

Stone walked about ten feet away and dragged his heel through the dirt to make a line in the soil. "Shoot from here."

"Stone, answer me."

He laughed. "I am your master, child, not the other way around. Enough prattle. You wanted training, and this is it. Now that your blood is moving, let's get started. Come over here and shoot from this line."

She took a deep breath for patience—so much for giving him a piece of her mind—and glanced over her shoulder. "Where do you want me to shoot? Through the hole?"

"Obviously."

She grimaced. "Look, I need to learn real magic. I need to learn techniques that can win a fight, not...whatever this is."

"That will come. For now, you're to hit that target by shooting a fireball through the gap in the bricks. If the fire is too large, it will knock over all the bricks. And if that happens, you have to restack each one by hand before you can try again. It won't be easy, either, since you have to stack them such that the hole is in the same place."

"That's mundane."

"It's your training. Take it or leave it."

Kara groaned. What a terrible teacher. She wished she had Braeden back. At least training with him was fun.

Her dream flashed again in her mind. She blushed. Braeden—she couldn't think about him right now. She had trouble focusing as it was without her heart racing at the thought of the man she loved.

"Why do I have to stack them by hand?" she asked.

"Because it will frustrate you, and it's harder to focus on the task at hand when you're angry. You must learn to control that temper."

She huffed. "Is that why you threw the brick through my window? You designed a training exercise around pissing me off?"

"That's one way to put it."

Kara shook her head and walked to Stone's line in the dirt. Flick jumped off her shoulder and trotted to the edge of the forest, as if he knew she needed the freedom of movement. Often, she figured he understood everything.

Stone shifted out of her way as she reached the line, so she turned to face the wall. She could barely see the opening in the bricks, much less the red target beyond.

She sighed. Whatever.

A breeze whistled by, and she borrowed some of the air to feed a spark in her hand. Fire blazed to life, hovering above the creases in her palm. Magic coursed through her, warming her veins with its vigor. A second pulse thrummed in her chest, an energy she had begun to recognize as magic itself.

With each beat of her heart, the fire grew. It flickered and crackled, burning the energy she'd kept pent up inside. The flames licked her fingers, but fire made by magic would never hurt its master. If anything, it tickled.

She frowned and held her breath in an effort to scale back the flames. They shrank ever so slightly, and she shrugged. It would do.

The brick wall loomed ahead, the tiny hole her only hope of getting to try any useful magic. It should be simple enough compared to what she had already accomplished. Kara killed shadow demons and escaped entire armies on multiple occasions. She rescued a prince. She was tortured and left in poisoned chains for days on end. She faced Death himself and came back alive.

She could hit a stupid target.

Kara aimed for the gap, took a deep breath, and threw the fireball with every ounce of strength she had.

The fire crashed into the bricks to the left of the hole. Dust billowed into a cloud that hovered like a swarm of flies. The bricks tumbled, clattering to the ground in a heap.

Stone tisked. "Wrong. Restack and do it again."

Kara grumbled under her breath and strode over to the pile of charred bricks. She rummaged through them, looking for any brick with a circular indent in it, and set those aside when she found them. The rest, she began to stack.

And with each *clack* from every brick she set back on the pillar, she resented Stone just a little bit more.

✳

Thirty minutes, two bruises, and several curse words later, Kara walked back to the line in the dirt. She had only just reset the bricks scattered by her first attempt. Now, she once more needed to throw a fireball through the tiny hole in an effort to hit the target on the other side.

"This is stupid," she said.

"Aim more carefully, then," Stone answered.

Flick curled up in the shade at the edge of the field to watch. He stretched his tiny paws and yawned, apparently bored. The black stripes on his spine contrasted with his red fur, shimmering in the low light under the trees as he rolled onto his back.

Kara wished she could join her pet and just take a nap. Instead, she sighed and lit another fire in her palm. It crackled, but she resisted the urge to relish its energy. She needed to suppress the power, or it would get too big to sail through the hole.

She aimed, all the while keeping her focus on making the flame small. After a few seconds of inner debate, she hurled her fire at the wall and held her breath in the hope it would sail through.

It didn't.

The fireball hit the opening, a full six inches too large. Bricks flew in all directions. More dust sprang into the air. Some crumbled to bits, raining to the ground like hail with the odd *thunk*. Other blocks sailed into the trees along the edge of the clearing, and some even flew farther into the forest.

"Wrong," Stone said again. "Reset."

"I destroyed some, though!"

"I brought extra."

Stone nodded behind him. Sure enough, three stacks of extra bricks sat just beyond the forest line, cast in the canopy's shadow. He had enough to rebuild the original pillar four times over.

Kara cursed.

"Reset," Stone repeated.

꙰

Kara spent four hours shooting at and resetting the brick wall. She shot eleven fireballs, and every one of them failed. Her temper grew with each clack from every block. Tension pulled at her shoulders, her fingers, her neck—but it wasn't from magic. She just wanted to scream.

Clack. What a stupid exercise. *Clack.* What a waste of time. *Clack.* She had so much potential. *Clack.* How could she save Ourea if she spent all of her time stacking cubes?

Clack.

She cursed under her breath. "I'm done."

"What's that?" Stone asked.

"I said I'm done!" she snapped.

"No, you aren't. I haven't released you."

She jumped to her feet. "I couldn't care less, Stone! This is a waste of my time, and you clearly don't know what you're doing. I want to train, yet here I am, stacking bricks. Ourea is about to go to war. I need to make the Bloods respect me, not learn how to blow apart baked clay!"

"This is training."

She forced a laugh. "No, it's monotonous! Training is sparring. Training is fighting. Training is learning techniques and how to duck and how to hit an opponent hard enough to cripple him. This brick thing is nothing but a waste of time!"

"It's hardly—"

But Kara wasn't having it. She raced for the village, her boots pounding along the trail. She ran so fast her lungs hurt. When a sting tore down her throat and her body cried out for a rest, she made herself run faster.

Cottages blipped into view from between the trees. At least she wasn't alone with her mentor. She was the second Vagabond, master of the legendary Grimoire, and that meant recruiting other vagabonds to join her if she wanted to survive. She'd been reluctant to drag others into her life of distrust and near-constant death, but she couldn't deny her gratitude for no longer being alone.

The village center—a circle of paved stones that connected the first Vagabond's tomb with Kara's mansion—appeared in the distance. Kara pushed herself to run faster. She didn't really know where she was going. She didn't care. She just had to get away from that stupid isen of a mentor.

Someone called her name, but her feet pummeled onward. Anger coursed through her, stronger now than it had been in the clearing. Rage, frustration, and annoyance propelled her through the treeline and into the village center, where groups of her vagabonds sparred in small huddles of four or five. Some turned and waved, but most didn't look up from the sparring matches in front of them.

Good. Her vagabonds didn't have much time to train. They had to take advantage of every remaining second.

She followed her feet and bolted up the steps to her home— the Vagabond's mansion. The three-story building sprawled across the grounds, and her mind wandered the many rooms inside. She could go to her room for some peace of mind, or maybe slip away to the war room.

Instead, her legs carried her to the study. She threw open the doors and slammed them behind her, only stopping for breath when a silent command slid the lock into place with a *click*.

Kara leaned her forehead against the door and sucked in air. Her lungs screamed for a rest, but her pulse raced. She couldn't sit. She couldn't move. She just stood there, brow to the cold wood as she tried to calm herself.

Only, her body wouldn't listen. Her heart raced harder. Sweat licked her neck and palms. She tightened her hands into fists and gritted her teeth.

She cursed again, loud enough for the word to echo once off the large windows covering the far wall of her vast office. The stacked bookshelves on the other walls absorbed what remained of the sound.

Kara glanced around the same office she'd seen a hundred times. The oak desk faced the door, centered beneath a pair of floor-to-ceiling windows. Papers and a few unlit candles littered the polished wood surface. The chair hovered by the window, pushed slightly back to where she'd left it the last time she left.

The office was her second home. She could think here. Her

heart settled ever so slightly.

She was the Vagabond. A protector. A hero. Ourea didn't have much time left before Carden did something to expose the Bloods so he could kill them. That was inevitable unless she convinced the Bloods to trust each other—to trust her. They had to unite against Carden, or he would tear them apart. Who knew what would become of Ourea then? This world was brutal, but it was the only home she had left.

Yet here she was, throwing fire at bricks. She needed real training if she had any chance of success.

"Screw Stone." Kara raised her hand to the window and pulled on the curtains with her mind. The fabric flung closed, casting half the room in shadow. She shifted her focus to the other window in the room without even looking over. The curtains closed there as well, sucking the light from the room with a rush of air.

The study plunged into darkness. A ray of light broke through the curtains here and there, but Kara could barely see the outline of her own fingers. A bead of sweat rolled down her cheek. Her pulse slowed.

Kara crossed to the dim outline of her chair and sat. She leaned back. The chair's wooden frame dug into her shoulders, but she relished the pressure. A deep breath filled her lungs, and she waited for her heart to settle further.

She peeked through one eye at her darkened study. The silhouette of an unlit candle on her desk caught her attention, and she grimaced. Of all the ways to handle conflict, she chose to sit in the dark and sulk. Her face burned with embarrassment. She was being silly. She'd overreacted, just as Stone predicted. Once she relaxed, she would talk to him about getting some real training. None of this sensei nonsense, either.

Kara glanced again at the candle and focused on lighting the wick. Tension pulled at her mind and shoulders. At her command, a flame blipped into life on the candle. The flame blossomed and flickered, casting an orange glow on her fingers. It sparked. Hissed.

It grew.

More fire followed. In seconds, flames roared to life from the base of the wax, engulfing the entire candle in an inferno that raced for the ceiling.

A wave of heat blew against Kara's arms. Her hair billowed from the force, the ends missing the flame by inches. She reeled back in surprise. The fire spread to papers on the desk. Puddles of melting desk polish pooled along the work area. Black smoke curled toward the ceiling.

Water!

Kara reached for the element with her mind, not caring where it came from. Panic tore through her. Fear dried her throat. She would not burn down her own home.

Gallons of water materialized from the air above the desk. It all dropped with a splash and the weight of a waterfall. Kara's skin stung and fractured like a desert's surface, suddenly dry. She must have taken all the moisture out of the air to put out her flaming mistake.

Her eyes adjusted to the darkness. She inched backward and tugged ever so slightly on the curtain. It inched open. A thin stream of light illuminated what remained of her desk.

A lingering smoke trail spiraled up from the soot and damp ashes that had once been her notes and jotted thoughts. The white ceiling now sported charred smudges. Small streams of water poured off the desk wherever an indent or fissure in the surface let it flow.

The last puff of smoke dissolved into the air. Kara coughed. The rivers of excess became a steady *drip, drip* of water on the hardwood.

Kara's fingers twitched. She turned, her shoulders and legs numb. With a sigh, she sat on the floor in the middle of the room. She crossed her legs and bit her lip to keep from crying.

Adrenaline surged through her veins. Her nerves crackled. The hair on her arms stood on end. Her breath came too quickly. She tried to take deep breaths, but she couldn't control her lungs. She couldn't stop the sweat pouring down her neck. She couldn't slow her racing heart. And she could no longer ignore the lingering frustration of what she had become.

Crack!

Kara flinched, only to recognize the familiar snap Flick made when he teleported anywhere.

In her selfish tantrum, she'd left her pet back at the clearing with Stone. How horrible could one person be? She curled her knees under her chin, sulking in a blurry cocktail of tears and shame.

The little creature batted his tail against her back, but she didn't turn. In her peripheral vision, he trotted into view. He purred and rubbed his head against her hand, so she relented. She reached an arm around him and hugged him close, apparently forgiven.

She might have one heck of a temper, but it couldn't be indulged. There was no time for that anymore. Like it or not, she was the Vagabond—a vigilante gifted with the power of the Grimoire and its endless knowledge. She had seen every surviving yakona kingdom in Ourea. She'd spoken with kings and queens and even the demigod-like beings that were the muses.

In her travels, one truth became painfully clear: the leaders of this world expected her to restore peace. Somehow, even after all the near-death experiences and lost allies, she expected as much of herself as well. How she would do it escaped her, but Kara always believed she would figure out how to live up to the responsibility she received when she opened the Grimoire all those months ago.

But that was before she became an isen. That was before she lost control. Every day, she sacrificed a little more of herself to the power surging within.

Flick butted her chin with his head. Her eyes snapped into focus and flitted around the dark room, taking in the shadows of bookcases and the ray of light shining on her smoldering desk.

She couldn't even light a candle anymore without destroying something. How could she possibly save the world she'd grown to love?

❧CHAPTER TWO

THE FORGOTTEN DOOR

Braeden cursed, his voice echoing through the trees. Birds hushed. A gust tumbled through the canopy, knocking leaves together in a rush. Beams from an orange sun illuminated the forest, but he didn't intend to quit just yet. He had a mission.

He stood in a clearing, hot rays beating down on his neck as he fought to rein in his frustration. A six-foot-wide stretch of stone wall towered over him, nothing but an eyesore he couldn't seem to destroy. This wall formed a gray archway in the middle of the woods, but dark stones filled in what should have been an easy passage underneath. Two marble statues framed the structure: a dragon and a sea serpent. Each stood upright, its body twisted around itself until it ended in a massive head with glittering jewels for eyes. Each curled its chin toward its chest, mouth open in a silent scream.

A lichgate lay in between the layers of this wall—a lichgate that would take Braeden to the Stele. He'd found notes about it in an ancient journal he stole from Ayavel's royal library a week ago, and he'd finally found the damned portal. The problem was he couldn't break through the enchantments that kept anyone from using it. According to another book he found in the library, locked lichgates were a recent development made only in the last eight hundred years, so Braeden's key to the Stele only unlocked lichgates altered in the last few centuries. In ancient Ethos, they only knew of one way to lock a lichgate: a magical barrier like this wall.

For the past half hour, Braeden badgered the wall with everything he could muster, including some newly acquired

Stelian techniques. A few months ago, he would never have used one, but the time had come to embrace his Stelian bloodline. It was part of him, even if most of Ourea feared him for what he was. His cruel father didn't define him. Braeden made his own future.

He took a deep breath to calm himself, but it didn't work. He'd already wasted precious time trying to demolish the seal blocking the lichgate. He'd shot at it from every angle and with every technique he had. The lichgate wasn't even visible from the other side. The wall encompassed it entirely.

Another curse bubbled in his throat, so he hurled a gray ball of flame at the giant wall. Its black stones absorbed the fire. Ashes popped and fizzled into curls of smoke, but not so much as a charred streak remained once the haze cleared.

Unbelievable.

He curled his hands into fists and stared at the wall. He didn't know what else to do but cling to what was left of his patience. His mind raced, grasping for any ideas of how to break through. According to the journal he'd stolen, this barrier went up after the fall of Ethos. The diary belonged to the Ayavelian Blood of the era—Blood Grizwold—and the number of secrets in the little book made Braeden dizzy the first time he read it. But of all the entries, one stood out: the day Grizwold banished the Stelian Blood—whom he wouldn't name—and sealed every known lichgate into the "vile kingdom."

"Vile kingdom"—those were Grizwold's words for the Stele.

Since Stelians traveled to and from the kingdom all the time, some of the sealed Stelian lichgates were somehow opened after the fall of Ethos. Others, however, seemed to have been forgotten entirely. This wall contained one of those forgotten portals.

Braeden's chest burned with frustration. He needed to get into the Stele unnoticed, and this forgotten lichgate was his best option. Arguably, his only option. Not long ago, he scouted the known lichgates into the kingdom, and every one of them now had dozens more guards than he'd ever seen before. Braeden could only guess why, but it likely had to do with his last visit home. He'd tricked Carden into stumbling into an ambush and nearly killed the man himself, though Braeden endured days of torture to get that far. And in the end, he failed.

He shuddered. Carden's torture nearly robbed Braeden of his free will. The only way to escape a life of servitude was to kill his father and take his place as the Stelian Blood. Braeden didn't enjoy the prospect of ruling, but he didn't have much of a choice.

Gray fire ignited in his palm and raced up his arm. Smoke curled around his face, snaking upward in hundreds of thin coils. He bent the hovering wisps with his mind until they each took the shape of a dagger. At his command, they all twisted toward the wall in a single blur. His army of blades hovered midair, every point aiming for a different crack in the mortar. The smoking knives fizzled, shifting in the low light of the forest as Braeden doubled his focus. The edges of the small swords sharpened.

Stelian techniques required concentration, but that effort was always rewarded with an incredibly powerful attack.

Braeden released the flurry of knives. A hundred smoke daggers shot forward, whizzing by his ears. He held his breath as they flew toward the barrier—waiting, hoping he'd done it right this time.

Nothing is unbreakable. You just have to find its weakness, he thought.

The daggers hit the wall with the force of a lightning bolt. The ground shook. Braeden's hair stood on end. A tremor raced through the stones. Dust shook from the ancient wall in a cloud that hovered in the air. Braeden dug his nails into his palms. Breath caught in his chest.

But when the dust cleared, the wall still stood.

Braeden cursed yet again and shot a ball of fire at the dragon statue. It sailed into the dragon's open mouth, the gray flames casting a pale glow from between the beast's teeth. The ruby eyes brightened.

A blip of panic skittered through Braeden's chest.

The dragon regurgitated his attack and shot the fire back at him. He dove into a somersault to avoid the blow. Even though fire he conjured couldn't hurt him, he had no way of knowing if the statue's magic could alter it somehow.

Something roared behind him. He turned in time to see the flame hurl toward a six-foot-tall, black creature with silver talons—his vyrn, Iyra. Her eyes went wide. She lunged into the forest, the fire missing her rear end by inches. The blast ignited a nearby bush, engulfing its leaves in seconds.

Braeden sighed and stifled the fire with a wave of his hand. The flames faded into nothing, but the bush's charred trunk sizzled. A few black coils of smoke slunk into the sky.

Iyra shot a wave of air through her nose and growled.

Braeden frowned. "Sorry. It's not like I did it on purpose."

He stepped back and examined the stone wall, a new idea forming on the tip of his tongue. Hitting the wall with attacks had done nothing at all. Hitting the statue, however, got a reaction. Fire in a dragon's mouth worked. But why? He must have missed something in the journals. There had to be a clue here somewhere.

He glanced at the other statue—the sea serpent. Besides extinction, these beasts only had one thing in common: magic. Dragons were creatures of fire, just as the sea snakes were creatures of water.

A smile crept across his lips. So what if he repeated himself, but shot water into the serpent's mouth before the dragon could shoot the fire back?

He inspected the sea creature, trying to gauge the angle he would need to make this work. If he leaned forward just right, and dove away at the end—

Iyra nudged his back and kept her nose against his shirt, since physical contact was the only way the two of them could communicate.

Calm down, Prince. You're going to get us killed, she said.

"But I think I figured it out. You might want to step back, Iyra."

She huffed again and trotted off to the treeline. Her rear hit the forest floor with a *whump*.

Braeden cracked his knuckles and tensed. If he didn't get this right the first time, it would probably hurt.

※

Braeden didn't get it right the first time. Or the second time. Or the fifth. He managed to burn most of the foliage within a quarter-mile radius before his sixth attempt, when he somehow managed to get fire in the dragon's mouth and water in the sea serpent's mouth before both shot back out at him.

"Finally!" he yelled.

He waited on the tips of his toes, ready to dodge the attacks again, but the forest settled. The air stalled. Nothing moved through the trees. Nothing chirped or squeaked. Somewhere behind him, Iyra caught her breath. Braeden didn't dare breathe for fear of jinxing his only idea of how to break the seal on this irritating lichgate.

The dragon's ruby eyes glowed. The sea serpent's sapphire eyes glimmered not long after. A shiver raced through the statues, knocking dust from their scales.

The crunch of splintering stone broke through the clearing. The sea serpent's neck slithered, unwinding itself from its perch. It moved like a living creature, save for the incessant groan of rock scraping against itself. Dust fell from its body and hung in a cloud around its face. From the recesses of its throat, the statue's mouth glowed blue.

The dragon dropped to all fours. The ground shook. Braeden spread his arms to brace himself. The dragon darted to the wall and stopped mere feet from it, claws digging into the dirt. Orange light spilled from the corners of its mouth, casting a warm glow on the wall. It tucked its wings in close and tensed like a hunter preparing to attack.

Braeden inched backward, not wanting to attract either statue's attention.

The serpent drew up next to the dragon and braced itself as

well. Both statues hissed, something within their bellies crackling. A gust swept through the trees, but the stone creatures' humming overpowered it with a sudden roar of thunder.

Flame shot from the dragon just as a spiral of water burst from the sea serpent's mouth. Both streams hit the wall in the same spot. Steam raced through the clearing like a dense fog.

Braeden coughed and tried to wave the mist away, but it clung to him the more he tried to lift it. He took shallow breaths in an effort to not breathe much of it in. Seconds crept by, too slow for his comfort. Nothing happened. Nothing moved. Not a single cracking twig broke the thick silence. It was all he could do to stand still. At any moment, either statue could barrel through the haze and turn its magic on him. He didn't know what he would do if that happened. If they were anything like the wall, no magical technique he knew could stop them.

Finally, a pale ray of sunlight broke through the white steam. A few more followed suit as the cloud dissolved. Braeden sucked in a deep breath, but he didn't dare relax. A trickle of fear swept down his spine as he examined the thinning fog. Not far off, the silhouettes of the two statues caught the light, both hunched toward the ground, frozen in a bow. Neither moved. Braeden inched closer, step by tiny step. An archway appeared just beyond them, two streams of light now blazing across the black stones that still blocked Braeden's way.

A hot breath rolled over Braeden's neck. He turned, tensed for a fight, but Iyra's massive black eyes stared down at him, inches from his face. He sighed and shook his head, brushing a hand across her nose so that he could communicate with her.

Don't sneak up on me like that, he snapped.

Sorry.

Braeden took two cautious steps forward with Iyra on his heels. As he neared, a dull glow snaked across the stone wall barring the archway. The glow became two strings of light: one red and one blue. As he watched, the lights became snakes, each blazing with the intensity of a star. They wound around each other in the crude shape of a clover, their tails intertwined. Their heads met in the middle.

Is that—? Iyra asked.

Braeden nodded. *I think that's the symbol of Ethos. I don't think I've ever actually seen it. I've just heard it described.*

It looks like the Vagabond's clover symbol.

I wouldn't be surprised if he got some inspiration from Ethos.

The snakes slithered away from each other. Braeden tensed and stepped back. The two beams of light raced around to the other side of the stone bricks. As soon as they disappeared, cracks broke along the mortar. A rumble began somewhere deep in the wall. The charred remnants of nearby trees rattled. Pebbles fell from the black stones first, followed by entire blocks.

Iyra grabbed a loose bit of Braeden's shirt with her teeth as the rocks continued breaking apart. She tugged him backward. He allowed it, transfixed as he was on the tumbling seal keeping him from the Stele. His jaw tensed as he watched the melee, hoping with all his might that this would somehow work.

The rumble faded. Pebbles and the occasional brick still tumbled to the ground, so he and Iyra kept to the outer rim of the clearing. It took a few minutes for the air to clear, but each grain of dust glittered like a small fire as the sun's orange glow trickled through the haze. The clearing glimmered with light.

Braeden shielded his eyes with his arm until the glow faded. When the brilliant light finally disappeared, he relaxed and let himself look, daring to hope he'd done this right.

The archway still stood, but only mountains of black rubble on either side of the lichgate remained of the wall that once blocked his way underneath. The muted blues of a lake appeared through the lichgate, diluted by the portal's sheer face. Braeden peeked around the archway for good measure, only to find the endless forest beyond. No lake. He couldn't find a recognizable piece of the statues, though he suspected the four gemstones that served as their eyes lay somewhere beneath the piles of rocks.

He grinned. "About time we got past this!"

Iyra grunted in agreement.

He'd really done it. A sigh of relief crept into his throat, only to die midway. He'd done it, which meant he would actually have to go back into the Stele to spy on his father's troop movements and uncover any new fortifications. Even though this was his idea, a small and terrified part of him had expected to never make it this far. He feared returning to the Stele when his father ruled it—at any moment, he could walk into a trap.

Braeden took a deep breath and squared his shoulders. If he would ever be free of his father, he would have to face the man again. He would have to fight, and he would have to kill. Otherwise, he would forever be his father's slave.

Iyra nudged Braeden's arm and knelt. He forced a smile and hopped onto her back, preparing himself for what lay ahead. He would have to return at least a dozen times over the next few weeks to track the Stele's progress, so he might as well take it easy today. He wouldn't go too far. He wouldn't stay too long.

Iyra walked through the lichgate and into the Stele. Blue light flashed in Braeden's peripheral vision, and his stomach twisted with a sudden burst of nausea. Though he recognized the telltale signs of walking through a lichgate, another tremor shot through him as his body recognized its home. Without a doubt, he'd just walked into the Stele.

Great.

They stood on the edge of a lake high in the mountains. Flies buzzed near the water. An otter dipped out of sight, leaving ripples on the still surface. The sun blazed overhead, its rays setting the lake's surface ablaze with shimmers of golden light.

The Stele offered all its subjects protection, but the grounds spoke to Braeden in an entirely different way. Without ever having visited this lake before, he could sense a submerged network of caves in its depths. And though the distant crash of a waterfall drifted toward him, he knew it would be exactly three quarters of a mile to his left. It was instinct. He and the kingdom shared a connection, one he guessed it shared with every royal before him as well—even Carden.

A silent command for troops to assemble outside the barracks drifted through the Stele from none other than Carden himself. A weight settled on Braeden's shoulders to obey—by right, he was Carden's general and should be leading those soldiers. The desire to sprint toward the castle flickered within him, but he suppressed it just as quickly. At least he could disobey his father, even if the desire to obey became stronger when Carden was close. The other Stelians had no choice.

If Braeden's plan to attack the Stele worked, he would kill his father and finally know freedom. And when the Stelian people were his, he would allow them their first taste of independence as well.

CHAPTER THREE

INHERITANCE

Someone toyed with the locked handle to Kara's office. The latch wriggled, metal scraping against the gears, but Kara didn't move from her place on the floor. She sat cross-legged, shoulders hunched as she stared at the cracks in the hardwood. Flick, however, jumped out of her lap and trotted to investigate.

The rattling stopped. With a click, the lock slid back. The handle turned, sliding open at whatever silent command came from the person in the hallway. Kara bit her lip in annoyance—that was a charmed lock, one that shouldn't open for anyone except the person who locked it. But she figured one isen would know how to unlock it anyway: Stone.

She wanted to tell him to go away, that she wouldn't stack another stupid brick, but she kept silent. She still hadn't recovered from lighting her own desk on fire. She didn't trust herself to talk yet. Or move. Or be near people.

Kara closed her eyes. The door creaked open. Footsteps thudded along the wood floor panels. The door shut. The footsteps stopped by the entrance, as if inspecting something. The hair on the back of Kara's neck stood on end.

A frame scraped the wall. Stone must have adjusted a picture hanging there. All she could think of was the portrait of the man she still didn't recognize.

"What do you want, Stone?" she asked.

He chuckled. "You're just like your grandfather."

She cringed and snapped her head around to glare at him. "Don't compare me to that murderer."

Her grandfather—Agneon—murdered too many Oureans to count. Isen, yakona, drenowith—he killed them all. Murder was the only thing he could do well. He even killed her grandmother. Kara didn't want to be compared to such a vile man.

Stone shook his head. "When he killed, your grandfather was merely obeying orders. You know an isen must do as his master commands, and Niccoli wanted those people dead. In most cases, Agneon had no choice. It's the same as saying if I wanted you to kill someone, you would have to do it. So he did as any slave does. When he couldn't cope with the murders, he found an escape to avoid the guilt. At first, it was women in general. Over his centuries...well, I'm sure you don't want the details. But when he met your grandmother, he found love for the first time in his life. He—"

"He killed her," Kara interrupted.

"He *loved* her. More than anything or anyone. They were passionate, hot, and testy, but it was love. And in his passion, he lost himself. He lost control. Yes, he killed her. But it was an accident."

Kara grimaced. "How do you accidentally kill the person you love? I could never do that."

"You didn't intend to knock over those bricks for four solid hours, either."

"That's different."

"Hardly. You couldn't control yourself enough to do something so simple as hit a target. Agneon couldn't control his power, either, and your grandmother was unfortunate enough to be in the way. How are the two of you any different?"

Kara's jaw tensed. She didn't answer.

Stone cleared his throat. "I wasn't trying to shame you. I just want you to you understand. Why have you taken to moping? It's not like you."

She stared at the bookshelf across from her. "I don't want to hurt people, Stone."

"Then focus. If you're paying attention, you won't."

"Of course I'm focused. You think I want to hurt people?"

"That's not what I said."

She pointed at the charred remnants of her desk. "I set that on fire trying to light a candle! I was calm. I was clear-headed enough. But this new power isn't manageable, Stone. I'll kill people!"

She walked to a window and leaned her forehead against the glass pane. The hot glass burned her skin, but she sucked in a deep breath and forced herself to endure the heat. Forty feet off, trees swayed in a summer breeze while Kara waited for something in her life to make sense again.

Stone sighed. "Life is not simple, Kara, but you are strong enough to overcome this. It's a setback. Your grandfather went through it, too."

She gritted her teeth at being compared yet again to the murderer, but she didn't say anything.

Stone stepped a little closer, and she looked over her shoulder. The old isen stood in the middle of the room, hands in his pockets, eyeing her. His salt-and-pepper hair and mustache made her think yet again of Shakespeare, but she could never see Stone creating art of any kind. He was a scientist. He dissected anything and everything he could until he understood it.

He crossed to her window and examined the forest. "Your grandfather went through just as much self-doubt and fear, Kara. This is your family's curse, and it's yours now. When you became an isen, your body fine-tuned itself. You're stronger and designed to manipulate magic. Thanks to the bloodline you inherited from your grandfather, you function in a unique way. There isn't another isen like you. Energy is constantly flowing into you, and it builds up when you're not using it. So when you do use a technique, it explodes. You lose control."

"Then what's the point of this wrist guard?"

"It limits the intake of energy, but nothing can stop your magic completely. The guard teaches you to control the power over time."

Kara nodded to the burnt desk. "This thing's not teaching me anything."

Stone crossed his arms and stared at the singed remains of her desk. Kara leaned against the wall. Angst and energy burned in her gut, but she couldn't go there. She needed to stay calm, even when trapped and hoping for an answer she wasn't sure would come.

Stone caught her eye. "May I show you something?"

"Depends on what it is."

"His home."

Kara balked. "Agneon's? Didn't he live with Niccoli's guild?"

She didn't want anything to do with Niccoli, and she would never go near him again if she could avoid it. He controlled a powerful group of isen—his guild—and rumor had it he ran the largest and most powerful guild in Ourea. That vile isen told her what she was, and he only wanted her for her power. He wanted to make her a true slave, one who killed as often as her grandfather. If Stone hadn't awakened her as an isen and became her master, Niccoli would have managed to do it eventually.

Stone shook his head. "Sometimes, Agneon and your grandmother would run off to a second home. It's where he kept most of his things. It's also where he killed her."

Kara narrowed her eyes. "Why the hell would I want to see that place, then?"

"He left something for his daughter. For his heirs. I want you to see the pain he endured every day. Once you do, I think you'll realize you two aren't so different after all."

Kara hesitated. When she did finally speak, her voice was almost too low to hear. "I don't think I want to know that."

Stone inched closer. "He wasn't evil, Kara. Neither are you. I just can't help you anymore. I can't understand why you react the way you do. But maybe if you see what he endured, you will be better equipped to handle this new energy. Will you go?"

Without answering, Kara set her forehead on the window once more. Heat crawled over her skin like a fog, soothing her racing thoughts. For a moment, she relaxed.

She did want answers. She did want help. She couldn't control herself. If Agneon lost control and killed the woman he loved after centuries of learning to master himself, what was stopping Kara from doing the same to Braeden? Her shoulders sagged. She would do anything for Braeden, even if it meant learning she was more like her grandfather than she wanted to believe.

"When should we go?" she asked.

Stone nodded, as if she had finally seen reason. Perhaps she had.

"We should leave now. It's quite a trek from here, and you'll need all the time you can spare to sort through the house. Let's fly. Pick your mount."

"Shouldn't we use Flick? He can teleport."

"He can't teleport through lichgates, which would leave us walking through three portals in dangerous areas. We should fly."

"All right, then. Let's take the black dragon from the Grimoire. I think he can fit us both."

Stone shuddered. "I don't ride mounts if I can help it. I'll be fine."

Kara laughed. "It's not like you can fly, Stone."

"There are several perks to having stolen a drenowith's soul." He grinned.

Kara's smile fell. She gaped at the old isen, comprehension spreading over her mind like a frost.

"You can change form?" she asked.

Stone nodded. "Summon your mount, but Flick cannot come. You need to experience this house alone. We should leave now."

Kara straightened her back and snapped her mouth shut. One of the few people she trusted had kept yet another secret from her. Her mentors didn't seem to trust her with the truth.

She crossed her arms. "Why wouldn't you tell me you can change form? That would have saved the long trip here after you turned me."

He shrugged. "I never wanted you to return here. You weren't ready, but you wouldn't shut up about it. I figured a longer journey would give you more time to learn to control yourself, but my ploy obviously didn't work. And there is much you don't know about me, child. I doubt you will ever learn it all."

"Then why—"

"Kara, there is no time for this. Your vagabonds need you to master your power. I'm offering you a chance to learn how to accomplish the task. Are you coming or not?"

She took a deep breath and nodded. "I'm sorry. Let's go."

❦CHAPTER FOUR

MEMORIAL

Braeden sucked in a sharp breath to calm his nerves. After four hours of scouting the Stele and an overnight trek back to the golden city of Ayavel, he stood at the front doors of the palace. At least he was allowed passage through the main lichgate without question anymore. The guards knew him and always let him and Iyra through. But after they entered the city this time, Iyra ran off into the forest to relax after their trip. Braeden would wait a few days before looking for her again. He owed her as much for her help.

Before him, two golden doors framed a set of glittering stairs. Eight guards lined each side of the palace gates, two on each step—four more than last time he'd come in this way. What a welcome.

He began up the staircase. With each step, white light glimmered in the stone under his boot, and the air hummed as if he'd stepped on a piano key. He shook his head. Only in Ayavel would this sort of thing exist.

The palace's front doors groaned and opened at a snail's pace, their hinges grating as the palace begrudgingly welcomed him. No one wanted him here. He was Heir to the Stele, after all. He represented the darkness of his father's empire, even if he wanted nothing more than to end the old man. If Braeden were anyone else, the gates would have been open and waiting for him long before he stood on the front step.

It took another minute for the doors to open enough to slip through. A respected guest would have waited. A prince would have been received. But as his only company was the guards who wouldn't look at him, Braeden didn't bother with propriety or courtesy. Since the doors weren't open when he arrived, he wouldn't wait for the slow formalities for fear he would be an old man before he stepped foot inside.

Once through the croaking doors, his boots tapped against the golden floor tiles. Clumps of mud fell off his boots, leaving a trail of dirt and leaf fragments in his wake. He didn't care. All he wanted was a meal and a warm bath.

The white hallway went on forever. Gold trim lined the floor and ceiling, breaking whenever an identical hallway turned off in another direction. Each corridor led to a distant wing of the massive castle, but Braeden never tried to learn the entire layout. He never had time. Even now, he barely recognized where he was. He eyed the hallway to his right. A flash of recognition snapped through him, but he couldn't place exactly why this particular passage seemed familiar.

A sob shot past him, breaking his train of thought. Another followed. Someone whimpered—a soprano note that could only belong to a woman. He hesitated, looking around, and followed the weeping down a hallway to his left. The crying stopped as he found a pair of double doors, one of them set slightly ajar. He peeked inside, only to find four golden thrones set on a platform at the far end.

He cursed. Someone was crying in Ayavel's throne room, of all places. He hesitated, waiting for confirmation. Sure enough, the mystery sobs began once more and drifted through the open doors.

Braeden's fists tightened. He hated to set foot in the room. Not long ago, Gavin and the other Bloods chained him, threw him to his knees, and sentenced him to death in there merely because he was Stelian. He'd managed to earn some of their trust back since then by demonstrating his mutual hatred for his father, but he had never regained their respect. He doubted he ever would.

He sighed. However much he hated that room, he couldn't just walk by when someone obviously needed help. He hadn't yet met an Ayavelian who willingly showed public emotion in such a way. Something had to be very wrong.

Braeden peered in and shifted to get a better view. A woman's slippers appeared to the left, most of her obscured by the door. A blue gown spilled around her ankles, its threads shimmering in the sunlight pouring through the windows above.

He rapped his knuckles on the door. His knocks echoed in the vast chamber. The sobs stopped. A woman sniffled. The shoes slipped out of view, so Braeden pushed the door open. His breath caught in his chest.

Evelyn lay on the stones, her knees tucked underneath her with that blue dress spilling out across the floor. Her classic Ayavelian skin reflected blue and green specks of light as sunlight hit her through the windows. Straight hair framed her face, its white glow accentuating her almond eyes as she stared at him. Ayavelians had three pupils in both eyes, each of which could convey a different emotion. But now, Evelyn stared at him with only a deep-rooted sorrow. His throat tightened.

Before her, the statue of a woman towered halfway to the arched ceiling above. Her white marble face glistened as she stared through the skylights, her eyes nothing but a solid sheet with no detail.

Evelyn wiped her own eyes with a sleeve. "You're back early."

"What's wrong, Evelyn?"

Her lip trembled. Her eyebrows arched upward. A dimple appeared in her cheek, as if she bit it to keep herself from crying.

"Aunt Aislynn's dead," she said.

Braeden's shoulders sagged. The air left him in a rush, and for a moment, he couldn't think. The last time he saw Aislynn, he nearly attacked the queen for trapping Kara and using her as bait to catch a muse in some half-brewed plan, nearly killing everyone involved. He hadn't given Aislynn the time of day to explain herself and refused to even look her in the eye after he discovered what she'd done.

But...dead?

When he was a boy, Aislynn saved his life. She took him to Hillside and gave him a second chance at life. She even stood up for him in this very throne room when the other Bloods sentenced him to death. Had he been too unforgiving to someone who helped him so much in life?

He knelt next to Evelyn and sat on his heels, shoulders hunched. Only then did he notice a plaque below the statue's feet: *Aislynn, last full Blood of Ayavel.*

"Is this her memorial?" Braeden asked.

Evelyn nodded.

"What do you mean by 'last full'—"

"I wasn't given the bloodline naturally, and I am therefore not a full Blood. She's the last of her bloodline. I'm a forgery."

Braeden's jaw tensed. He didn't know what to say.

They sat in silence for a while. He watched her from the corner of his eye, never looking at her directly. Her hair fell around her, hiding her face. Streaks of dried tears crusted along her cheeks, dulling her skin's reflective nature.

After a second, he cleared his throat. "I thought memorials weren't supposed to go in the throne room. In Hillside, we have a park for Bloods' memorial statues."

A pang of regret tore through him. Braeden couldn't say he was a part of Hillside anymore. Gavin disowned him and took his key to the kingdom when Braeden's Stelian ancestry was discovered. Even though he'd spent twelve years in Hillside and grown up with Gavin as a brother, he was no longer a part of the Hillsidian world.

Evelyn frowned, snapping him from his thoughts. "It's my kingdom, Stelian. If I want to honor my aunt's memory in the throne room, I have every right to do it!"

Braeden tensed as he was reminded of one of the many reasons he disliked this girl, but he took a deep breath. She was obviously grieving. He needed to be forgiving and patient.

"I meant no offense, Evelyn. I was merely curious."

She cleared her throat. "I'm sorry, Braeden. I'm just—I—"

He caught her eye. "You're hurting. It's okay."

Her lip trembled again. "Why would she leave me? I'm not ready for this, Braeden. Being awoken as the Blood—it hurt so much. I couldn't walk for nearly a day afterward. I can sense the moods of my people. I can actually control them, make them do things they don't want to do. I can command them, and they have to obey. I don't want so much power!"

Braeden wanted to inform her it was far too late to back out of her responsibilities now that she'd taken the bloodline, but he kept silent.

Evelyn took a deep breath. "The drenowith killed my aunt. They took her from me too soon, before she could teach me. I just know it."

"What makes you think so?"

She groaned. "Don't be an idiot. It's obvious! They led her to the Stele all those years ago and nearly got her killed in Carden's dungeon—you know the story all too well. And a week or so back, when she tried to get her revenge on them by stealing some muse's blood, they decided to end her once and for all. It's the only thing that makes sense!"

Braeden couldn't deny her logic. Aislynn tried to kill a muse named Adele and almost succeeded. Braeden didn't have any theories of his own, and if anyone killed Kara, he would get revenge in the same way. For twelve years, Aislynn had been his mentor and, for the longest time, she was the only one alive who knew of his double life. But the moment she'd threatened Kara and used her as bait, he disowned her. He had to admit he would have killed her himself if she'd gone too far and taken Kara from him completely.

"The drenowith might be involved, but we can't know for sure," he finally admitted.

"Oh, I'm certain," Evelyn spat.

"How?"

She shook her head. "There's just no denying it, Braeden. What she did started a feud between the drenowith and the Ayavelian race. I'm not saying I'm proud of her choice, but I will never forgive the muses for taking her from me."

"We already have a war on our hands, Evelyn. Don't start another one with creatures as powerful as the drenowith."

"I won't. I'm not stupid. But I will never trust a drenowith again, nor will I let one live if I find it."

Braeden sighed. He couldn't blame her for that hatred, even if it wasn't healthy.

A sob pricked his ear. Evelyn cradled her face in her hands, shoulders hunched and shaking. She cried into her palms, the dam apparently breaking in the middle of her throne room.

Braeden patted her back. "I shouldn't have intruded. I'll leave you alone."

Instead of nodding or ignoring him completely, as he'd expected, Evelyn wrapped her arms around his torso. She burrowed her cheek into his chest and hugged him so tightly it hurt.

His voice caught in his throat. His shirt absorbed the young queen's tears as she held onto him, apparently forgetting their years of mutual disdain. She trembled, the nails of her thin fingers digging through the fabric on his back.

Kara flashed across his mind. What would she have said if she walked in at this moment?

Unsure of the right thing to do, he continued patting Evelyn. She sobbed and leaned in closer. He sighed and slipped his arm around her, trying to imagine what Kara would want him to do.

He cleared his throat and let his mind wander back to Evelyn's theory. Something about this story didn't sit right with him. While he could believe Garrett would kill Aislynn out of revenge, he didn't believe Aislynn would be so naïve as to expose herself. She would have stayed close to the kingdom, all the while knowing full well Garrett was out for blood.

"How did Aislynn die?" he asked.

Evelyn mumbled a response through his shirt.

"What?"

The queen lifted her chin enough to answer. "No one knows."

"How is that possible?"

"Last I spoke to her, she was going to her room to rest. A few hours later, I woke up screaming and in the worst agony of my life. I didn't even realize I was being awoken as the Blood until one of the generals mentioned it. They sent a small army to Aislynn's room, but no one was there."

"Has anyone else gone missing?"

Evelyn wiped her eyes. "General Krik. No one knows where he is, either. Some rumors say they were lovers, and something went wrong on a rendezvous, but that's treasonous. If my aunt had a lover, he wouldn't be secret. She would never have hidden such a thing from me."

Braeden glanced at the floor and kept silent. There was plenty Evelyn's aunt had kept from her. He had no idea how the girl could still have such faith in the dead queen.

"This doesn't add up," he said.

"What do you mean?"

"Aislynn was smart. She wouldn't have exposed herself to the drenowith after what she did. She wouldn't have left the kingdom."

"No one wanted her dead but the drenowith."

"I'm sure Carden wanted her dead. There are plenty who would have killed her. It's unwise to focus your hatred on the drenowith when this could be something else entirely. Your safety could be at risk."

Evelyn sank back onto her heels, her eyes shifting out of focus.

Braeden couldn't suppress the selfish thought to use this moment. Evelyn was a major player now. With her on his side, he might even get Kara back into the council. The Ayavelian girl simply had to get past her hatred of drenowith. If Garrett really had killed Aislynn, it would never happen. There was only one way to find out for sure.

Braeden ran a hand through his hair. "I'm only saying you shouldn't assume this was the drenowith's doing. I think you should speak with Garrett. With Kara's influence, I think you can find out the truth."

Evelyn's eyes snapped to him. She frowned. "How dare you

suggest I speak with one of those creatures as if he is capable of telling the truth! If he did it, he would lie."

He shook his head. "The muses helped me more than once. Maybe if you spent some time with one, you'd realize how wrong you are about them. They care about life. About us. They saved me from Carden. They helped me save the Heirs after the Gala. They—"

"I've heard enough." Evelyn shot to her feet and stormed toward the door.

"Evelyn, wait a minute! You're angry, and—"

She hesitated by the exit, one hand on the open door. "No, my mind is crystal clear. I won't be a pawn, Braeden."

With that, Evelyn disappeared through the door, her blue dress swishing along the floor. Her footsteps disappeared the moment she passed into the hallway.

Braeden sighed and slumped back on his heels. She must have known he was trying to use her. Disgust bubbled in his gut, swirling with the shame of his selfishness. He might have been a prince, destined to rule the Stele one day, but he wasn't a very good politician. His failed attempt at a political play just cost him the one ally he could have possibly found in this traitorous arena.

He forced himself to his feet. By default, he headed toward his office. He wandered out of the Ayavelian throne room and through the halls, but his mind raced in a different direction. He should visit Kara. Get away from Ayavel for a bit. Talk strategy. Compose a new game plan.

He laughed. He couldn't even lie to himself. He didn't want a new strategy. He wanted an escape, and Kara always brought him freedom. But she needed time to master her isen abilities, and he couldn't interrupt her training. Not much could hurt Braeden, but Kara could kill him if she didn't master herself. Her newfound power had no limits. And if she ever stole his soul—however accidentally—he didn't think even he could fight her.

❧CHAPTER FIVE

THE COTTAGE

Rain battered Kara's face, each drop hitting her skin like a needle as she zipped through the sky on the black dragon's back. She squinted, trying to see through the gray haze of fog and thunder, but the wind stung her eyes and tore at her hair. Her dragon surveyed the mist around them, its white teeth face frozen in a toothy smile that always sent a shiver down her spine.

A white owl flew just ahead of them—Stone. Once they left the village, he'd shifted form and taken off without a word, though Kara still couldn't figure out why he chose to be an owl. Maybe he just wanted to keep a low profile, or maybe he enjoyed the symbolism of wisdom. Kara grunted. Stone wasn't narcissistic enough for that last one. Whatever his reason, he managed to keep up with the dragon. Only that mattered.

Stone pulled ahead, his white feathers shifting in the gusts of air. A crack of thunder shook the sky. Rain fell harder. Through the fog, the snowy tip of a mountain loomed suddenly into view. Crags broke away from the peak like spikes stuck into the rock, ready to tear open anything unlucky enough to fall on them. Pines blanketed the lower slopes, but everything beyond dissolved into the mist of this storm. Kara could barely see more than fifty feet on either side of her, and she had no idea where they were.

The white owl dove. The dragon plunged after it without waiting for an order from Kara to follow. Her stomach twisted. She clutched her beast tighter, wishing with all her might that they could just find the house already. But Stone banked around the mountain, and yet another came into view. He twisted around that as well, the dragon mere feet behind. One after another, the mountains zipped by as the three travelers sped through gaps in the peaks. Snow clung to the mountains, a melting blanket clinging to the biting chill of the high altitude. A shiver snaked its way through Kara's body.

Finally, Stone dove again and aimed for a flat ledge at the tip of a mountain. As he flapped his wings to slow his landing, a tremor raced through his body. His torso stretched outward. His wings became arms. The white feathers receded into his hairline, leaving behind the white beard that reminded Kara of Renaissance actors. His feet brushed the stone slab just as the last of his claws disappeared. Without breaking his stride, he walked toward the mountain and brushed a bit of snow from the steep rock.

Kara breathed a sigh of relief and nudged the dragon down toward the ledge. It landed with a less than graceful *thump*, but Kara slipped off as soon as its feet touched the ground. She patted her mount's neck, wishing it back into the Grimoire with the silent command she used on all her mounts. The black dragon flashed its white teeth and dissolved into black dust that drifted away on the next gust of wind.

Eager to be done with the rain, she ran to Stone's side just as he finished wiping snow from a bit of the mountainside. She leaned in, only to see a small carving in the rock. The engraving reminded her of a star, with five spikes jutting from a central point. Each line rounded out to a sharp tip and curved such that it almost touched the one to its left.

Stone reached into his shirt collar and pulled a chain from around his neck. A pendant slid along the metal, a mirror image of the emblem carved into the rock.

"What—?" she asked.

Stone shouted over the rain. "This house has been sealed for you, Kara, preserved as it was when Agneon left it. This will break the seal."

Without another word, he pressed the key into the carved

lock. Something groaned deep in the mountain. Clicks and hisses fumed from somewhere beneath their feet.

The mountain shook. Kara knelt for balance, but Stone never even flinched. With a boom as loud as thunder, a crack traveled from the lock and wandered in a circle, creating something of an archway in the rock. Kara shot to her feet and shuffled backward, teetering on the edge of the platform. Another gale whipped by, pushing her off balance, but she widened her stance and eyed the growing crack in the cliff.

With a final hiss, the splitting rock shifted and broke away from the mountain. It rolled a few feet to the left and stopped, exposing the tunnel it guarded. The ground stilled, and Kara finally regained her balance. She inspected the new passage, but the low light only illuminated the first few feet of darkness. Stone stepped into the tunnel and hesitated on the threshold. Kara followed.

Steam radiated from Stone, the water evaporating as he no doubt used some technique to dry himself.

"How are you doing that?" Kara asked.

Stone shrugged and waved a hand across her face. Steam radiated from her, and her clothes dried within seconds. Water dissolved from the crevices around her eyes, and her hair regained its shine.

"Neat. Will you teach me?" she prodded.

"There are more important matters to address, Kara. I will teach you this later if you remember to ask."

Kara sighed. "Fair enough. What was that around your neck, then?"

"A key."

"You just happened to have the key to my grandfather's cottage with you?"

"I use it for many things, not only this cottage. It can keep out the unwanted. Nothing and no one can break its seal—I've tested it."

Without another word, Stone walked into the darkness. His

shoulders disappeared first into the gloom, and the rest of him followed shortly thereafter.

Kara took a deep breath and joined him. She probably managed to annoy him with too many questions again.

Stone's breathing echoed through the tunnel, magnified by the absolute silence. Her footsteps mingled with his. Tension pooled in her shoulders as she sensed the cave walls pressing in on her.

A cool draft blew on her face. The tension in the air shifted. It seemed to break and peel away, as if they had just walked into a cave with a much higher ceiling.

"Let's get some light in here," Stone said.

He clapped once. The mountain groaned in response. Pebbles clattered all around Kara, raining from walls she couldn't see. Cracks splintered through the rock above. Light drizzled through the ceiling in curved rays. A perfect ring of sunlight snaked its way around the cave's dome, illuminating polished gray stone.

Rainwater poured from the new ring in the ceiling, crashing to the floor like a circular waterfall. Kara flinched. Out of instinct, she shifted her weight to the balls of her feet, ready to sprint when the water came barreling at them, but it didn't. Instead, the water tumbled into a gutter at the edges of the cavern and raced away into the recesses of the mountain. And while the perfect circle of light let in rainwater directly above where Kara and Stone stood, a small roof jutting over their passageway kept them dry. The rain cascaded toward the ground on either side of her like an archway and disappeared into the gutters. The rain continued, now a curtain of water along the outer ring of the cave.

Though the fog reduced visibility on their way over, even the low light shattered the dark cave. A polished wall circled them in a perfect dome. The ceiling towered a hundred feet above. Kara took a step back. It was like looking at a life-sized snow globe.

A house sat in the center of the circle: a two-story wooden cottage with white paint and two brick chimneys. The roof came to a point, its gray shingles glinting in the cave's cold light. Its blue shutters creaked as gusts of wind peeled away from the rain. A porch wrapped around the entire first story, with three rocking chairs positioned by the door. The chairs creaked in the breeze.

Stone crossed his arms. "Welcome to the Walnut."

"The what?" Kara couldn't help herself. She giggled.

Her mentor rolled his eyes and began toward the house. "Agneon named this the Walnut—he said the house had a hard shell but held the most precious people in his life at its center. I suppose even the strongest man has his soft moments."

The smile dissolved from Kara's face as she trailed behind him. "Strong" wasn't the word she had in mind for her grandfather.

"This was his haven," Stone continued. "He and Miriam could find peace here."

"Miriam?"

"Your grandmother."

Kara nodded. She didn't know what to say.

Stone stopped at the foot of the porch steps. "You should lead. This is your home to explore, not mine."

A gust of wind blew the hair away Kara's neck. The cool breeze dried the nervous sweat already brewing on her neck. She eyed the blue front door, painted the same color as the shutters. A brass handle waited for her. She took a deep breath and started up the stairs.

A rocking chair creaked again. It leaned forward and fell back in a constant rhythm, a few fingernail scratches along the white paint of the arm rest. Kara brushed the crevices with her hand.

Gold dust sprang from beneath her finger. It bred and engulfed her, spinning around her until the cold gray of the cave dissolved. A warm glow replaced the fog, the light enough that she had to shield her eyes with her arm.

When she lowered her hand, a man sat in the rocking chair. His long blond hair hung in a braid down his back, and his squared jaw reminded Kara of someone she couldn't quite place.

His skin glittered with the gold dust clinging to the air.

A small girl no older than five sat in the man's lap. She wore a green dress with black embroidery, her blond hair in loose curls that frizzed at the end. She stared off into the distance.

Neither the man nor the girl looked at Kara. Part of her was grateful.

The girl sighed. "I'm glad you're home, Papa. I missed you."

The man smiled. "I missed you, too, Ellen."

Kara's breath caught in her chest. Dread spread to her fingertips, weighing them down. She forced herself to breathe.

Ellen—that was her mother's name.

"Where did you go, Papa?" little Ellen asked.

The man's arms tensed from their place around his daughter. "Business."

The dust dissolved with a *poof*. The gray gloom returned, and Kara found herself staring at the empty rocking chair, still not quite able to breathe.

"What...?" she asked in a small voice.

"One of Agneon's memories," Stone said.

Kara glanced at the porch railing. Stone leaned against it, arms still crossed. He looked at her over the brim of his nose, as if judging how much he should say.

Her voice lingered in her throat, much quieter than she intended. "That was a memory?"

Stone nodded. He unfolded his arms, a folded piece of paper now in his hand. Since his clothes didn't have many pockets, Kara couldn't help but wonder where he'd kept it.

He handed her the page, and she took it. And when her skin brushed the paper, more gold dust poured from beneath her fingers.

The gray world dissolved again, but she now stood in an office. Bookshelves lined the nearest wall. A wooden desk sat in the corner, glittering with the haze of yet another memory. Sunlight streamed through a window along the far wall, shining its light on two men.

Stone stood by the desk, looking out the window. His skin glittered in the golden vision, but he didn't look a day younger than the isen Kara had come to know.

Another man sat at the desk, his shoulders hunched over a piece of paper. A blond braid hung down his back, just like the man in the first memory. Kara inched closer until his already familiar squared chin came into view. This had to be Agneon.

Her grandfather sobbed and dropped a quill. Ink splattered on the paper. A few half-formed sentences littered the page. Two had been crossed out.

"You must focus," Stone said.

"Tell Ellen I'm sorry," Agneon whispered through a sob.

Stone nodded.

But Agneon continued. "I'm sorry I can't be there for her when she grows up. I'm sorry I can't hate her suitors and listen to her cry when they break her heart. I'm sorry she will have to go through the curse of our lineage without me."

Stone shrugged. "She doesn't have to. You don't have to let the drenowith destroy you just because you killed Miriam."

Agneon choked on another sob. Kara burned with annoyance and anger, though she wasn't sure the emotions belonged to her. Thoughts whizzed through her mind, some of them in languages she didn't understand. Regardless, Stone didn't have to be so callous. Agneon already felt terrible enough as it was.

But Agneon shook his head. "I can't live with myself. Not now. Ellen saw what happened. She saw everything. She ran away when I tried to explain. I found her running toward the cave exit. She didn't want me to touch her. She was trembling and..."

Agneon bit his knuckle. He didn't say any more.

Stone shifted his weight. "And you think embedding your memories in your home will teach her how to deal with this curse even though you failed?"

Agneon nodded but didn't look up. "Maybe she can learn from my mistakes."

"I doubt she will ever want to come back to this life."

"Then let her find happiness somewhere else. I hope she never becomes an isen. I hope Niccoli never finds her. She barely has the isen scent, so who knows? Maybe she doesn't have the gene. Maybe isenhood skipped her. I hope it did. If she forgets me, if she never comes back to Ourea, she might be better off. But if she does find her way back, I want her to know I tried. I tried to be a good man. I tried to love. I simply failed."

Stone nodded. "We should begin, then."

Agneon's picked up his quill. "Will I lose the memories when you embed them in the house?"

"Yes."

"But I won't be stuck here, right? Just my memories, not my soul."

"Correct."

Agneon nodded. "Good."

The golden light imploded on itself. Once more, Kara stood on the porch of the house in the middle of a mountain, staring at the isen who somehow pulled memories from her grandfather.

Her legs wobbled. She lowered herself onto the stairs and set her head in her hands.

Stone sighed. "Kara—"

"Hush. I need a moment."

※

Kara didn't know how long she sat on the first step of her grandfather's cottage, but she needed to get her bearings. The letter crinkled in her hand, still unread.

She saw her grandfather cry. The isen known to Ourea as the greatest mass-murderer of the last few centuries sobbed and lost himself to remorse for killing the woman he loved. That was *not* the way she had imagined him. She couldn't quite wrap her head around the idea that he could feel anything but hatred.

Stone sat beside her. The stair creaked beneath his weight, but he remained silent.

"So you embedded his memories into the house?" Kara finally asked.

Stone nodded. "He asked me to do it. I believe you now know why."

"But how? How did you even do that? I thought only the Vagabond could see others' memories."

"And who do you think taught him?"

Kara caught Stone's eye. "Really? You taught him to see others' memories?"

Stone nodded. "I wanted him to be safe. Knowing another's most influential memory shows you what drives them."

"I didn't think you cared about anyone's safety, even his."

His shoulders sagged ever so slightly. "I didn't expect you would."

She rubbed her face with her free hand. "I'm sorry, Stone. That's just how you come off."

He shrugged. "I don't care about many, but Cedric has always been like a son to me. And now you have become like a daughter. You two are the only family I have ever known and the only family I suppose I will ever know. An isen's life is not a happy one, child, and that's what you must understand. You have the same rare power as your grandfather. You must see what he endured to understand the temptations and limitations of your new power. If you don't, you will destroy your family just as he destroyed his."

Kara's jaw tensed. Her eye stung, but she couldn't tell if she were about to cry. Though Stone hadn't lost his monotone, this was the closest he had ever come to sharing his emotions.

"All right," she whispered.

"Don't open the letter until you've seen the entire house. Will you wait?"

She nodded and handed him the folded paper. He took it and gestured to the front door.

"Go on," he said.

Kara pushed herself to her feet. She passed the rocking chair on her way to the front door and resisted the impulse to touch the armrest once more. She wasn't sure if she would relive the memory, but she had plenty of others to worry about as it was.

Her fingers hovered over the brass doorknob. She didn't know if she was really ready for this. Agneon could have embedded a memory in nearly anything, including the handle. With each step, she wouldn't know what memory would come next—it could be a happy one that made her smile or a terrifying one that brought her to tears.

But such was life. She took a deep breath and turned the handle.

The door opened onto a living room. Off to the left, a loveseat faced a stone fireplace. A wooden dining table with a red tablecloth filled the space to her right. A kitchen counter peeked through a doorframe in the far wall. Beside it, a hallway ended in a closed door.

Kara took a step farther into the room and closed the front door behind her, leaving Stone on the porch. He hadn't moved from his place on the first step, and she doubted he would enter while she explored.

She glanced around the living room, taking note of anything that might contain a memory. A glass globe sat on a coffee table near the couch. A blanket lay draped over a chair in the corner that Kara hadn't previously noticed.

A thin table sat against the wall under the stairs, its surface covered with framed sketches and a few items that glittered as she moved. Kara inched closer, and the glimmering items turned out to be jewelry. A diamond necklace lay spread in the center of the table, blue and green light reflecting from its jewels. A few rings sat nearby, their gold just as bright as the gems. A brooch, a comb, and a bracelet—all of them lined with sapphires or some other colored stone—glittered from their places on the counter.

Kara shuddered. That table had to be a minefield of memories.

She peeked through the open doorframe and into the kitchen. Granite countertops reached across three of the four walls. Oak cabinets filled the space beneath the counters, while cupboards with glass doors lined the space above. An island counter with a sink lay in the very center of it all.

Kara walked into the kitchen, her hand brushing something cold as she entered. She turned even as the gold dust sprang from beneath her fingertips. A black iron oven sat in a massive fireplace by the door. As the glitter enveloped her, she sucked in a breath to steady herself. A soft hue took over the air once more, and Kara disappeared to another time.

A small woman with red hair leaned over the stove. Her hair pooled over one shoulder, caught on the neck hem of a blue gown. A white apron stained with beige smudges covered most of the dress. She opened the oven door and smiled, her eyes creasing as she glanced over whatever filled its trays. The scent of cinnamon and sugar tickled Kara's nose. She grinned. That had to be her grandmother.

Ellen—she had to be six or seven, now—ran up and tugged on the woman's apron. "Are they ready yet, Mama?"

"Not yet, baby. Five more minutes," the woman said.

Agneon skidded into view from behind Kara. He grinned, and his entire face lit up with the smile. "Can't we have one now? No use waiting when your family's hungry, Miriam!"

Miriam bit back a smile and shook her head. "You impatient man."

He reached his arms around her waist and nuzzled her neck. "Just one, please?"

"I got them, Papa! Run!" Ellen shouted. She squealed and darted out of the room holding a towel in her hands. Two cookies lay on top, the air above them steaming.

"That's my girl!" Agneon shouted. He thundered after her.

"You two are trouble!" Miriam yelled, but she burst into laughter before she could finish the last word.

The gold dust imploded yet again, and the cold kitchen snapped into view. Kara took a deep breath and laughed. Trouble indeed. There was no question where she got her mischievous nature.

Nearly three hours later, Kara sat on the stairs and rubbed her face. She had touched nearly every item she could find. She probably witnessed fifty memories, just on this floor alone.

The first floor had been a relatively happy place; she witnessed an argument or two, but most memories showed her the blissful moments Agneon had treasured.

She witnessed little Ellen's first birthday and Agneon's lopsided excuse for a cake on the occasion—he'd conceded to letting Miriam bake all the family's sweets after that. She saw Agneon carry a four-year-old Ellen on his shoulders as they hiked through some unknown forest for the first time. She smiled as she watched the family play a game on the coffee table...a game of cards that reminded her of the rainy nights spent with her own mom and dad in the Tallahassee house.

So many of her mother's passions—hiking, games, food— came from Agneon. Kara wondered if her mother ever realized that.

Kara glanced up the stairs to the empty hallway above. If the first floor had been happy, the second had to house Agneon's dark memories. She took a deep breath and stood.

Bring it on.

❧CHAPTER SIX

AGNEON

Kara didn't know what she expected to find on the second floor of her grandfather's cottage. Bedrooms, perhaps, and a closet or two. Maybe an office. But not blood. She hadn't expected to find that. Streaks of blood stained the white walls, dark red and a little crusty. It had been allowed to dry before the house had been sealed.

She swallowed hard.

The stairs led to the center of a hallway. Three doors lined the hall to her right, with just two to her left. The streaks came from the last door to her right and carried halfway down the stairs, where they disappeared.

Kara figured she wasn't quite ready for whatever lay in that room.

Instead, she turned left and opened the last door in the hall. A desk filled a corner, with bookshelves along the near wall. A lonely window on the far wall let in light. Shadows danced along the wall like waves as the waterfall crossed in and out of the low sunlight streaming in through the ring in the dome above. A leather chair sat against the wall nearest to the door. She narrowed her eyes and tightened her grip on the door handle. This was the room from the memory attached to the letter Stone had given her. This had to be Agneon's study.

She crossed to the desk but didn't touch anything. A few quills crowded a corner, each laid perfectly next to the others. An ink jar stood by them, its lid closed. A neat stack of blank paper sat on the surface near the wall.

Kara turned toward the bookcases. She glanced over every

shelf, taking in the various items set in front of the books. A green orb the size of a marble rested in a wire holder. Yellow smoke sizzled inside the orb, snapping at its edges like bolts of lightning. A gold nugget sat on another shelf, and letter opener on yet another.

A rusty old nail lay beside the letter opener. Kara furrowed her eyebrows and leaned closer. What an odd thing to leave on a bookshelf.

She touched it, knowing in her gut that it held a memory. When the gold dust jumped into the air from under her finger, she smiled. Maybe she was getting the hang of this after all.

The memory pulled her from the office and into a forest. Agneon sat on a branch, hammering planks of wood to its limbs. He had already fashioned a crude box between the tree's limbs in what Kara assumed was a tree house. A ladder leaned against the far side of the tree.

Agneon straddled the branch and held a nail against a board. He aimed the hammer and drove it toward the nail, only to smash his thumb instead of the iron spike. He cursed and chucked the hammer into the woods. It crashed through the foliage at least fifty feet away. A string of curses poured from his mouth, some of which Kara didn't even understand.

The isen stuck his injured thumb in his mouth and threw a left hook at the board he was trying to nail into the tree. It splintered into a dozen pieces. Shards flew in every direction. Cracks spiraled down the other boards he had already nailed into the tree. Something snapped. The tree house groaned. Agneon grabbed a branch, but not in time. The house collapsed in on itself. Nails and planks rained to the ground. Agneon landed on his shoulder with a thud.

He pushed himself to his feet. His scowl deepened. Wrinkles bore into his forehead, turning his glare sour. His cheeks reddened.

Kara shivered. His anger had apparently dipped into cold hatred. She didn't recognize him as the man holding his daughter in the porch rocking chair anymore. This was the look of a murderer—one who would kill anything that moved. There seemed to be a fine line between his two personas.

A spark jumped along the tree's trunk. Kara flinched, half-believing she imagined it until an orange flame burst from one of the boards. More fire sprang from the planks littering the ground. A green glow skittered over Agneon's skin. It pulsed, growing dim and brighter with a steady beat. The isen gritted his teeth. His eyes narrowed.

Nails levitated, shaking. They shivered and inched free of the planks. The green light on Agneon's skin grew. It cast murky shadows on the grass around Kara's feet. She squinted, trying to keep an eye on the scene as the light grew, but she finally squeeze her eyes shut. She raised her arm to cover her face and heard one last curse from her grandfather.

A pulse of energy blew past her—no, through her. She was a ghost in this memory. Trees toppled. Fire crackled on timber. The green light faded, and Kara lowered her arm.

Roots of fallen trees stuck out of the ground, some easily taller than her. Flames tore across the forest's canopy, eating away at any tree still standing. Only a charred trunk and piles of ashes remained of the tree Agneon had once used for the tree house.

Her grandfather stood in the middle of the clearing, the earth beneath his feet smoking. He stared at the burnt tree, his eyes out of focus. His shoulders relaxed, and he let out a quiet breath. He rubbed his neck and shook his head, but never once took his eyes off the smoldering remnants of the tree.

"I only wanted to do something nice for her," he said under his breath.

The dark office returned in a rush. Kara collapsed into the chair by the door. Annoyance churned in her gut as she gripped the armrest. He burned down a forest because he hit his thumb with a hammer. That wasn't a temper. That was just childish.

She shut her eyes and forced herself to take a deep breath. She couldn't be a hypocrite. After all, she did burn her own desk to bits in much the same fashion. She was all too familiar with

Agneon's frustration. His anger bubbled out of control, as did hers.

Sunlight caught on something yellow, blinding her for a moment. A table sat beside the chair, and on it lay a dagger in a brilliant blue sheath. She leaned closer. A golden hilt protruded from the sheath, its end curving to a rounded point. Carvings wove across the metal in tight circles, giving off the appearance of tiny hills and valleys.

This was the first weapon to surface in the house. She reached for it, curious as to what kind of memory it held, when she noticed what had actually glimmered: a small golden medallion the size of a quarter. It rested beside the dagger, its chain hanging off the edge of the table. The image of a man covered the medallion's face, a halo around his head. The words *Saint Nicholas* stretched along the top-most curve of the metal.

Kara picked up the medallion without another thought. Gold dust spiraled from beneath her fingers, and curiosity ate at her. What memory could a relic from the human world hold?

Blood.

Before the dust engulfed her completely, the memory began to play out. Blood sprayed into the air without a source. Kara gagged, but the world blurred with blues and greens and yellows. Rot and rust stung her nose. She stepped back, trying to get her bearings, and the world snapped into focus.

Agneon spun a sword in his hand. Fury stained every inch of his face, distorting it into a grimace of hatred. He glared at something just past Kara.

She swiveled. A Kirelm soldier rushed toward her, his white wings outstretched. Sweat dripped down his silver skin. He let loose a battle cry and sailed through her body on his way to Agneon. Her grandfather just smirked and shoved his blade clean through the Kirelm's gut. The yakona retched, and Agneon flung him off to the side.

Soldier after soldier ran toward him. Each man swung weapons in a slow arc. Everything moved in slow motion, and each swing of Agneon's sword found a vital organ. Kara flinched with every blow. After minutes of nothing but death and blood, she nearly screamed with the desire to escape this memory.

Green light pulsed on Agneon's skin, just as it had in the memory with the tree house. The glow hovered over his body, illuminating his victims' corpses with a growing radiance. It bubbled and grew, until finally Kara had to shield her eyes.

Men screamed. Horses followed suit. Metal clanged. Something roared. The patter of skin smacking against the earth over and over rolled through the clearing. Smoke wafted by, choking Kara as she tried to clear it from her lungs. She shuddered, but she couldn't escape until the memory ended. She had to wait it out.

The light faded, but she hesitated. Without a doubt, she did not want to see the aftermath of whatever attack Agneon just used. But when the memory didn't fade, she peeked over her arm.

A sea of dead bodies filled the clearing. Corpses littered the ground. Pools of silver blood soaked the grass. Some survivors moaned, but dread shot through Kara's gut. She doubted they would live.

She turned back to her grandfather, hatred boiling her blood. Instead of a gloating victor or the smug smile of satisfaction, she found him on his knees. His eyebrows twisted upward as he stared at the dissolving soldiers around him. The anger in his face faded. It was as if he had been possessed before and could only now understand what he had done.

He frowned and twisted his head to the left. Kara followed his gaze. Niccoli stood on the edge of the field a hundred feet away. The ancient isen crossed his arms and grinned.

Agneon sighed, stood, and sheathed his sword. He reached into the collar of his shirt and pulled out the medallion—the one Kara had touched—and kissed it.

"I'm sorry, Miriam," he whispered.

Kara's throat tightened. The office returned once more, its cold gray a relief from the endless death she just witnessed. She leaned forward in the chair and hugged her knees. Deep breaths filled her lungs, but spots lined her vision. If she didn't settle her breathing, she would vomit. What a disgusting vision. She rubbed her face as her heart rate settled. There had been so much blood. She eyed the dagger. If a medallion housed a memory filled with so much death, what kind of memory would an actual weapon hold?

She swallowed hard and hesitated, but she'd come this far. Judging by the memories from the first floor, Agneon's life contained as much good as it did evil. This was her curse, now, and she had to learn to control it. With a deep breath, she reached for the dagger. If it meant she could learn to control her power, she would force herself to see every memory in this house.

More glitter sprang forward and spiraled around her, painting a completely new world in shades of brown and green. A wooden bar counter appeared before her, and a stool sprang upward to give her a seat. Oak barrels the size of horses rose from the floor behind the bar. Other stools blipped into view up and down the room. People filled them. Chatter rippled through the room as framed paintings popped into the memory along the walls.

Agneon walked behind her and sat in the seat to her right. A brunette in a tight green dress smiled at him, and he grinned in return. His eyes never left her face, though her shirt hung low enough to entice the imagination. Kara couldn't quite figure if this woman was human or Hillsidian.

"What can I get you, honey?" she asked.

"Whatever's good," he answered.

She nodded and walked toward one of the oak barrels behind the bar.

"Nice place, isn't it?" Agneon asked.

He turned toward Kara. Panic snaked through her chest. He couldn't possibly see her. After being ignored in every memory thus far, she couldn't possibly be able to interact with him. She didn't want to, not after watching him murder all those soldiers.

"I guess," someone said from beside her.

She sighed with relief and spun to see her neighbor. His salt-and-pepper beard gave her a start. Of all people—Stone sat next to her, wrapped in a brown cloak as he nursed a silver mug.

Kara swiveled on her barstool and examined the men and women filling the pub's tables. Swords covered most surfaces. Half of the men had a scar of some sort across his face, but almost everyone wore a dark green tunic. Some laughed and pointed at each other. Others frowned and inched their fingers toward their belts, likely in search of weapons Kara couldn't see. This had to be an Ourean bar. The bartender stopped by and set Agneon's drink in front of him. She winked and walked off.

Agneon nodded to Stone. "What are you having, stranger? I'll have to try it next."

Kara furrowed an eyebrow. Stranger? Unless this was Agneon's poor attempt at humor, it had to be the memory of how he and Stone met.

Stone sighed. "I haven't smelled one of our kind in a while, boy, but we're hard to mistake. I know what you are, and I have a pretty good idea of why you're here. You might as well get to the point."

Agneon grinned and sipped his drink. "Works for me."

He reached into his shirt and set a familiar dagger on the counter. Its bright blue sheath and the brilliant gold of its hilt contrasted with the earthy undertones of the bar.

"I'm here to kill you," her grandfather said.

"You're not doing a very good job of it," Stone answered.

Agneon shrugged. "I don't really want to kill you. From what I've heard, you deserve nothing but respect. I mean, who escapes his master? How does someone like us even achieve such a thing? But Niccoli...well, he holds grudges."

Stone nodded. "That he does."

Agneon frowned, and his grip on the beer tightened. "How did you do it? Escape, I mean."

"And why should I tell you?"

"What have you got to lose?"

"I fail to see what I have to gain from it, either."

Agneon leaned over his drink. "There's nothing for you to gain. I just don't want to kill anymore. I despise what I've become. I want a way out, but I can't kill myself. I have a family. There's no way out for me unless you tell me what to do."

Stone didn't look up. He swirled his mug.

Agneon sighed. "I should kill you and get it over with."

"I doubt you would get very far."

"You don't know what I can do, old man."

"Of course I do. I know who you are. I've heard the rumors. Many know your name, even if they don't survive a run-in with you. I'm surprised they let you in here."

"Me, too. I think everyone's too drunk to recognize me."

"Yet they could any minute. Do you have a death wish?"

Agneon hesitated. "I don't know."

Stone grinned. "I hear a yes."

"My wife is pregnant. I can't leave her."

The elder isen sighed. "Ours is not the best life for a family. I had an adopted son, once. I outlived him."

"I'm sorry to hear it."

"It's quite all right. We still talk sometimes."

Agneon glanced over to Stone, eyebrows furrowed in confusion. Kara laughed. Her mentor must have visited the Grimoire in the centuries before she found it. She doubted the Vagabond ever appeared for him, but Stone probably talked to the chained book anyway.

"You're a little odd, aren't you?" Agneon finally asked.

Stone grinned. "You speak your mind. I can admire that."

"Do you admire me enough to tell me how you escaped Niccoli?"

"I stole a drenowith's soul."

Agneon flinched, as if surprised asking a direct question had worked. "Wait, what?"

"That's how I broke my tie to Niccoli. I stole a drenowith's soul. He can't control you if you're stronger than him."

"And how did you steal a muse's soul?"

"The trick is to make it trust you."

"Well, ain't it that easy," Agneon said with a snort.

Stone shrugged. "You asked. I answered."

Agneon downed the last of his beer and scooted the mug closer to the bartender. "I still have to kill you, you know. An order's an order."

"It is."

"I'll do it next time."

Stone nodded and stood. "I can live with that agreement. But boy, watch out for your child. What we are is inherited, as is your—well, gift. If your kid has power even remotely like yours, Niccoli will want your child same as he wants you. He will want your children more than he wants anyone else, and he'll turn everything you love into leverage if he has to."

The smile faded from Agneon's face. "I know, old man."

The warm glow of the bar snapped away. The dark office returned. She leaned back in her chair and shook her head, a grin stuck to the corners of her mouth. Relief sent a rush of adrenaline straight down to her toes—at least it hadn't been a violent memory. She sighed.

Three memories down, and a whole second story to go.

�֙

After going through the memories in the office, Kara didn't even bother keeping track of time. At some point, the gray sunlight faded. Stone came in and handed her a lit candle in a lantern before returning to his place on the porch, all without saying a word.

Kara explored nearly every room—all except the one with the trail of dried blood coming from it. As a child, her mother slept beside Agneon's office, her bedroom complete with white wicker furniture and stuffed animals. The chamber next to

Ellen's was Miriam's personal space, filled with books and sewing materials. The room between that and the blood-soaked door was an armory.

The second story contained much darker memories than Kara prepared for. She witnessed Miriam cross-stitching while Agneon lay in her lap, confessing his recent murders. The woman had grimaced, but remained silent. Kara also pressed herself against the wall in yet another memory, when Agneon screamed at the top of his lungs in his armory, his anger boiling over after a recent battle. He'd killed families. Mothers. Children—even one who looked remarkably like Ellen. He'd come home and sent the girls on a picnic only minutes before he hurled an axe into the armory wall.

Memory after memory sprang forth from the various objects upstairs, each more hateful than the last. It seemed like they got worse as Kara moved toward the blood-stained door. She wondered if the blood had been left on purpose, to steer her toward the office first. But now, Kara stood before the last door, her lantern's candlelight casting flickers on the paneled wood. Part of her didn't trust herself with a candle after her episode in her own study, but it wasn't as if she had a flashlight. She could probably make one of those explode, too.

Her grip on the lantern's handle tightened. She steadied herself with a deep breath and straightened her back.

Here goes nothing.

She reached for the polished handle, and a pang of relief shot through her that no blood managed to get on the doorknob. The door creaked open at her touch. The lantern's flickers swept into the darkness, bringing the shadows to life. A mirror on the opposite wall snatched the candlelight and shot it across the room. The corners of a dresser popped into view. Near its feet, a shattered vase and wilted flowers lay on the floor in a circle of carpet one shade darker than the rest. The posts of a bed appeared beside the broken vase, a white down comforter across the mattress. Though exhaustion tugged at Kara's eyes, she wouldn't dream of lying down in her grandparents' bed.

Carpet fibers muffled her footsteps as she walked in. She

peeked back at the smeared blood on the hallway wall and followed it inside. It wrapped around the doorframe and slid to the carpet. Halfway up the wall and shy of the smear was a bloodstain the size of a torso. Drip lines covered the stain, blurring its edges.

Kara's stomach clenched. She gasped and took a step back. The rug dipped, and she fell back into the wall behind her. She spread her arms to regain her balance.

Black soot marred the rug beneath her feet. Melted fibers formed an oval a quarter inch lower than the rest of the floor. Rays of burnt carpet stretched away from the burn spot like light glinting off a lake. Kara glanced back to the bloodstain and took a stunned step forward. Her foot landed in the middle of the burnt carpet. Gold dust sprang from under her feet.

She cursed and shuffled toward the bed. Despite everything she already witnessed, this had to be something she wouldn't want to see. She cringed as the dust enveloped her. It was too late to escape the memory now.

The room brightened—not only from the golden glow of Agneon's memory, but also from an influx of sunlight that didn't exist in Kara's time. Everything in her grandparents' old room reset itself. The flowers on the floor bloomed and jumped back into their vase. Droplets of water split away from the dark spot on the carpet and filled the pot, all before the vase returned to the dresser. The soot in the carpet dissolved. Wrinkles appeared in the bedspread, and a corner flipped back to reveal the sheets. A curtain opened, letting in more light.

Agneon appeared beside Kara, standing on the once-scorched carpet. He frowned and yelled at the wall near the bloodstain.

Miriam appeared as well, her frown just as deep as her husband's. Her red hair curled around her face, and she yelled right back. "Ellen will not become a tool!"

"You're not listening, woman!" Agneon shouted.

"I have done nothing but listen for fourteen years! I listened to your stories of how Niccoli shoved you into battle. I listened as you confessed to all those murders. How many thousands have you killed? Hundreds of thousands? It's effortless to you, and it will be effortless to Ellen when she's old enough to survive being awoken as an isen. Niccoli won't let her live a normal life. He will make her a slave, just like you!"

Agneon reeled back as if she had slapped him in the face. Kara bit her lip—that had been a low blow.

"You think I don't know that?" he asked.

Miriam grimaced. Tears poured from the corners of her eyes. "Of course you know that. But you don't care! We aren't safe here, Agneon! Niccoli is biding his time until Ellen is old enough to turn. He'll be unstoppable if he controls you both. Let me take her some place safe!"

Agneon tightened his fists. "Niccoli knows where you are, and that's the only thing keeping either of you safe. I know what he wants, and I have a plan to protect you both. But you have to be patient! Our family's safety depends on him keeping tabs on Ellen. On me. The moment either of us disappear, he will kill you!"

"I don't care. All I want is for Ellen to be safe."

"I don't have a choice, Miriam!" Agneon screamed.

Green light pulsed once along his skin, much like it did in the memory attached to the medallion where he'd killed so many Kirelm soldiers. It flickered over his arms like lightning, but Miriam didn't seem to notice his anger. She took a step closer.

"My parents will look after her. Niccoli doesn't know where I came from. When he tries to find us, he won't know where to look. My plan will work!"

"I have a plan, Miriam, but I need you to trust me."

"You've had eleven years. I think that's enough time. What's to stop Niccoli from turning her when she's fifteen? Twelve? What's to stop him from taking her now? I can't let my baby become a monster!"

Both Kara and Agneon flinched at the insult.

"JUST LISTEN!" Agneon roared.

The green light blurred again across his skin. It pulsed with renewed life. Static charged the air.

Kara reached out to stop him. He was losing control again, like he did with the tree house. But her hand sailed through his shoulder. She knew what was coming, and she could only watch.

Sparks blurred over his shoulders. Electricity arced across him, hugging his body as if he was a conductor. Miriam stood up straight, brows set and head high. She was no doubt ready for whatever came next. In the split second before all hell broke loose, Kara couldn't help but wonder if this was all a ploy. Miriam knew her husband would lose control. She knew he would feel guilt afterward and hide Ellen, just as she'd asked. But had Miriam truly known how far he would go?

Green light erupted in the small, white room. The glare blinded Kara, yet the blast itself sailed right through her. She covered her eyes. Glass crashed against something solid. Water splashed. A small scream escaped Miriam, but a thump cut her short. Something heavy hit the wall. Something else snapped.

The green pulse faded until only the brilliant sunlight filled the room. A gust of wind rocked the shutters. Kara peeked through her fingers. Agneon stood as he had, the carpet beneath his feet now burnt. He stared straight ahead, his mouth frozen open as he gaped in horror. He tried to form words, but only half-uttered whimpers escaped.

Miriam lay in a heap, still as a corpse. Red blood covered the wall behind her, so thick it dripped down the wallpaper.

A door creaked open. Someone in the hallway screamed. Kara glanced up in time to see Ellen—maybe ten or eleven—run back into the hallway. Ellen's scream snapped Agneon out of his shock. He ran to Miriam and lifted her head in his hands. Blood dripped through his fingers. Her neck bent too sharply away from her body. Her eyes never opened.

Agneon sobbed. His mouth opened again between his gasps for breath, but he never managed to say anything.

The gloom and candlelight of the present day snapped violently back into view, pulling Kara from the memory. She stood by the bed, one arm holding her side as she stared at the dried bloodstain. A tear rolled down her cheek, but she couldn't bring herself to wipe it away. The movement required too much effort. Horror crept over her body, freezing every muscle.

A ball caught in her throat, and she didn't resist. She curled against the bed post and pulled her knees to her chest. She let herself cry—for her grandmother, for her mother, and for the grandfather who only ever wanted to protect those he loved. She cried for his failure and for the fear that she would fail, too.

Kara wiped away the final tear sometime later. Tension she hadn't noticed before lifted from her shoulders, and she could breathe a little easier.

She pushed herself to her feet and headed to the porch. Even if there were other memories in the room, she didn't have the energy to see them. She saw everything she needed to witness.

Once downstairs, she opened the front door and stepped outside. The first rays of a sunrise peeked through the gaps in the ceiling. A fresh breeze tore through the cave, and she took a deep breath of the cool mountain air.

Stone sat on the first step, his arms crossed as he stared into the distance. She didn't bother following his gaze.

"You went in every room?" he asked.

Even though he couldn't see her, she just nodded.

"Do you know why he failed?" Stone continued.

Kara hesitated, her mind wandering over the various memories she endured. Sleep tugged at her eyes again, and she longed to curl up in her mother's old bed, stuffed animals and all.

"No," she finally admitted.

"It is my belief Agneon never trained his mind. He mastered his body, but he always assumed the magic would become easier to control with time. He was wrong. As his power grew, the wrist guard became useless. Especially in the beginning, he should have meditated more than he trained. He should have tried to understand the reason behind his power surges, rather than fight them. He never accepted what he was.

"But you have a chance to overcome, Kara. You can learn from his mistakes. This is why I wanted you to focus on controlling your magic enough to hit a target through stacked bricks. You need to control yourself. When you do, you will control your magic as well."

Kara nodded again. She sat beside him and hugged her knees. "I won't fight you anymore. I'll listen."

Stone nodded and let out a long sigh. "Thank you."

"Can I read that letter?" she asked.

Stone handed her the folded paper, even though she hadn't noticed it in his hand before. She must have been more tired than she realized.

When she touched the paper, the memory of the two men in the study flashed across her mind. Thankfully, though, the gold dust and full flashback stayed dormant. She took a deep breath and unfolded the parchment.

The first two lines had been crossed out, and a splotch of ink stained a corner of the page. This had to be the letter Agneon was writing in the memory.

Ellen—

Apologies can never undo what has been done. They are never good enough. I cannot make the world right. All I have ever done is destroy, and for that, I do not deserve this life any longer. But trust me when I say every moment of every day that has passed since the night we lost your mother has been filled with nothing but remorse.

You have a chance. You can be greater than me. And if you truly love those in your life, you will find a way to succeed where I failed.

If this letter finds another of my heirs instead of my daughter, then I am happy. It means Ellen loved and lived and escaped Ourea. So to my new heir, I wish you the luck I never had. You will need it.

—Papa

"History remembers the legend and forgets the man," Stone said.

"I guess he wasn't so evil after all." Kara rubbed her thumb against the paper.

Stone shrugged. "We're all a little evil."

Kara rubbed her eyes. She hardly wanted to get into a philosophical debate, so she changed the subject. "What happens now?"

"We return to the village. You need to hit the target before I'll let you go out in the world again."

She smiled through her tear-stained eyes. "Fair enough."

❧CHAPTER SEVEN

SURPRISES

With a groan, Braeden finally sank into the familiar armchair of his temporary office in Ayavel. His attempt to sway Evelyn into allowing Kara back into the council failed dismally. He wasn't even able to bring it up—he failed by simply implying the drenowith weren't inherently evil.

He surveyed the room, not quite willing to get back to his attack plans yet. Everything appeared as he'd left it: in complete and utter disarray. Piles of maps and charts littered his desk. Three floor-to-ceiling windows adorned the wall across from it. Light spilled through the open curtains, illuminating the once-organized library shelves along the far wall. The bookcases held tomes in all the wrong order, some stacked on each other instead of aligned neatly along the rows. To anyone else, this must have looked like chaos, but it all made sense to him. He could find anything in the mess. Not that anyone visited him.

Braeden sighed and leaned back in his chair, closing his eyes. Maybe he should regroup and head out on another reconnaissance mission to the Stele. As long as Kara remained in the village, he had nothing better to do but spy on his father.

Someone knocked on the door, the hesitant raps barely resonating through the wood. Braeden eyed the threshold, wary. No one even brought him food during his planning sessions, so he didn't know who this could be.

"Come in," he said.

The door inched open. Braeden tensed, not sure what to expect. But instead of a Blood or perhaps a maid, a slender Kirelm woman tucked in her only surviving wing and ducked into the room.

"Aurora?" Braeden asked.

She caught his eye and stiffened, her hand still on the door knob. "Am I still allowed to come in?"

"Absolutely not. I don't want to be anywhere near you. Why are you even here? I helped you escape from a Stelian prison, but you repaid me by knocking me into a mob of Stelian soldiers. You're not here because you enjoy my company."

She wrung her hands. "I know. I don't deserve a second of your time, but please, hear me out."

Braeden frowned. "You have thirty seconds."

"I betrayed you. I'm not proud of that. I was afraid. I know you didn't torture me. You didn't leave me with a stump of a wing. But to realize you were a Stelian terrified me. I couldn't think. I was still recovering from the torture. Just know that I'm sorry. All I can do is hope you forgive me."

He crossed his arms. "Stelian or not, I was saving you. Why betray the person who helped you escape? It's stupid."

Aurora glanced to the floor. "I thought it was a trap. I wasn't thinking straight. Father never told me political secrets, so I didn't have any information to give up during torture. But Blood Carden didn't believe me, and I was afraid he'd come up with some clever trick to get me to share information I didn't have to someone I trusted during the rescue. I'm sorry."

Braeden stared out the window, not wanting to look at her even as he'd already begun to forgive. He'd gotten soft if he could forgive her for nearly landing him in the prison from which he rescued her.

The princess took a step forward. "When I was in the Stele, I couldn't protect myself. I was completely vulnerable."

"Most people are when faced with Carden's hatred."

"That sounds like firsthand experience."

Braeden caught her eye but didn't say anything.

She nodded. "I don't ever want to feel helpless again, Braeden."

"I don't blame you."

"That's why I want you to train me. Please," she added.

Braeden laughed. "Train you?"

She frowned. "Don't laugh. I have every right to save myself if I need to."

"Then training is something your father should arrange, not me."

"He would never allow it. Heir or not, I'm just a woman. He wouldn't waste the effort."

"This really isn't my fight, Aurora."

"I have no one else to go to, Braeden. Please help me. I need to know how to defend myself."

"Ithone would be furious if he found out."

"That's why he can't know. Hopefully, I'll never have to fight, and this will just be our secret. But I can't ever be the victim again."

"Even soldiers can lose. Winning a match is all about your opponent's strength and your ability to match or outwit him."

"Maybe. But I need to have something to build on. At the very least, it will be a start."

Braeden sighed and rubbed his face. "I'll think about it. I want to talk to Gurien first."

"Absolutely not! He would tell Father in a heartbeat. You will never tell him about this, or anyone for that matter."

Braeden's eyes snapped toward the princess. "Don't ever speak to me like that again. I don't owe you anything. You have no right to give me orders, especially when you're asking for my help."

Aurora frowned, her eyes narrowing. "I apologize, but you don't need to go about asking permission."

"I trust the general a great deal more than I trust you, Heir. Don't forget it. And I'm not asking for permission. He's a friend, and he would understand the consequences of this training better than you."

She took a deep breath and headed to the door. "Very well. I cannot force you to teach me, Braeden. I appreciate your time, but I hope you'll sleep on it rather than talk to Gurien. He's a good man, but I don't want to risk him telling Father."

"He won't."

"I hope you're right."

The princess slipped into the hallway, and the door shut behind her with a click. Braeden rubbed his neck. What had he gotten himself into?

Braeden wandered Ayavel for about an hour, not really sure where to find Gurien. The Kirelm general rarely ventured far from Blood Ithone, so Braeden hadn't rushed to find him. He needed a plan to get Gurien alone, but so far he had no ideas.

After a while, he headed outside. The sun baked the summer air, and sweat clung to his shirt almost instantly. Just behind the palace, a cluster of roughly twenty Kirelms circled two soldiers in an impromptu sparring ring. The match reminded him of his days he spent in the Kirelm capital, disguised as one of them in an effort to protect Kara on her goodwill mission to meet with Blood Ithone. He sparred with Gurien then, back before they were friends—more importantly, before Gurien knew what he was.

Two Kirelms with white wings wrestled in the center of the ring, apparently forgoing magical attacks in favor of a physical competition. One of the men spun and pinned his opponent to the ground.

Gurien.

The general held his soldier to the grass, twisting the Kirelm's arms behind his back. The guard grunted, trying to wriggle free. After a minute of immobility, Gurien's victim hung his head and sighed.

"You win, General. Again," the man said.

Gurien laughed. "You'll beat me eventually."

"Not at this rate."

The soldiers lining the ring laughed and clapped. Gurien stood and helped the guard to his feet, catching Braeden's eye through gaps in the bodies.

"What can I do for you, Heir Drakonin?" he asked.

The Kirelms hushed and turned to face Braeden. Smiles faded into thin lines, and many stared at him. A few soldiers crossed their arms. Others stretched their wings as if tensing for a fight.

"Enough of that!" Gurien snapped.

Most of the soldiers relaxed their shoulders or stepped back to give Braeden space, but none of them smiled again. Braeden had been welcomed as a brother back in Kirelm when he was disguised, and no one knew who he really was. But now, only Gurien showed him any real kindness.

"Break off into pairs," Gurien ordered.

The Kirelms rushed to obey, dividing into groups of two and assuming fighting stances. Some began their sparring right away, while others eyed the newcomer as they circled their opponents.

"Warm welcome," Braeden muttered when Gurien joined him.

The general shrugged and lowered his voice. "Sorry about that. They're having trouble seeing you as more than a Stelian. Don't worry. Once they see you in battle, they'll respect you again. Most don't even know you and I dueled back in Kirelm. Doesn't seem right to mention it."

"Good choice."

"Do you need something?" the general asked.

"I do. Can we talk in private?"

"Of course. Follow me."

Gurien headed toward the nearby forest line with Braeden in tow. They crossed into the trees, stopping just under the canopy's shadow. A cool breeze tickled Braeden's neck. Relief shot through him as he escaped from the summer heat.

"We should be fine here as long as we keep our voices low," Gurien said.

"All right. I have to ask you about Aurora."

Gurien tensed. Desire flitted across his face at the mention of the princess. "Oh?"

Braeden laughed. "You're so transparent."

"Not really. It's obvious once you know."

"If you insist."

"So what about Heir Aurora?"

"She came to me earlier to ask for training. She wants to learn how to fight."

"What? Why?"

"I think you know why."

"Her wing?"

Braeden nodded. "More importantly, the time she spent in my father's torture chamber."

Gurien sighed and rubbed his face. "I would give anything to undo what happened to her."

"But you can't. That's why she wants to learn to fight—so it never happens again."

"Understandable."

Silence settled between them. Braeden took in the warm evening. Sunlight filtered through gaps in the forest as the sun made its descent.

"Why did she come to you?" Gurien finally asked.

"Desperation, I think. She says you're a good man, but she thinks you're too loyal to Ithone to help her."

Gurien laughed. "If she only knew."

"What do you mean?"

"I've been trying to convince Blood Ithone to instruct her for years. Woman or not, she will be our Blood. She needs to know how to fight and strategize."

"But if I train her, won't Ithone be angry?"

"Furious. He won't have it. So you'll have to be quiet about where and when you give lessons."

"You think this is a good idea, then?"

"Only if Blood Ithone never finds out. If he does, I'll have to pretend I have no idea what's going on. If he forces me to tell the truth, though, I'll lose everything. I'll lose my title, my position, and my betrothal to Aurora. I don't enter into this lightly."

"Understood. But what will he do if he finds out?"

Gurien shrugged. "He'll make your life hell, for one. He'll banish Aurora back to Kirelm. I don't think he would leave, though. He has too much riding on this alliance."

Braeden sighed. "I respect where Aurora is coming from, but I don't think teaching her to fight is worth the risk."

"Please do it."

"But you just—"

"I've wanted her to learn to fight for three years now. I didn't like the idea at first, but it just makes sense. I don't want her to have to wait until her father dies to have the freedom to protect herself. I'm afraid by then it will be too late."

Braeden frowned. "I don't even know where we could train in secret."

"While looking for any sort of sparring arena—which they don't seem to have—I found a clearing in the back of this forest, one that doesn't seem to be used at all. It's a trek, but you'll have privacy. You can have a real match without attracting attention. I'll keep an eye on Blood Ithone and try to keep him away from the area whenever you spar."

"Why don't you teach her, then?"

Gurien tensed his jaw. "Blood Ithone specifically forbade me from it. I can, however, teach her theory. That would give you time to continue planning your attack on the Stele without hindering her lessons."

Braeden took a deep breath and leaned against a tree. "You sure this is a good idea?"

"No, but she needs it. I would be forever grateful if you would teach her."

"It's what friends are for," Braeden said with a grin.

Gurien laughed. "I suppose you're right. If I can ever repay the favor, I will. Would you or your woman perhaps like to learn a bit about Kirelm techniques?"

"You don't have to worry about Kara. She's training already."

"I'm glad to hear that. How is she?"

Braeden crossed his arms and glanced into the forest. "Fine, I guess. She'll be safe as long as she stays away from this mess."

"I'm sorry for what happened to her in Ethos. I didn't find out about Blood Aislynn's plan until afterward."

"It's not like you would have done anything. We weren't friends yet at the time."

Gurien sighed. "I suppose not. I still feel guilty for implicating her. She's only a girl."

Braeden shook his head but kept his mouth shut. Powerful new magic had awoken within Kara. The woman he loved was so much more than an ordinary girl, and he sometimes wished it wasn't the case. He could handle a human, but an isen—he would have to be careful.

"I should get back to my men," Gurien said.

"All right. I'm still undecided as to whether or not I'll help Aurora. I think I need to sleep on it."

"That's reasonable. Find me when you've decided."

Braeden nodded, and the general jogged to his troops. They grinned when he approached, talking to him in low tones Braeden couldn't understand. He walked toward the palace, keeping within the treeline so as to remain unseen. After the welcome he'd just gotten from the Kirelms, he wanted some time alone.

His mind raced as he walked, thoughts blurring by too quickly for him to focus on any one in particular. At first, he mulled the risks and consequences of training Aurora. If Ithone found out, he would likely banish Aurora to their home city and might even attack Braeden out of spite. But for Gurien to ask him to do it anyway—Braeden sighed. He didn't have many friends, and he didn't want to let the general down. As long as he was careful, Ithone would never have to know.

Braeden walked into the castle and, after a while, came to a stop. He blinked himself out of his thoughts and glanced around. An archway stood before him, the thin stones around the entryway shaped to resemble book spines. A pair of wooden doors hung open beneath the arch, the room beyond littered with endless bookshelves.

The Ayavelian library had served him well in his hunt for information on the Stele. Few visited, which meant he could enjoy quiet without being banished to his tiny office. More importantly, the room held the knowledge of the entire Ayavelian race. Many secrets from the time of Ethos survived here.

Guilt tugged at the back of Braeden's mind. Right. He already stole an ancient journal from the library, even though no books were allowed to leave the room. He should probably copy and return it before Evelyn realized it had gone missing, though he doubted she would. He never once happened across her down here.

He entered the library and scanned the shelves without a subject in mind. The Legendary Creatures section caught his eye, so he turned down the aisle. He eyed the book titles from an author named Clehm Gaehr: *Flittered Fancy; Forgotten Drowng Legacies; Griffons of Kirelm; The Lost Creatures*. Braeden continued, discovering titles about everything from ice demons to flaers, large dog-like creatures that could walk through walls.

He turned a corner and scoured the shelf for a plaque describing its subject matter. His heart leapt into his chest when he found it.

The Drenowith.

He ran his eyes along the sparse titles. Though the entire shelf was dedicated to the drenowith, empty space filled most of the twelve-tier bookcase. Spider webs dotted the corners. A few lines sat in the dust on the shelves, evidence that at least a few interested souls had thumbed through a book or two from this section.

The remaining titles reminded Braeden of Aislynn's hatred for the drenowith race: *Drenowith Magic Gone Wrong; Immortal Truths of an Evil Race; Liars, Thieves*, and *Immortals*. Braeden couldn't help but wonder if Aislynn had cleared the shelves of all but the most negative titles. He stepped back to glance over the upper levels far above him, but found only empty space. He sighed. Waste of time.

A shadow in the topmost shelf caught his eye. He examined it, squinting into the top right corner. The tip of a book spine peeked over the high ledge. Its black cover nearly blended in with the dark wood, save for the one line of faded silver lettering.

Curious, Braeden borrowed a bit of the stale library air and threw it toward the volume, commanding the breeze in circles until the book shifted forward. Magic burned through his veins, warming his palms as he focused. Inch by inch, it crept toward the ledge as Braeden's magic swirled about. After a moment or two, it finally tumbled off the shelf in a flurry of dust. Braeden caught it by the spine.

He examined the front cover for a title. The faded cracks of silver lettering read, *Conversations with a Drenowith*.

Braeden grinned. This book must have somehow survived a purge of drenowith knowledge from the Ayavelian library. It helped that the book resembled the shadows in which it was hidden.

He tucked the tome under his arm and headed to his study. This was probably one book that would never make it back to the Ayavelian library.

⚜

Braeden didn't sleep much that night. Instead, he tore through the old book long after the rest of the castle had retired, examining every handwritten page with as much focus as he could muster in the early hours of the morning. Every word consumed him.

This journal was a recorded conversation between a

drenowith and an ancient yakona named Yori. Judging by the brittle pages and strange spelling of common words, the book had to be thousands of years old. How an Ayavelian managed to convince a drenowith to speak with him baffled Braeden, but their conversation kept him turning the pages.

Yori and the nameless drenowith—referred to only as "my friend"—discussed everything from the creation of drenowith to the magic behind lichgates. According to the drenowith, lichgates could not be created or destroyed. They could, however, be altered, but the drenowith refused to tell Yori how to do such a thing. He said yakona would discover the magic when they were ready. He did offer a clue: every lichgate had its own brand of magic, which had to be understood before any changes could be made. Braeden whistled under his breath, marveling at the drenowith's knowledge. Yes, yakona had eventually figured out how to lock lichgates and create specialized keys for those locks, but nothing further. How much more did they not know?

About halfway through, the book's conversation trailed to the origin of life in Ourea. Isen, yakona, and humans apparently all descended from a single ancestor who roamed the part of Earth now dominated by humans. Over time, some of those ancestors migrated to Ourea, where they evolved into yakona and isen. While the yakona remained in Ourea, isen chose to live in both worlds. Since then, most of the three species shared lineage was forgotten despite the fact they were more alike than any could believe.

Braeden hesitated, rereading this section of the conversation without registering the words. His thoughts raced ahead. If yakona and isen weren't that different, why could isen steal yakona and human souls but not fellow isen? Certain differences between species were inevitable, of course, but the magic of yakona and of isen were virtually identical. They even looked similar. Humans and isen could obviously have children, though he'd never heard of an isen falling in love with a yakona before him and Kara. Could an isen and a yakona bond the way yakona lovers did? Why not? Despite their differences, they apparently had as much in common.

He frowned. Every yakona was born with a lifeline wrapped around the right arm in a pattern resembling a tattoo. It allowed each to bond with another of the race. When bound to a soul mate, both lifelines would merge to create a new pattern on the right arm of each lover. Isen, however, didn't have the lifeline. Kara had never acquired any sort of tattoo on her arm after being awoken. It was entirely possible that lifelines evolved in only the yakona, but it might not matter. He and Kara could still be together. Considering their similarities, they might even be able to have a family.

Braeden sucked in a breath at the thought of children and sat back in his chair, not quite sure what to make of all this new information. He hesitated, not yet convinced yakona could bond with other creatures. For a moment, however, he let himself hope. Bonding was an ancient tradition held in the highest regard, especially for Bloods and their Heirs. An Heir born of a bonded couple always held more sway over his people. Since Braeden finally accepted his future as a Stelian Blood, he wanted Kara to share a bit of his culture with him.

Before Kara, his idea of success was keeping his head down and living his lie as Gavin's adopted brother. As long as no one discovered his Stelian bloodline, he was fine. But with her, he experienced the kind of laughter that made him happy to be alive. She affected him in a way he never thought he would know. Her love gave him the strength to escape mindless slavery to his father. Through her compassion, he finally realized the Stelian people weren't evil but simply reflected the moral fiber of the Blood who commanded them. After a lifetime of hating himself, he grew to accept his right to the Stelian throne. He finally believed he could rule the Stele.

He'd never wanted a woman as much as he wanted Kara, and he was prepared to spend forever with her if she wanted him as well.

Braeden stood and pulled aside the curtain covering his window. With no moon to illuminate the horizon, the dark sky stretched out forever. Pools of stars dotted the sky, the pinpricks of light offering him his only scenery through the window.

He wanted to know what Kara would think of bonding with him. Was it too soon? He certainly didn't want anyone else. They survived a horde of shadow demons together. Kara saved him from his father when Aurora betrayed him during their escape. Though his new life was filled with the disdain and hatred of his fellow yakona, Kara gave him the strength to keep going. To fight. To survive.

What he would give to go visit her. He needed a dose of the sanity and peace only she could give him. But he couldn't. He had to wait. When she'd mastered herself, she would find him. If he rushed her, he would be a distraction. It would unravel anything she had accomplished in her time with Stone.

He pressed his head against the cool windowpane and let out a long breath. The next time he had her alone, he would ask her what she thought of being with him forever. Hopefully the prospect of a lifetime with him wouldn't scare her away.

❧CHAPTER EIGHT

A NEW MASTER

Braeden awoke with his cheek on a desk. Sweat glued his shirt to his torso. His body slumped over the polished surface, back and legs contorted in an effort to make his chair comfortable.

He groaned.

Conversations with a Drenowith lay open on the table a few inches from his nose. He stretched and craned his neck until it cracked. Relief swam down his spine. He jumped to his feet and shook his limbs, trying to regain feeling in his fingers.

He'd read through the book once and started again, though he couldn't remember where he stopped. He must have dozed off mid-sentence. Though he'd spoken with drenowith often enough since meeting Kara, he never had the opportunity to ask them this much about the history of the world and the ways of magic. With the book, he had an edge on the other Bloods—including Carden. He smirked. The journal was like his own little Grimoire, albeit lacking the instant-answers and small zoo of creatures.

As much as he wanted to race to the village and steal Kara away to talk about what he'd learned, he couldn't. She needed to train, and he had a heaping pile of his own problems. Namely, the Kirelm princess with one wing and a vendetta.

Aurora. Braeden needed to decide whether or not he would teach her. And why should he? He didn't owe her anything. He had enough to do, what with planning the attack on the Stele and scouting its borders. It wasn't like he had spare time.

He grumbled. He could make time if he wanted. It wasn't healthy to live and breathe war. If anything, Aurora's training would be a good distraction from the constant planning and scouting missions. It might do him good. It wasn't like he had many friends, and the one Kirelm general he trusted was adamant for him to help her.

Braeden rubbed his face. He might as well instruct the Kirelm princess. He might gain an ally that could work in his favor down the road, and it would please Gurien. The three of them just had to be careful. If anyone else caught wind of this, Braeden would be a dead man.

He sighed and headed to his room. He needed a bath and some fresh air.

An hour later, Braeden ran into Gurien as the general left the main dining room. They walked together down another hall, both silent until the chatter of idle conversations dissolved into the distance.

It took a few minutes of walking until they found an empty hallway. They ambled along without direction. Braeden wondered if they could speak here, or if Evelyn had eyes everywhere. In Hillside, the castle seemed to speak to its royalty. Having a conversation in the castle was as good as sharing it with the Hillsidian Blood. Was it the same here in Ayavel?

The hair on the back of his neck stood on end, as if a dozen eyes watched the two of them walk through the corridor. He cleared his throat and suppressed a shudder.

"Have you decided?" Gurien eventually asked.

Braeden just nodded.

"And?"

"I'll do it."

Gurien smiled wide. "Thank you, my friend. I will get everything ready."

Braeden nodded, too nervous to return the smile. "When should we begin?"

"Tomorrow. I need time to prepare," Gurien replied, his tone neutral.

From his lack of detail, the general must have sensed the same discomfort scorching Braeden's nerves. Braeden glanced around, looking for the source of his anxiety, but could find only paintings and the occasional closed door. Light spilled in from the many windows, illuminating the hallway. Dust floated in the beams of sunlight, peaceful and still until the two men passed.

Someone had to tell Aurora about his decision, but he didn't know how to word the statement without being obvious. "Should I—?"

"Yes," Gurien replied.

Braeden nodded. Good enough. To distract whomever may or may not be listening to their conversation, he launched into a discussion about Gurien's lessons with his soldiers. He didn't really listen to himself talk, nor did he really hear Gurien's answers.

His mind raced ahead to his new mission: school an obstinate princess whom he didn't really like. He would push her. Whereas he admittedly went easy on Kara during her training, he would not be kind to the Kirelm princess. Aurora would have to prove herself, and he would test her dedication by seeing to it she bled.

꙰

That evening, Braeden found Aurora in the Ayavelian gardens under a cherry blossom tree. He whispered instructions regarding where to meet him the next day and told her to find trousers. She would eventually need to learn to fight in a gown, since that's what she always wore, but for now a dress would hinder movement. After he delivered his orders, she didn't answer. Instead, she nodded and bit her lip to hide the smile.

She wouldn't be smiling for long.

After Braeden fell asleep, he tossed and turned with nightmares of being discovered. In each dream, Ithone stumbled upon their sparring arena. The Kirelm Blood went into a rage and set the trees on fire, all before snapping Braeden's neck.

Braeden shot up in bed after the last nightmare. Unable to endure yet another, he went to his study and read through

Conversations with a Drenowith until the sun rose.

The day sped by. Braeden began work on his Stelian attack plan, but his quill seemed to write his thoughts for him. His hand swept over page after page of maps and battle notes, sketching troop movements and areas of risk without his knowledge. He'd memorized the maps, and his subconscious simply filled in the gaps after his last trip to the Stele.

He would have to go again, of course. Several times. Troop movements changed. New battlements could go up at any moment. He had to keep an eye on his father for fear the attack plans would unravel at the last minute. Only the element of surprise could win this final fight.

Braeden only ate once, around noon. His mind wandered, half of it focused on the maps while the other half lost itself to thoughts about where he would begin his lessons with Aurora.

Eventually, daylight faded into dusk. The last traces of sun trickled in through his windows, the burning light casting a red glow on his papers. He sat back and stared into the growing shadows of his study, not yet willing to light candles to keep working.

In an hour, he would have to go meet Aurora for the first time. By then, the arena would be ready. Gurien would distract Ithone, and Aurora would finally learn what it meant to be a Blood.

✣

Braeden leaned against a tree in the clearing Gurien mentioned those few days ago. He eyed the stars above to distract himself from the dead quiet, searching for the moon that wouldn't appear. A gray fire burned in the center of the clearing, surrounded by a circle of rocks he laid to keep the flame in check. Flickers of dull light cast shadows over the grass as the flames crackled.

Footsteps crunched dry leaves in the distance. Braeden sighed. The princess would have to learn stealth, too.

Aurora gasped and stumbled into the clearing. The familiar

gown was gone, replaced by a fitted shirt and brown pants. Her boots caught on a branch. She tripped. Her one wing shot out to help her balance, but the lack of a second wing to spread the weight sent her tumbling to the grass. She landed on her palms and cursed.

"How graceful," Braeden said.

Aurora scowled and pushed herself to her feet. "You could have helped me find this place. I trekked through a mile of—"

"You don't get help anymore. You will be absolutely and completely independent from now on. I'm not going to coddle you or be gentle. My primary duty is planning the attack on the Stele. You will always come second, even when we're out here. On nights when I'm scouting, you'll have to practice on your own."

"But what if I go with you? I can—"

He laughed. "Absolutely not. For starters, you can't even walk through this forest without everything in the trees knowing where you are. I'm not risking both our lives by bringing you along."

"But I can help!"

"Not in the Stele, you can't. The answer is no. Stay focused on this training or risk losing me completely."

She bit her lip and stared at the ground.

Braeden continued. "While we're out here, I will not refer to you by your title. In this clearing, you're a girl with a lot to learn. You will not ask for a hand to help you up when you fall. You will not complain. You will do exactly as I say the moment I tell you to do it. I am your master now, and you will obey me. Are we clear?"

Her jaw tensed, and she frowned. Her fists tightened. The remaining wing shifted closer to her body, the feathers rustling against her shirt.

"I do not repeat myself," Braeden snapped.

"We're clear," Aurora said.

"Good. Come here."

Aurora hesitated, but her boots eventually stomped toward him.

"Are you an elephant? Be quiet. Walk on the balls of your feet. Avoid twigs and anything capable of crunching underfoot."

She frowned but glanced down. Her eyes trailed the ground as she tiptoed toward him.

Braeden summoned a gray flame. It hovered over his palm, crackling. Aurora glanced up. Braeden cocked his arm to throw the fire. The princess's eyes went wide. She shifted, but overcompensated with her wing. She barely moved. He threw. The fire sailed into her shoulder and knocked her backward. She twisted around and landed on her stomach.

Aurora smacked the earth with her fist. "What was—?"

"Keep your eyes up and stay alert. Anything can happen at any time. You're not allowed to be caught off guard anymore. Nothing will surprise you by the time we're done."

Aurora sat up, a six-inch hole torn in her shirt sleeve. Her silver blood stained bits of the cloth and grass where she fell. Soot lined the hole's edges, but as she was a Blood, the skin had already repaired itself from Braeden's attack.

Her eyes narrowed. "Is this revenge for you? I can heal instantly, so you think you can burn me and beat me until—"

"We're going to spar. We're going to fight. You're going to get hurt. I thought it was obvious."

She frowned and pushed herself to her feet. She wobbled. Her wing shot out again, and she fell to her knees.

Braeden eyed the wing. "You need to regain your balance."

"Obviously."

"Resist the impulse to be a spoiled princess. We have to pretend we're equals in the palace, but don't be disrespectful if you want me to train you."

She took a deep breath and nodded. "I apologize."

"Forgiven. Stand."

She pushed herself to her feet. Again, she wobbled.

"Tuck your wing in," Braeden said.

She obeyed. Her stance evened.

"Good. You need to find a new center of gravity. Before, it probably sat right in your middle, here"—Braeden tapped his abdomen—"but now it's shifted to the left. You need to compensate."

Her wing pulled in close, so tight to her body only the tip appeared above her head. She stood with ease.

Braeden nodded. "A good start."

"What I would give for my wing back," she said under her breath.

"Don't waste time on wishes like that. Focus on the now. You're missing a wing. Deal with it. Accept it. Own it. Use it as a weapon. People will underestimate you and assume you have no balance. Lure them in with your perceived vulnerability and break them once they're close."

A smile spread across the princess's face. "Yes, Master."

Braeden suppressed a grin at her use of his new title. "Good. Let's get started."

He conjured a blade of air, careful to create a weak one. It would hurt enough to make a mark without killing her. He aimed and shot it at her leg within a second. His attack flew too quickly for Aurora to duck out of the way. The blade sliced through her pant leg and cut down to the bone. Silver blood spurted from the wound. She screamed and knelt.

As soon as the wound materialized, her body stitched itself back together. Muscle inched over the exposed bone. Skin stretched over the injury, covering it with a dome of silver flesh as she healed beneath it.

"A little warning would be nice!" Aurora yelled.

"You may not get warnings in a fight. Like I said, you must always be ready, even if your opponent lulls you into a sense of security. And besides, I did warn you. I said we should get started."

She grumbled under her breath. Her wing curled toward her

body, and she stood with ease. Braeden smiled. Aurora seemed to learn quickly. This might not be as difficult as he originally thought.

He shot a bolt of green lightning at her face. She twisted to the left and fell to the ground, out of the way. The bolt sailed into a tree. A sharp crack tore through the night. The trunk splintered. Branches swayed. Everything above his attack toppled into the clearing, leaves rustling as they fell. The tree landed beside Aurora with a *thump*.

She shot to her feet. Ice covered her hands. She raised her pointer fingers and pressed them together, aiming for Braeden. An icicle emerged from the tips of her fingers. Water dripped from the ice, already melting in the hot summer night. She smirked, and the shard of ice flew toward Braeden on her silent command. But as it sailed through the air, it curved and fell to the dirt five feet in front of him.

So Aurora knew a few techniques after all, however unimpressive they might be. Braeden grinned and conjured another bolt of lightning. Time to see what she could do.

He aimed again, too far to the right in an effort to trick her into the path of his next move. She ducked the zap, but he followed his first bolt with a second aimed right for her stomach. She flew backward and smacked against a tree trunk.

His least favorite memory of the princess flashed through his mind. Aurora elbowed him in the gut. He fell. A horde of Stelians grabbed his arms while she escaped, leaving him to rot. He relived that betrayal twice in the blink of an eye. Anger burned in his stomach. Hatred contorted his thoughts.

A flash of adrenaline shot through Braeden as he debated what to do to her next. His fists tightened. His mind raced. Fire burst to life in his palms. Magic coursed through his body like a second pulse. He savored the energy.

Why should he forgive Aurora for such a betrayal? She nearly sent him back to a lifetime of slavery to his father. Kara would have died if Braeden succumbed. He would have lost everything. He didn't want to forgive. He wanted blood. And out here, he could have it. Out here, she belonged to him.

His eyes narrowed. He smirked.

Aurora gasped. Her lips parted. For a moment, she didn't get back on her feet. She watched him. Her body shook, but she never once looked away.

Kill her.

A jolt of panic flooded his chest after the vile thought. He shook his head and cursed. The anger simmered in his gut, urging him to sink his blade through her throat. Instead, he rubbed his face and inched away. He forced himself to turn his back on her in an effort to calm down. His lungs sucked in a deep breath. His mind cleared.

He set his arm against a tree trunk for balance. His heart settled. The desire to kill simmered below the surface. He acknowledged it. It would always be there. His natural love of pain and fear would never go away, no matter how much he wanted it to disappear. His inner masochist would survive regardless of how much he loved Kara or his people or anything else. He was Stelian, after all. This hatred was a part of him, as much as he loathed it. He couldn't allow it to rule his life. He couldn't let it take over and make him do something he would regret.

When his pulse evened, he turned. Aurora stood by the fire pit, arms crossed.

"Let's try that again," Braeden said.

Braeden spent three hours in the clearing with Aurora. He expected a temper as hot as Kara's, but the princess remained focused. After her brush with Braeden's darker side, she didn't speak except to acknowledge him whenever he corrected her. She kept her wing in tight throughout most of the sparring and often repeated mistakes only once or twice. Silver blood stained most of her clothing by the end of their sparring session. Rips and holes covered a good deal of the fabric, but she didn't seem to care. Though Braeden attacked without reservation, he was careful to aim such that the princess could maintain her modesty.

Her years of doing as she was told and biting her tongue manifested in fierce determination. The princess had a focus even Braeden envied. She pushed through every drill, absorbing his criticism like a sponge. He taught her only a few techniques, but she promised to practice them in her time alone. Braeden had no doubt she would improve quickly.

Time sped by. Every day, Braeden planned his grand attack on the Stele. And every night he wasn't on a scouting trip, he trained Aurora in their clearing. She never again asked to join him on his trips, which he figured had something to do with his outburst. His anger seemed to scare her into submission. He had two similar incidents during those first few days, but he kept himself in check. The anger didn't own him, and he didn't want to kill her. He began to admire her dedication, though he didn't quite like her yet.

After one week, Aurora could finally dodge most of Braeden's simpler attacks. After two weeks, she could improvise during a fight. Her strategies weren't altogether clever, but Braeden had high hopes for her. After three weeks, the princess landed her first hit on Braeden's toe. It only nicked him, but he grinned with pride nonetheless. By week four, Aurora learned eight techniques and managed to burn the hem of Braeden's shirt twice.

Meanwhile, Braeden's Stelian scouting missions grew more interesting with every trip. Seven new guard towers emerged overnight in some pockets of the Stelian forests. Troops gathered in remote areas, away from the castle. Patrols along the main fortress walls waned, as if Carden was preparing for a fight at the far edges of his kingdom. Braeden tracked the movements in a journal, not quite sure what to make of the changes.

The attack plan itself came along nicely with his growing arsenal of information from his scouting trips. He often had to force himself to work, though, since the pull to outline new lessons for Aurora distracted him. He managed to balance his two projects well enough.

On occasion, Gurien and Aurora would sneak to Braeden's study and play chess or discuss war strategy while he studied his notes on the Stele. He could ignore them, but occasionally glanced up when a lull settled on the couple's conversation. He sometimes found Gurien admiring Aurora as she focused on her next chess move, but he once caught Aurora smiling at the general with a hint of desire in her eyes. Braeden tried not to look up again. He wished they could meet in some other room, but his was the only one from which the Bloods were banned.

Aurora's progress—and her attitude—improved every day. But throughout her lessons, Braeden's nightmares grew worse. He frequently dreamed of Ithone's hands around his neck. The forest burned behind the Blood, who glared at Braeden with cold hatred. And every night, the crack of his own neck breaking in the dream jolted Braeden awake.

❧CHAPTER NINE

A VOW

After Kara returned from her grandfather's abandoned home, it took her two weeks to master the brick wall. When she finally shot a fireball through the hole and hit the target on the other side, she ran a victory lap around the entire village before she came back to Stone for her next assignment. She figured she'd graduated to the next level of training. Instead, he made her tackle the wall again. And again.

With only a few exceptions, Kara succeeded every time.

Her success came once she discovered the trick to her patience: Braeden. When her temper rose, she imagined his smile. Her heart would settle, and she could focus after a few deep breaths. Considering the depth of Stone's training, Kara needed all the warm thoughts of Braeden she could muster. In the week after she conquered the bricks, Stone revealed an endless array of new exercises. Each tested her patience more than the last.

Every day, Kara woke up before the sun rose and went to bed long after everyone else. Flick always watched her lessons, but he and Stone were her only company. She barely interacted with her vagabonds. With her new regimen, she didn't have time to do more than train. And considering her grandfather's failures, she didn't mind sacrificing relaxation with friends if it meant she would learn control. She left the tasks of leadership and governing to Twin and the ghost of the first Vagabond, who made himself visible to the yakona in her village.

Instead of raising morale or welcoming new recruits, Kara withdrew to focus on Stone's training. In the solitude of their forest, she and her master ran drills, meditated, and explored the depths of Kara's magic. She tracked her mentor's movements blindfolded, chased squirrels, and even cooked her own meals with nothing but the flame in her hand. If she burnt the food, he forced her to eat it anyway. It only took a few days of crispy dinners before Kara figured out how to rein in the fire. After that, she had to cook Stone's meals, too. She still ate whatever she burned.

Stone also taught her to levitate solid objects by curving the air around them. Her first attempts on branches ended in splintered wood, as the force of her focus blew the timber to bits. But as she improved, she graduated to bricks, logs, and eventually liquids. The day she could levitate water without it dribbling all over the ground, Stone took a cup from the kitchen and set it at the top of the mountain. For several hours every morning, she had to carry a floating ball of water up the nearest mountain and drop it in the glass multiple times. If she had any surplus, she carried it back down to the well in the same manner.

No matter what Stone demanded of her, Kara never groaned. She never rolled her eyes. She obeyed and listened to everything he said. Witnessing her grandmother's murder had changed her. Seeing her mother's childhood gave her hope. To avoid becoming Agneon, Kara would do whatever it took to master herself, and Stone's endless lessons were her last resort.

※

After taking water to the cup at the top of the mountain for the four hundredth time, Kara collapsed under a tree near the clearing that had become her training ground. Stone stood just inside the treeline somewhere, but she couldn't lift her head to look for him.

Her body ached. Thanks to four weeks of solid training, her muscles screamed with every movement. It didn't matter that she only threw fireballs or cooked food; the focus necessary to control herself took as great a toll on her body as sparring.

"I'm impressed," Stone said.

Without looking his way, she gave him a thumbs up. She wasn't sure what impressed him, but all she really wanted was a bed.

The sun sank along the horizon and burned the sky beyond the village's mountain range. A crescent moon peeked through the clouds, as if waiting for the sun to disappear so it could truly shine. Eventually, Stone would have to let her go to sleep.

"I'm afraid I'm out of ideas," Stone said.

Kara glanced at Stone as he seated himself next to her. He crossed his legs and straightened his back, all without looking her in the eye.

She laughed. "You? Out of ways to torture me? Nonsense."

"I suppose I do have one more."

Kara forced herself upright. "Let's hear it."

"I am going to insult you, and you cannot say anything. You also won't be allowed to move or leave."

She narrowed her eyes. "What?"

Stone shrugged. "When your emotions run rampant, you lose control. All of these exercises taught you to control your magic, but they also taught you to temper your frustration. Yet you cannot rely on physical activity to distract you from the root problem—your temper."

"So you're going to try to get a rise out of me?"

"Yes. I'm quite good at insults, too."

"This will be interesting."

"Are you ready?"

"Guess so."

He sighed. "What a pathetic answer. Weeks of work, and you can't even commit to something as basic as the next task. Don't waste my time."

Kara bristled. She spent the last month working on his mindless tasks, so of course she could commit to this. A flash of anger shot through her stomach. Tension pulled on her shoulders, but she resisted the impulse to snap at him. This had to be the insult. He'd begun, and according to his rules, she couldn't respond or debate him.

He scanned her face. "But you are a waste of time, aren't you? It's in your blood. It's who you are. You don't learn. Look at your past. Your mother died because you couldn't help her in time. You killed your father with your own stupidity. It's your fault you're an orphan."

Kara stared at the ground. Her temper surged. A burst of electricity raced along her arm—vicious and free. She bit her cheek to keep from saying something she would regret.

This is just a test, she told herself.

Stone laughed. "Your life is rather pathetic when you think about it. I could make you do anything at any time. I could order you to burn this village to the ground if I wanted, like the way Niccoli commanded your grandfather. You're a slave, same as him. Did the obvious fact even cross your mind? You were an idiot to trust me back in Scotland. You should have run, but you followed me like a dog. And now I'm your master forever. You even led me back to the famed Vagabond's village. I have endless souls, here, powerful souls I can steal at the drop of a hat. It's a buffet. I could even make you join me. Would you like immortality, endless power? It's what we isen do best. In the long run, what good are your vagabonds to me alive?"

Electricity snaked along Kara's skin. Sparks popped by her ear. A green glow washed over the ground. She grabbed her knees and tightened her fingers until they bleached from the effort. Her breath all but stopped. Clumps of dirt shook at her feet.

The green glow became a mist. It crackled over her skin like transparent fire, blurring the freckles beneath it.

A jolt of panic broke through her anger. She sucked in a breath. Her heart skipped beats, and her fingers trembled. That same green light preceded every major disaster in Agneon's life. It even killed his wife. In that glow lived her family's curse, and if she let it free, it would kill everything nearby.

She squeezed her eyes shut. She wouldn't lose herself to the power. She would never become her grandfather. With a deep breath, she conjured Braeden's face in her mind. His olive skin and dark eyes snapped into focus. He broke into a smile the moment she visualized him. Her pulse slowed. A wind picked at his hair. His eyes softened. Her panic dissolved, as did the sting of Stone's insults.

Her mentor's voice continued, low and just out of reach. Kara didn't try to understand the words. She didn't want to.

"...and what do you think, child?" he asked.

Kara blinked herself back to reality. Stone squatted before her at eye level, his elbows resting on his knees.

She smirked. "I'm sorry. Did you say something?"

He smiled. "Not bad."

"Is my reward a bath and an early bedtime?"

Stone laughed. "I think you've earned that much."

She sat upright. "Really?"

"There's nothing else I can do for you, not in what time we have left. You should go back to your vagabonds and discuss strategy. You're not done, of course—you need to keep practicing on your own. But I do think our work together will give you a strong foundation on which to build."

"Thank you, Stone." Kara hugged him.

He grunted. "Please don't."

She nodded and pushed away, but couldn't keep a smile from spreading over her face. She'd done it. She could control herself, at least mostly. She could be the Vagabond again, which meant she could finally get back to Braeden.

"You're not done," Stone repeated. "But you should enjoy your evening. The real work starts tomorrow when you face your vagabonds again."

⁂

The next morning, a bird tapped on Kara's window. She groaned and shoved her face under a sheet. Last night, she promised herself she would get up with the sunrise and check in on Twin, but so far she'd spent the last three hours of daylight burrowing back under the covers. The world could wait five more minutes.

Whump!

She flinched. Something had definitely banged against her wall. Her eyes fluttered open. Her bedroom door bled into view, its edges blurry. She rubbed her face.

Bang!

The door rattled. The knob shook.

"I don't care!" someone shouted in the hall. A man.

"Let her sleep!" someone else yelled. A woman. Twin?

Kara pushed herself to her feet. Blood rushed from her head. White specks dotted her vision, and the room spun. She grabbed the bed post to brace herself, but as soon as the room came back into focus, she crossed to the door and swung it open.

Richard stood in the hallway, mud still stuck to his traveling boots. He had his back to the door, his full focus apparently on Twin. She stood close behind him, a green dress flattering her curves. She caught Kara's eye and frowned.

"You've gone and woken her up, Richard!" Twin said.

Richard twisted around and glanced Kara over. His brows furrowed, but Kara couldn't figure out if it was anger or worry.

"What on Earth is going on?" she asked.

Twin shook her head. "Richard just got back from giving those last Grimoires to our final recruits. I told him what happened with...you know..."

"You're an isen!" Richard shouted.

A flash of fear squeezed Kara's heart. She explained her isen nature with the other vagabonds when she first returned from her time at Stone's home. In the matter of a few hours, she told them everything about her grandfather, her new power, and her isen mentor. Some of them left because of what she was. Some yakona wouldn't fight for an isen, even if she was the legendary Vagabond.

She'd forgotten Richard wasn't there to hear the news. He *hunted* isen. Murdering soul suckers was what he did best.

Before Kara found Ourea, Richard taught Braeden how to be one of the best isen hunters in the world—Richard hated isen. He always cherished the legend of the Vagabond, but Kara doubted that would be enough to sway his hatred for what she'd become in his time away.

She straightened. Her hand tightened into a fist, but she didn't say anything.

He arched his back and sniffed the air, eyeing her the whole time. "You even smell like one. You really are an isen. I can't believe it."

"Is that a problem?" she asked. Sweat licked her palms.

His eyes softened. "But how...?"

Kara shook her head. "I didn't know, either. Only a few did, and they didn't tell me until it was too late."

"You didn't choose this?"

"I didn't want to turn, but I would have been forced into this life eventually. It happened the way it needed to. I'm an isen, Richard, but I'm still the Vagabond. That will never change."

He broke eye contact and rubbed his neck. Kara let him simmer. Interrupting him or rushing him would only push him away.

Richard turned to Twin. "Are you sure she's really her?"

The Hillsidian girl nodded. "She was tested before we let her back in the village."

Kara cringed and suppressed a shiver. The test wasn't something she wanted to relive.

"Will you stay?" Kara asked Richard.

"Does what she is really matter?" Twin added.

The retired king leaned against the wall and crossed his arms. "I've hunted isen all my life, so yes, this is important to me. But I know you, Kara. Your race doesn't define you. Deep down, I wanted to be sure. I had to know. I never imagined the Vagabond would be an isen. I was always told they were evil beasts with no souls of their own."

Kara flinched and glared down the hall.

Richard sighed. "But with all you've done, Kara, I couldn't possibly hate you simply for what you are. You're more than the horror stories. You're the Vagabond, and I trust you. Those who left were fools to go."

Relief pooled in Kara's shoulders. "Thank you, Richard."

He offered a thin smile in return. "Of course, my girl. We apparently have a lot to talk about. I brought you more vagabonds, and they're itching to meet with you. But before you go down to them, I have a few things for you."

Richard lifted a sack from the floor. With the anxious reunion, Kara must have overlooked it before.

Twin crossed her arms. "Can you be ready in an hour, Kara? Now that Richard's back, we need a plan. Fast."

Kara nodded. "Just let me get dressed. Richard, I can meet you in my office if—"

He laughed and slipped past her into the room. "Not necessary. This will only take a minute."

She caught Twin's eye and frowned. Once a king, always a king. Pushy man.

Twin smiled and shook her head. "I'll see you downstairs in a bit."

"Sounds good."

The Hillsidian turned back down the hallway and headed off toward the stairs. Kara shut the door, leaning against it as she examined the retired king. Richard stood with his back to the window. When he caught her eye, he smiled and tossed the bag on the bed. Metal clinked. Despite the smile, his eyes narrowed a bit more than they used to. His stance remained tight, shoulders tense and squared. He crossed his arms, but left his hand free— probably so he could grab the sword tied to his waist if need be.

"Are you nervous?" Kara asked.

His jaw tensed. "Old habits. You smell like an isen. It's intense."

"It's what I am."

"Does Braeden know?"

"Of course."

"How did he react?"

Kara smiled. "He tried to kill me at first. Thought I was Stone."

"Who?"

"My master."

Richard cleared his throat and eyed the floor with sudden interest.

She suppressed a groan. "If this is going to be a problem, we need to clear the air now."

"I'll be fine. I need time to adjust."

"Suit yourself. What's in the bag?"

"A few things you left in Ethos after the Gala unraveled. One of my Hillsidian friends grabbed them for you."

Kara untied the drawstring and peeked in. Light glinted off of silver. She pulled out a small box on clawed feet. Several other boxes sat at the bottom of the bag. Recognition tugged at her mind.

"Are these the presents I got at dinner during the Gala?" she asked.

Richard nodded. "I figured you would want them. Who knows? They may come in handy."

"Maybe." Kara set the silver box back into the bag. She would deal with the gifts later.

"I have to say, Vagabond, I'm impressed you let those vagabonds leave. A Blood would have had them killed."

She shrugged. "We're vagabonds. We value freedom. I don't feel I had much of a choice but to let them go."

"Well, at least they don't remember where we are. That's a plus."

Kara glanced up. A thread of worry pulsed in her chest. "What are you talking about?"

Richard frowned. "No one told you?"

"Told me what?" Frustration bubbled in Kara's stomach. He

didn't have to be so cryptic.

He sighed and sat on the edge of her bed. "Apparently, Remy rounded the deserting vagabonds up by the lichgate in what he claimed was an expedition to lead them safely back. Instead, he used some technique I've never heard of before. It knocked them unconscious and blurred their memories in such a way they won't remember where they've been or who they were with. It's a bit like the aftermath of a night of heavy drinking, only this mars the entire memory of the village. I'm pretty sure he and Twin dumped each of them near their respective villages afterward."

Kara grumbled. "When exactly were they going to say something?"

Richard shrugged. "It's my understanding you haven't exactly made yourself available, my girl. Remy tried to get your attention a few times but said you never gave him the time of day."

"He could have found me. I never flat-out ignore anyone."

"Perhaps not intentionally."

She thought back over the last few weeks, but her memories mostly involved training, burnt food, and sleep. Though—she sighed. Perhaps that wasn't true. On more than one occasion, she'd heard someone call her name as she focused on the brick wall or when she'd run away from Stone on her first day of training. She hadn't had the willpower to lose focus, so she'd carried on. During her training, she hadn't been there for her vagabonds at all.

"I guess I can't be angry," she said.

"You really can't. Remy was only protecting the village. He was looking after you and his fellow vagabonds. You gave all of us a second chance. We're free for the first time in our lives."

She nodded. "Well, I'm here now. I won't ignore anyone again."

Richard stood, set his hands on her shoulders, and smiled. "I meant what I said, earlier. Isen or not, you have done far too much good to be evil. Never forget it."

Kara's mind drifted to Agneon's cottage, to the memories of

him burning and destroying the family he always tried so hard to protect. She patted Richard's hand, and her eyes snapped back into focus.

She smiled. "That means more than you know."

"I'll let you get ready. We have a long road ahead of us."

He headed to the door, but Kara stayed by the bed. The door clicked shut as he left, a cold echo that shot through the room. Her training was over, and suddenly that seemed like the easy part. Until this war ended, she would not have a peaceful moment to herself.

It took a few minutes for Kara to throw on clean clothes and a pair of boots. She tied her hair in a ponytail and headed downstairs for some breakfast. If she had to spend the entire day making war plans and meeting with people, she might as well enjoy the morning sunshine and a good meal first.

A plate of fruit, some ham, and a few bread rolls later, Kara strolled through the village center. For the first time in a month, she could just relax and enjoy her new home.

She walked across the stones outlining the village center, her boots clacking on the rocks as she traveled. Her mansion stretched out behind her, its endless rooms and hallways already memorized. The first Vagabond's tomb loomed ahead, set perfectly apart from the main house. Smaller cottages lined the paved circle where she walked, each of them filled with bustling yakona. One Hillsidian woman set two loaves of steaming bread on a windowsill. Through the open door of the next cottage over, a Kirelm man hammered at the blade of a sword. His black wings twitched as he hammered, while rivers of sweat dripped along his silver arms.

Throughout the village center, about fifty vagabonds clumped in circles of three: two sparred while a third critiqued. Hillsidians ducked and swerved, living up to the stealth and speed for which their race was famous. Kirelms used their wings to outmaneuver their opponents, flapping them to throw other races off balance. Lossians bobbed their blue heads, dancing around blows with practiced grace. No Ayavelians stood among those sparring, though. Kara paused for a moment, suddenly uncertain as to whether Ayavelians could fight at all.

Light reflected off of something in her peripheral vision. She spun. Eight Ayavelians trotted down stairs in front of the Vagabond's tomb as the great stone door swung shut behind them. Sunlight flashed along their skin, shooting red and blue beams onto the grass nearby.

Kara smiled. Aislynn—the Ayavelian Blood—may have betrayed her, but that didn't make her people any less stunning to watch.

A short and slender Ayavelian among the group waved. The girl's white hair curled over her shoulders, giving her sharp chin an even more pronounced point. Kara waved back. The door to the Vagabond's tomb opened once again, and Richard slipped out into the sunshine. With a wave of his hand, he beckoned her over.

She took the last bite of her bread roll and ran toward the group. If Richard was giving them a tour, those had to be his latest—and final—recruits.

Sure enough, Grimoire pendants bled into view around their necks as Kara got closer. When she finally stopped in front of them, the group smiled almost in unison.

Richard patted her back. "In case you hadn't guessed, Kara, these are our last vagabonds. Every Grimoire pendant has now been filled, even those from the yakona who left when they found out...uh..."

"We don't care if you're an isen!" one of the Ayavelians shouted. The girl slipped to the front of the line and stood a full foot shorter than Kara. The Ayavelian's hair sat in a long braid down her back. Her smile stretched over her face.

Kara grinned. "I appreciate that. What's your name?"

"Rieve. It's an honor to meet you, Vagabond. I always dreamed I would!"

"My little sister's not the only one. Most of us have," another

Ayavelian said.

He elbowed Rieve and smiled, but quickly glanced back to Kara. He was about six feet tall, with broad shoulders. Rieve pushed him back and laughed.

"Well, make yourselves at home," Kara said.

Richard opened his mouth as if to add something, but shouts erupted across the field. A woman screamed, and someone else barked orders Kara couldn't quite make out. The sparring matches broke apart. Vagabonds ducked into cottages. Those who couldn't find shelter hovered along the edges of the nearby forest, waiting.

Everyone looked up at the sky.

Kara followed suit in time to see wings blip into view on the horizon. Something large and brown soared toward them at a speed too fast to track. In a matter of seconds, the blip became a dot the size of a dime.

Whatever this was, it knew exactly where they were.

A pang of fear raced through Kara, but she swallowed it. This was her home. She would kill anything that threatened it or her vagabonds.

"Spread out and stay at the edges of the clearing!" Richard yelled. He pushed the Ayavelians backward into the treeline.

But Kara stepped out onto the now-empty stone circle. The fingers of her left hand hovered over the wrist guard that kept her true nature at bay. She wouldn't take it off unless she absolutely had to.

Details appeared on the creature as it neared. Tufts of brown fur. Off-white fangs. Black eyes. A ten-foot wing span. Body shaped like a bullet. Clawed feet tucked under its hairy stomach. Whatever it was, this thing had evolved for speed.

The creature slowed as Kara stepped into its path. Its wings shoved the air aside, loosing a gale that ripped through her hair. Kara didn't flinch. She kept eye contact with it even as the creature uncurled its feet to land not ten feet away.

But as it began to land, the claws on its feet became boots.

The thin legs stretched and thickened into brown pants. A tremor raced through the wings. They shrank into arms. Hands. The beast's fangs retreated into a tanned face with copper hair.

Kara grinned as recognition buzzed in the back of her mind. "That was a tad dramatic, Garrett."

A corner of the muse's mouth curved into a smirk, and he crossed his arms in response.

She hadn't been able to resist the joke, but Kara didn't let herself relax. Last they met, Garrett left her chained in Aislynn's company after the Blood used her for bait to lure Adele—the love of Garrett's life—into a deadly trap. He saved the unconscious Adele and barely hesitated before he'd torn out of the cave and all but left Kara to die.

She couldn't blame him, not really. He wanted to protect what he loved, and Kara wasn't on that list. Guilt churned in her gut as Adele's screams flashed again in her mind. Aislynn wanted to drain every drop of blood out of the muse in an effort to steal her power. As far as Kara could tell, it hadn't worked. But the fact Adele wasn't with Garrett now could only mean something terrible happened.

He could very well be here for revenge—and if so, she wasn't sure if even she could stop him.

Kara stood as tall as she could, shoulders back. A muscle in the small of her back burned from the effort.

"What can I do for you, Garrett?" she asked.

"You've been awoken as an isen," he said without answering.

She nodded. "I guess you knew, too?"

"We did."

Kara's fists tightened. Of course they did. If Stone and the Vagabond had known, it only made sense the drenowith did as well. She wished someone had actually told her.

He nodded toward the edge of the field. "They can relax. I'm not here to cause trouble."

She narrowed her eyes. "You sure about that?"

"Quite. I simply wanted to tell you what happened to Adele."

Guilt ripped through Kara again. "How is she?"

Garrett shook his head. "Not well. She's in a crystal coffin, which uses ancient magic to heal. But she hasn't moved since I placed her there."

"I'm sorry," Kara said. It came out more as a whisper.

"I know. She only ever wanted you to be safe. You trusted the wrong people, but I forgive you."

Kara glanced around the field. Her vagabonds stood along the edges, each poised to attack. She wanted to tell them to relax, but she still wasn't quite sure they should.

"Can we talk in private?" Garrett asked.

Kara nodded. "Follow me."

She led him toward the mansion. They walked in silence, Garrett staring ahead the whole way. Kara glanced around, keeping an eye on the vagabonds nearby. She passed Demnug—Braeden's best friend and once a captain in the Hillsidian guard. He placed a hand on his sword hilt, but Kara shook her head. He tensed his jaw and took a step back.

When Kara reached the front door, she held it open for Garrett. He walked inside, and she gestured to the vagabonds to resume their daily lives. They inched into the field, all a little tense, but Richard shouted to get their attention. He began barking orders Kara could barely make out, and she left him to it.

The door shut silently behind her. She walked around Garrett and toward the stairs—she figured her office would be the best place to have a quiet conversation. Besides, the war room still had weapons lining every wall. Even though Garrett wouldn't need them if he wanted to kill her, she didn't want to give him any help. The muse followed without a word.

"Where is that girl?" someone demanded from around a bend in the hallway.

Stone rounded the corner and stopped in his tracks. His eyes skimmed right over Kara and locked on the drenowith standing in the hallway. He cursed.

"You," Garrett seethed.

Cold panic shot through Kara. She froze, uncertain of what to do. How could she be so stupid as to not think this one through? She had been distracted, but she should have sent someone to warn Stone about Garrett. Muses were slow to forgive, and Stone took the soul of Garrett's closest friend—someone he and Adele still missed.

"I'll kill you!" Garrett shouted.

Kara stood between him and her isen mentor. "You won't."

"What makes you so sure?" The muse scowled. White light pulsed through the gaps in his fist.

"Because this is my home, and you will respect what I say or leave."

"It's not like he could manage it anyway," Stone added.

Kara elbowed him in the gut. "You're not helping."

Smoke billowed from Garrett's clenched fists. "He's a murderer, Kara. Killing him will finally free Bailey's soul after a thousand years. I can finally let my friend die in peace. Why would you deny me that?"

"Stone awoke me, and he has helped me overcome much of what I am. Not only that, but he tutored the first Vagabond. He and I both owe Stone quite a lot."

Garrett's jaw tensed, and his frown deepened. "If we had known the first Vagabond had ties to Stone, we would never have helped him. We would have never helped you."

Kara flinched at the revelation. The muse walked away, his hands shaking as if he was doing his best to control the raging hatred within him.

Despite the lingering sting of Garrett's words, she couldn't let him go. If he left, Kara would lose her last tie to the drenowith. She would never know if Adele died or survived. She would forfeit a powerful ally who, despite leaving her in the cave with Aislynn, had protected her and guided her when she had nowhere else to go.

"Garrett, stop!" she shouted.

He hesitated in the hallway, fists still smoking. He didn't turn.

He didn't speak. But he paused, and Kara counted that as a small victory.

She took slow steps toward him and kept her voice steady. "The First Vagabond—Cedric—he stopped talking to Stone when he stole Bailey's soul. He hated Stone for it and blamed himself for the tragedy more than anyone else. Bailey's freedom isn't my fight, and I don't want to get in the middle of it. But I am asking you to please listen. I can only imagine what you're going through, seeing Stone now. You must feel as much guilt and anger as Cedric did, all because you couldn't help your friend."

The smoke in Garrett's hands thinned. The light dimmed.

Kara took a deep breath—that had been a good sign, but she wasn't out of this yet. "Do you remember when we first met? When you and Adele helped me escape Carden? Adele said I reminded her of someone she failed—and I get it, now. I thought she meant the first Vagabond, but she meant Bailey. I wish I'd known him, I do. But I won't. What's done is done, and we can't look back."

"But I can free him. I can let him move on by killing that conniving son of a—"

"Not in my house, you won't."

"Then get to the point, Kara," Garrett snapped.

She lifted her chin. "The point is that even though Bailey may have needed you back then, I need you now."

Garrett's shoulders drooped. The smoke in his hands fizzled out with a *hiss*. He sighed.

Kara inched around to see his face. He stared at the floor, water clinging to the edges of his eyes. He swallowed hard.

"I'll make you a deal," she said, her voice almost too quiet to hear.

He glanced up and caught her eye. His brows twisted upward, shoulders hunched in a sorrow which made her breath catch in her throat. But she had to fight through this. She had to compromise, even though she wasn't sure which side she was on.

She forced a smile. "If you don't kill Stone now, I won't stop you two from going at it when this whole war is over. You can duke it out then, winner takes all. And I won't begrudge the victor."

"Glad I was involved in that decision," Stone said with a grumble.

Kara resisted the impulse to give her mentor the bird. "Is it a deal, Garrett?"

"I never want to see that vile isen again. Are we clear?" he asked under his breath.

She sighed. "He'll be in the same meetings. We can minimize the time you spend near each other, but I can't promise you'll never see him."

Garrett rubbed his face. The air around his fingers sizzled.

Without looking away from Garrett, Kara waved at Stone to shoo him into another room. In her peripheral vision, the old isen rolled his eyes and walked back around the corner.

"So you'll stay?" Kara asked.

"For now."

"Do you still want to have our talk?"

Garrett laughed. "Indeed. I believe we have even more to discuss than before."

⚜

Kara didn't try to keep track of time while she and Garrett caught up. For an eternally young creature with forever ahead of him, he could certainly accomplish a lot in little over a month.

Five weeks had passed since Kara was shackled with poisoned chains and dangled as bait to lure Adele. Kara shuddered. Up until then, Aislynn played the perfect queen so well. She was polite, patient, and kind. Kara never saw the betrayal coming, and yet...

She sighed and rubbed her face. She didn't quite know how she would face the Bloods again. When she did, she would have to bring an army to make them listen. She would have to terrify them into respecting her. She could do it, of course. She just wasn't sure if that was a smart thing to do.

Despite the cheery sunlight streaming through her windows, Kara couldn't shake her guilt. Shame pooled in her gut as she told Garrett about what really happened the day Aislynn lured her to be bait for Adele. The truth of the matter was Aislynn hadn't been the only one to betray her. Gavin, Frine, and Ithone had agreed to duel for the right to control Kara because they knew they would lose her trust after they tried to kill Adele. The losers would to split whatever they found in her village.

If Garrett helped her, he would be helping those who had tried to kill Adele.

Once she told him everything, silence settled into the room. He stared at her, eyes crisp and focused, but he didn't say anything. Eventually, he turned toward a portrait by the door. Kara sat in her chair, elbows on her desk. A few sunbeams cast spotlights on bits of the hardwood floor. The room darkened now and again as a cloud passed by the sun, but the light still glinted off gold lettering on various books in her library.

Garrett continued to stare at the picture. With his back to her, she couldn't tell if he was lost in thought or studying the portrait.

"What are you thinking?" she asked.

"I'm trying to figure out who painted this," he answered.

"Shouldn't you be more concerned with the fact that none of the Bloods are trustworthy?"

"I already knew."

"But if you help them—"

"I'm not helping them."

Kara sat back in her chair and waited for him to elaborate. He would continue when he was ready.

He crossed his arms. "I'm helping you. I'm helping the future generations of Ourea. I'm sick of seeing all the blood and death. Ourea is my home. I want it to be great again."

Kara nodded and let out a shaky sigh of relief. She relaxed into her chair. Neither of them spoke for quite a while, and she didn't mind. It was nice to merely sit and think, even if those thoughts did take her constantly back to the night she nearly lost one of her only friends.

"Can I see Adele?" she finally asked.

He shook his head. "I never show anyone my home, not even you. It's the only way to keep it hidden."

She nodded. "I understand."

"Do you know who this is?" he asked, pointing to the portrait.

A tanned man with black hair smiled back at her from the painting, an air of mischief about him. Maybe it was the way he tilted his head, or the curve of his eyebrow. Kara couldn't tell. She imagined he would be the sort of person who always had a thrilling story, or who could make her laugh whenever she needed to smile.

"No," she admitted.

Garrett snorted. "Figures."

She frowned. "No need to be rude. Who is it?"

"Bailey."

Kara sat straighter. "Why wouldn't Stone or the first Vagabond tell me?"

Garrett shrugged. "Probably because you never asked."

She leaned back but didn't respond. In all fairness, she'd been a bit distracted to ask about pictures.

"Have you ever heard of the Broken Trinity?" Garrett asked.

"No."

"It's the only artifact I know of that can subdue a drenowith. It renders us immobile when used properly. Aislynn had one, and she knew exactly how to use it. It's how she forced a muse as powerful as Adele in—uh, into..."

He cleared his throat and closed his eyes.

Kara wanted to give him a hug but refrained. "It's okay. If you could talk about what Aislynn did to her without showing emotion, I would think you were heartless."

He let out a quiet laugh. "Thank you."

She nodded. "So Aislynn used this artifact called a Broken Trinity? How did she get it?"

Garrett gripped the edge of the nearest bookshelf. A crack shot into the wood. "The only remaining Broken Trinities were with Verum."

Kara gaped. "With the drenowith leaders? Verum gave her one?"

"I went to the Council to find out exactly that."

"And?"

Garrett shook his head. "Verum didn't have any clue as to what happened, but someone else in attendance did. Mirrow."

A chill raced through Kara at the muse's name. While most drenowith preferred a human form, Mirrow appeared as a minotaur when she first met him. He hadn't spoken much, but he looked ready to kill her at any moment. She couldn't imagine why, but everything about him seemed off. Wrong.

Garrett stared into the crack he'd made in her bookshelf. "Mirrow confessed to giving the Broken Trinity to a messenger. A general of Aislynn's...one named Krik, I believe. Mirrow somehow discovered Adele and I were still helping you."

"Murder and betrayal seems like a harsh punishment!"

"It was. But he has always been Verum's enforcer. He ensures we obey the mandates Verum makes. When we lost Bailey, everyone was devastated. In his grief, Verum warned us helping other Oureans would mean death. We all took it as a warning against meddling...but not Mirrow. To him, it was a decree. So when he saw Adele slip away to help you again and again, he took it upon himself to enforce what he thought was law. He had to think I would kill myself in my grief, thereby finishing his work for him."

Disgust crept through Kara's chest. Her stomach churned. "What did Verum say about this?"

"Killing another drenowith is punishable by death, yet Mirrow acted in an effort to preserve our kind's law and order. Verum saw the wrong in both arguments. So instead of punishing either me or Mirrow, he let us punish each other."

Garrett stared at his hands, but he didn't say anything more.

Kara leaned in. "What does that mean?"

"We dueled. I killed him."

Despite the gravity of such a statement, a pang of envy punched Kara in the stomach. A drenowith battle had to be an amazing thing to witness, and she missed it.

"I'm glad he's dead," she finally admitted.

Garrett shrugged. "Revenge has been around since the dawn of time. No one is the better for it."

"Are you saying you forgive Aislynn? Stone?"

"Never in a million years. I will someday free Bailey's soul from your shameless isen master. And if I'd had the chance, I would have killed the queen. She was a menace."

"Wait, 'was'?" Kara asked.

Garrett caught her eye. "Aislynn is dead. Evelyn is now the Ayavelian Blood. The news didn't make it here?"

Kara shook her head even as relief washed through her. Aislynn truly lost her mind. Kara wasn't even sure if there was any good left in the woman at all.

"I've been training," she said. "I figure I'll get a briefing on quite a bit of news at the meeting the other vagabonds later."

"I suspect so," Garrett agreed.

"Will you come? I meant what I said, Garrett. I need your help. To make the Bloods listen to me, I have to bring one hell of a show of force."

Garrett nodded. "Adele truly adores you, Kara. In her honor, I'll do whatever I can to help."

Kara breathed a sigh of relief. *Thank goodness.*

❧CHAPTER TEN

MISTAKES

Deep in the dark Ayavelian woods, Braeden tightened his fist and smirked. Smoke billowed from the fire pit of his makeshift sparring ring, its gray tendrils curling into the midnight sky. His gray flames cast trembling shadows on the circle of trees lining the clearing, but the darkness swallowed everything beyond the first few rows of trunks. Clouds blocked out the stars, though the moon's glow illuminated one patch of clouds with a white backlight.

Aurora whimpered. She sat beneath a tree, cradling her arm. Her hand hung limp by her side. Silver blood trickled from a fresh wound on her shoulder. He'd thrown a fireball at her, and she tried to block it with a blast of air. Instead of redirecting his attack, her actions fed the flames until the fireball scorched her down to the bone. He figured it was a mistake she wouldn't make again. Her wounds served as the best lesson.

For some reason, Braeden expected the princess to be more resilient. She picked up techniques fast enough, but her years of palace living seemed to soften her tolerance for pain. Here she was, sobbing in the middle of a sparring match. He grimaced.

Time to call it quits for the night.

He cocked his arm to prepare a finishing move. He wanted something strong enough to knock the wind out of her without actually killing her. Magic burned through his veins. Black smoke clung to his hand, shifting like a shadow in his palm. He aimed for her face. When it hit, the smoke would blind her for thirty seconds—likely enough to scare her into ending their sparring a little early. Braeden would allow it because he wanted a bath and a bed.

With a deep breath, he shot the flickering smoke at the one-winged princess. The shadow blurred, racing toward her. Aurora's frown shifted into a smirk. She reached for it with her fingers. The blue veins in her palm glowed white. The quiet forest sprang to life. A gale pummeled through the trees, ripping leaves out of the canopy. Branches bent toward her. Black strands of hair danced about her face. With a flick of her wrist, Aurora redirected the smoky haze. It circled her body and flew back toward Braeden.

Braeden laughed. Clever girl.

He reached toward the smoke. Tension pulled on his arms, but he dug his heels into the ground for support. The attack sailed forward, maybe a dozen feet away now. He snapped his fingers, and the attack dissolved midair.

"I don't believe you learned your redirection technique from me, Aurora," he said.

"I sneak away sometimes to watch Gurien's soldiers spar. I stole some of their tricks and practiced on my own."

"Smart."

Braeden conjured three bolts of lightning from the static in the air and shot each at Aurora. The princess gasped, apparently choking on a retort. She twisted away, but two bolts hit her square in the back. She sailed into the treeline. Her head rammed into a trunk. Bark split away from the wood under her forehead. She slumped to the ground, shoulders hunched. After a groan and a couple curses, she pushed herself up with one hand. Her arm shook under her weight. A puddle of silver blood streamed down her neck.

With a groan, Braeden crossed his arms. "Don't—"

"I know, I know. Focus on the fight. No conversation," she snapped.

Aurora wheeled around, eyes narrowed. Her shoulders tensed, and she dipped into a fighting stance. Her fists tightened. She frowned, and the hair around her face levitated. Braeden paused. If this was a new technique, he had no idea what it would do or how to counter.

White dots cropped up on her skin, as if ice filled every pore. They grew until frost covered every inch of her body. She stared at him, blind to everything but whatever she was about to do. The breeze stilled. Aurora's lip twitched into a dark smile.

Boom. The frost shot away from Aurora in an explosion of ice. Hundreds of ice daggers sailed in every direction. Dozens struck trees, the icicles embedding deep into the bark. Dozens more shot toward Braeden. Out of instinct, fire ignited in his palms and flew over his body. The black flames melted much of the ice as it struck him, but a few of the thicker particles sailed through his shield. One stabbed him in the gut.

He cursed and fell to one knee. The fires covering his body hissed as they faded into nothing. He yanked out the few icicles stuck in his body, but he remained still as his skin stitched itself back together. That hurt.

Adrenaline barreled through him. Every muscle tensed. The ancient desire to kill resurfaced, but he drowned it with pride. She'd never landed such a powerful hit before.

Time to see what else she could do.

He tensed and spun, grabbing the wind in one fluid motion. Blades of air cropped up around him—dozens of them. Pressure gathered on his fingers, and he used the resistance to aim. The first blade of air flew like an arrow. It shot clean through Aurora's shoulder. She screamed and knelt, one hand over the wound as she cursed.

Braeden released another and another. Blade after blade shot toward her. After the weeks they spent sparring, she could absolutely block them. The question was whether or not she had enough faith in herself to do so.

Aurora raised her hands and gritted her teeth. A rush of air sailed through the trees and flew past her, toward the attacks. The clatter of leaves clapping against each other drowned out Braeden's thoughts. Wind stung his eyes until he had to squint. If his blades hit anything, the gusts ruined his ability to tell.

The raging fire lighting their arena flickered and faded in the tempest. Imprints of the light flashed in Braeden's vision as he tried to adjust to the sudden darkness. He blinked, tensing. Aurora's storm still raged in the forest.

He reached to light another fire in the circle of rocks, but something sailed into his chest. He flew backward and landed hard against a tree. The air shot out of his lungs. Embers burned in the fire pit, their light too weak to illuminate the sparring arena.

A pair of boots snapped the dry grass. Braeden gasped for air. What hit him? Aurora could barely duck the blades in time. He doubted she could have followed up with another attack so quickly, unless this had that been yet another elaborate trick.

"Father, no!" Aurora screamed.

The fire pit blazed to life. Red flame crackled in the night. Ithone stood ten feet away, eyes locked on Braeden. The Blood's eyes narrowed, and his lip twisted into a sneer of disgust.

"How dare you attack my daughter, Stelian!" Ithone barked.

They'd been discovered. The last of Braeden's breath escaped him. He didn't know what he would say even if he could speak. His mind raced. How did Ithone find them? Gurien managed to keep Ithone away from the sparring arena for almost a month.

Braeden shot to his feet. Sure enough, Gurien stood just within the forest, watching with a grimace. He frowned and mouthed, *"I couldn't stop him."*

Thick frost spread over Ithone's arms. "I should have killed you back in that throne room when you were in chains. All Stelians are the same. Why would you lure an innocent girl out into the woods and try to kill her? She's done nothing to you!"

Braeden hesitated. "What?"

"Don't mock me!"

Ithone conjured a ball of ice in his palm and threw it at Braeden's head. Braeden ducked. A jolt of fear snaked through his chest as he put the pieces together. Ithone thought he was trying to kill Aurora. The Kirelm Blood didn't realize Aurora came on her on accord to learn and practice. This was all a misunderstanding.

Braeden showed his palms in an effort to calm the Kirelm. "No, I wasn't—"

Ithone cut him off with a barrage of ice. Clump after clump sailed through the air. Fire climbed over Braeden's arms and torso, but not quickly enough. Three balls of ice crashed into his chest. Frost crawled over his skin, searing whatever it touched with a subzero sting. He cursed. Fire erupted over his body. The ice melted away in a rush. He eyed Ithone through the flames, unwilling to let down his guard.

"Stop!" he shouted.

"Not until you're dead!" Ithone screamed.

Braeden's fingers tensed. Fingernails dug into his palms. Adrenaline pumped through every vein. gray fire ignited in every pore of his body and pulsed against his skin. Ithone wouldn't listen. Ithone wouldn't stop. Braeden would have to beat sense into the Blood or kill him trying, and it would take every ounce of his power to do so. But dying—that wasn't an option. Aurora might become Blood tonight, but Braeden wouldn't die here.

He let go of his Hillsidian form and shifted into his natural body: the towering Stelian. His skin darkened to that familiar charcoal gray. His arms and back bulged with muscle. His shirt stretched against his growing frame. The fire on his arms thickened. And as he shifted back into what he really was, the desire to kill the Kirelm Blood grew within him. With every second, this fight became less about survival and more about murder.

Ithone would kill him out of a misunderstanding. And where was Aurora? Braeden grit his teeth. Useless girl. Weak. Fickle. She hadn't even tried to help beyond a pathetic scream. She yet again proved herself to be utterly worthless. He just wasted a month risking his life for a princess who would abandon him the moment her father intervened.

The hatred within him doubled. The rage living deep within ignited. His charcoal skin faded until it was black as the night. The fires on his arms burned dark gray. He would end the whole Kirelm line tonight. Right here.

With a sneer, he called on the darkest part of his soul: his daru. Smoke hissed from the pores along his neck and arms. With a rumbling laugh, he gave himself over to the depths of his royal Stelian power. Heat welled in his gut. His chest burned. The hair on his arms prickled. Red and black flames coursed over his skin, fighting for dominance.

Usually, his daru needed to feed on the fear of those around him. But tonight, it fed off of him. His hatred. His anger. His disgust for the Bloods who would never accept him. His own fear that he would never be good enough.

His peripheral vision blurred. The edges faded to black, until he could see only Ithone. The Kirelm stood by the fire pit, wings stretched into the air. A glossy sheen spread across the Blood's skin like a thin sheet of water. His pupils dilated until they filled his eyes with nothing but black. Claws grew from the king's fingernails. This must have been Ithone's daru, but Braeden didn't care. He wouldn't lose to a giant bird.

He lunged for Ithone. The Blood swung a clawed hand. Braeden ducked and shot a fist into the king's jaw. It hit. Ithone cursed and staggered backward. Braeden followed up with a fireball to the gut, but Ithone twisted out of the way and returned with a chunk of ice aimed at Braeden's face.

They ducked and swung at each other in a fluid dance with no end. Braeden's hatred fueled him. He itched to rip Ithone's head off. He wanted to throw it at Aurora and laugh at her failure. He would decide what to do with her later.

He grabbed the Blood's neck with both hands and shot a burst of lightning into the Kirelm's body. Ithone twitched and reeled backward. The king staggered but stayed on his feet. He eyed Braeden, hesitating.

Braeden grinned. He'd just won.

A flame ignited in his palms and billowed into the sky. He pulled everything he had into a final attack—one large enough to end a Blood. A king who tried to kill him. A king who tried to enslave Kara. A terrible monarch who raised a weak daughter and didn't deserve to rule the kingdom he'd been given.

Braeden threw the fireball at the Blood. In a flash, a thick wave of ice formed over Ithone's body. The ice preserved the man's features, right down to his wide eyes. Fool. He couldn't hide from death behind a wall of ice.

The fireball hit. Ice shattered. Shards fell like glass to the ground.

Nothing remained of the Blood.

A foot dug into Braeden's spine. Pain splintered through his back, up into his neck and clean down to his ankles. Every nerve screamed. He sailed headfirst into a tree. Spots littered his vision. Panic cooled the adrenaline in his veins. He slumped on the ground. The flames on his arms receded.

He forced himself to look back, even though the world spun around him. Trees leaned to the right, their branches somehow on the ground with their roots in the air. The sky tipped. Bits of starlight blended with the spots in his vision. Ithone stood just feet from him, leaning a bit to the right but completely solid.

The ice wall had been a trick, just as Aurora had tricked him earlier.

Braeden tried to stand, but his legs gave out. He tried to push himself upright, but his arms wobbled. His body wasn't healing fast enough—either that, or the attack had crippled him enough to delay healing. He slumped to the grass. Ithone knelt and wrapped a hand around Braeden's neck.

"I should have done this long ago," the Blood said.

"Father, I said no!" Aurora screamed.

A blast of air shot Braeden back into the tree. Another wave of pain ricocheted through his body. He cursed and stifled a scream of agony. He couldn't move. He couldn't breathe. He lay there, body writhing as it tried to heal itself.

A shadow fell over his face. He opened his eyes. Aurora stood with her back to him. Ithone lay on the ground by the fire pit, apparently also knocked over by the gale. His eyes widened as he stared at his daughter. The firelight danced on her skin, illuminating the rips and blood stains from her earlier sparring. A gash in her boot exposed the shin beneath. Her hair hung loose around her head, the braid she wore into the arena long gone.

Ithone gaped. "How dare you—"

"Braeden didn't try to kill me—at least not tonight. You tried to murder my master, and I won't allow that. He taught me to fight, Father. You have no right to harm him."

Ithone's breath left him in a rush. "Your master? Has he brainwashed you?"

"Hardly. He taught me to protect myself. It's more than you ever did."

Ithone's eyebrows twisted upward. His lip twitched. "What are you?"

"An Heir. Finally."

Ithone shot to his feet. "What is this madness? What happened to the little girl I raised?"

Aurora's fists tightened. "She died in Carden's dungeon, Father."

The two Kirelms examined each other, Aurora tensed for a fight. Meanwhile, Braeden's body twitched and molded itself together. His vision cleared enough to spot Gurien a few dozen yards off, sword drawn. He bit his lip, eyes on Aurora.

A tremor slithered down Braeden's back. Something clicked into place along his spine. He sighed with relief, but guilt churned in his stomach just as quickly. He'd finally healed, but this fight wasn't over.

However silent Ithone was, Braeden and Aurora wouldn't spar again. Ithone would likely send the princess back to Kirelm, and he would give Braeden hell until the Blood finally died. And no matter how often Braeden told himself he'd done the right thing, he would always wonder if this was really worth it.

Ithone rubbed his face and walked into the forest without a word. Gurien hesitated but followed not long after.

Aurora knelt beside Braeden. "Are you all right?"

He nodded. "Keep your eye on your opponent."

"Father left. It's over. We're safe."

Braeden caught her eye. She had no idea how wrong she was.

Braeden slumped over his desk and groaned face-first into the polished surface. He cursed under his breath and hit his forehead once on the wood.

Idiot.

He didn't regret training Aurora. Judging from her attacks in that final fight, she learned more in these four weeks than she let on. She absorbed every word he said. No, he was proud of her. He regretted getting caught. He'd been careful to stay alert out there, but Ithone's stealth matched the greatest Hillsidian trackers. He doubted even Gavin would have heard the Blood coming.

Someone rapped against the door—two light knocks.

"Come in," Braeden said.

The door swung open. Gurien slipped in and quickly shut the door.

Braeden frowned. "You'll get in trouble for being here."

"Maybe, but I had to thank you before we leave."

"We?"

Gurien frowned. "We. Blood Ithone is forcing every Kirelm to leave."

Braeden shot to his feet. "Over a sparring match? He's insane!"

"He's furious. He won't listen to reason when he gets this emotional. He's even slipped into his daru a few times in the last half hour from a lack of control."

"That's ridiculous."

"I agree." Gurien rubbed his neck.

Braeden sank back in his chair. This wasn't supposed to happen. Worst case was Aurora getting sent back to Kirelm. Worst case was dealing with Ithone's insults afterward. Worst case wasn't supposed to mean losing a powerful ally altogether.

His shoulders slumped. He stared at the desk, words on the

tip of his tongue as he searched for what to say. He had to fix this. He had to do something. If he didn't, it would unravel a good chunk of what he and Kara had achieved thus far. The Bloods' alliance was a bit frail, but it had to be stronger than this.

Braeden caught his friend's eye. "What do I do, Gurien?"

"There's nothing to be done, I'm afraid. Blood Ithone has made up his mind."

The general scanned the closest shelf and grabbed a book. Candles on the desk cast shadows on its gold binding. Braeden couldn't read the title, but he hadn't pulled many books off the shelves. He didn't recognize it.

"What are you doing?" he asked.

"Hope you don't mind if I take this. I lied and told Blood Ithone I needed to fetch something from my room, so I can't return empty handed. I also can't stay any longer. I'm sorry, Braeden."

"Why are you apologizing? I'm the one who ruined everything."

"Nonsense. You trained Aurora. You taught her the basics, and now she's going to practice in every spare moment she can find. You got her started, and that's more than I could ever do. Thank you, my friend."

Braeden sighed. "Whatever you say, Gurien."

"This will blow over. Just wait. We'll see each other soon."

"I hope you're right."

Gurien smiled and slipped out into the hall. The door clicked behind him. The Kirelms would probably be gone before Evelyn even heard what had happened. She would likely meet them at the gate and urge Ithone to stop, but he wouldn't. It was too late. Braeden ruined everything even though he only wanted to help a princess protect herself.

He set his chin on the desk and tugged *Conversations with a Drenowith* close enough that he could read it from this angle. His eyes skimmed the words, but he didn't pay attention. His thoughts raced ahead to everything that would happen. Evelyn would call a meeting to yell at him until she went hoarse. The other Bloods would probably agree to something stupid in their anger. His life might be in danger, but he doubted it. They needed him to manage the attack on the Stele. He groaned—now he would have to rewrite his plans for that. Everything he designed thus far required Kirelms in the final wave. To simply omit a massive component of his army would render the plan useless.

Braeden eventually gave up on reading and closed his eyes, his cheek resting on the desk. His neck would ache when he woke, but he couldn't bring himself to go to his room. If he left, he risked meeting someone in the hall. He couldn't face anyone at the moment, not even a maid.

He needed to get out of Ayavel. He needed to find Kara and take a vacation. He needed to curl up next to her and confess everything. His resolve began to fray. Yes, she needed to train. Yes, she needed to focus. But with every second, his determination to give her space weakened.

His eyelids drooped. He willed them open, but they ignored him. His body relaxed against the desk, and his mind wandered. Perhaps he would just take a nap. When he woke up, he could decide whether or not he would stay.

He reached for his book and used it as a pillow. His arms folded around his face, burying him in the ripped folds of his shirt sleeves. Maybe this chaos would make sense in the morning.

❦CHAPTER ELEVEN

PLANNING

Three hours after Kara spoke with Garrett in her office, she sat at the head of the table in the war room. Garrett leaned against the wall, arms crossed as he glared at the floor. Stone sat at the end of the table, as far from the muse as possible. Despite the drenowith's earlier threat to kill her mentor if they ever saw each other again, Kara needed Stone's input on what to do next. Besides, it would have been impossible to make Stone wait outside.

A wooden table filled the room, its massive surface supported by a dozen matching legs with clawed feet. Seventeen chairs circled the table, each filled with a body. A few extra seats waited along the edge of the chamber, ready to be put to use. Swords, daggers, and a myriad of other weapons covered the walls, all of them remnants of Braeden's first visit to the Vagabond's treasury. His effort to preserve the blades and rescue them from the loose piles in which they were left turned the war room into an armory.

Sometime during her training, each race within her vagabonds apparently elected three representatives to lead them. Those twelve vagabonds served as her cabinet and would communicate any concerns expressed by the rest of the troops. Those twelve officials sat with Richard, Twin, and Demnug at the table, each with his or her head turned to Kara.

To her left sat the Kirelms—among them, the isen hunter, Remy. He stretched his black wings as he settled into his chair, and Kara suppressed a shudder. Though she understood his reasoning, she couldn't quite forgive him for the painful way he made her prove who she was when she'd first returned to the village. A shadow of the shattering pain rippled through her bones at the memory. It would take a while to warm up to him.

Beyond Remy sat the Ayavelians. Rieve—the Ayavelian Kara met earlier that day—settled in next to her brother, whose name turned out to be Zimmermann. Kara still hadn't caught the name of the third Ayavelian, nor the names of the three Lossians who clumped to her right.

When everyone sat down and settled in, Kara leaned forward.

"Let's start with the latest news. I heard Aislynn is dead. Is that true?" she asked.

Demnug nodded. "Some rumors say she and General Krik eloped, and something went wrong along the way. But more reliable sources say a drenowith killed her out of revenge for what she did to that muse in Ethos."

Garrett laughed. "If only I'd had the chance. Believe me, I did not kill her."

"Who do you think did?" Richard asked.

The muse shrugged. "I'm certain she had more than one enemy."

Kara sighed. "We need to find out how she died, even if we don't share that information with the other Bloods. But we have a new issue to deal with—Evelyn is Blood now. Because of the way the bloodline was transferred to her, Evelyn will rationalize in much the same way as Aislynn did. Aislynn's morality will essentially become Evelyn's conscience, and that's the real problem."

Stone told her that once. A bit of Aislynn lived on in her niece, and the thought sent cold dread through Kara's core and down to her toes.

Richard leaned back. "I didn't know."

Kara nodded. "The stone table Aislynn used to give Evelyn the bloodline and, uh"—she shot a quick glance at Garrett— "well, the point is, there's much about that table we don't know. The theory is it works like isen do, and a bit of Aislynn's soul was actually moved into Evelyn. Thus, we should see new similarities between them that didn't exist before the transfer."

Twin whistled. "A scary thought."

"Exactly," Kara said.

Zimmermann leaned over the table. "Everyone is still in Ayavel—all the Bloods. They meet regularly, even Heir Braeden."

Kara sat a little straighter at Braeden's name. Her gut twisted. Heat flashed in her cheeks. The sudden desire to drop this whole war business burned within her, but she suppressed it with a deep breath.

Garrett crossed his arms. "I can't help but wonder if it's dangerous for the other Bloods to be there. Evelyn will monitor everything in her kingdom. There will be no privacy. As long as her home is their safe house, she has almost complete control over the other Bloods."

Demnug shrugged. "Ethos isn't safe, as we learned from the Gala. The only safe places to meet are the kingdoms, which will always give one Blood dominance over the others. They probably stay because they don't fear her or think she's a threat."

"That's a mistake," Kara said.

"I agree," Garrett added.

A Lossian leaned forward. "Let's focus on what we need to do. We have to make ourselves known to them. Kara, the world thinks you disappeared. They don't know what you've become or where you are. A few rumors claim Heir Braeden hid you away from the world, and others say you're dead. You have to make yourself public again."

Kara's heart skipped a beat in fear, but the Lossian was right. She had to prove once and for all that the vagabonds could not be tamed. But to do that, the Bloods would have to respect her. They might even need to fear her a little.

She nodded. "I need to go to Ayavel and interrupt one of their meetings. I won't wait to be summoned, and I won't play by their rules. Not initially, at least."

Richard sighed. "There was a time when I would have

disagreed with you, but you're right. At least with your first impression, you have to make a statement. You have to show no fear. You have to demonstrate your new power."

"But should she tell them she's an isen?" Twin asked.

Remy hunched over the table, his wings casting a shadow along the wood. "I believe she should. She may not want to announce her relation to Agneon, but her isen nature would explain her increased ability to use magic. Besides, they will likely know what she is the moment she walks in the door. The isen scent is unmistakable."

Kara fidgeted in her seat. Everyone seemed to catch the mixed perfume of lilac and pine on her that clung to every isen, but she couldn't smell it. In fact, she began to wonder if she'd ever smelled it, even on Deidre.

"I don't think telling them she's an isen is enough," Demnug said.

"It's not," Kara agreed.

Richard crossed his arms. "We need to show you're not alone. I think we should tell them you've made more vagabonds."

"But not how many," Remy added.

"Right," Richard agreed. "Or if they press for a number, tell them far more than is true. What's more, I think it's time for the vagabonds to re-assimilate. Everyone should go back to their kingdoms. We'll hide in plain sight, ready and waiting for the moment we're needed."

"But how will we vagabonds communicate with the others in different kingdoms?" Zimmermann asked from the far end of the table.

Something clicked in the back of Kara's mind. She grinned. "Richard, when you added those maps of the kingdoms' lichgates to your Grimoire, they appeared in all the others, right? So what's stopping us from using pages in the Grimoire to communicate with each other? The books never run out of pages. And all we would have to do to see the most recent note is ask for it."

Remy nodded. "True. You could communicate with us at any

point. But just in case, we should assign vagabonds around you to communicate the message in case you're detained."

"I agree," she said.

Rieve piped up from beside her brother. "I heard vagabonds can't hear silent commands from their Bloods. Wouldn't it be an easy way to find us out?"

Kara leaned back in her chair. "I don't know."

Someone rested a cold hand on her shoulder. Ice drilled through her skin. She flinched and twisted in the chair, but the first Vagabond's ghost smiled down at her. Her heart settled, and she cursed under her breath. What an entrance.

"I can answer for you," the first Vagabond said.

Rieve's face lit up. Except for Garrett, who scowled at his feet, everyone's lips parted in awe. Even Remy smiled, and the grin leaked a happiness Kara had never before seen in the stone-faced yakona. Apparently, all of her vagabonds respected the legacy her mentor left behind.

But more importantly, they could see him, too.

The first Vagabond crossed his arms. "In my day, we fabricated a rumor to protect suspected vagabonds. We used our networks to circulate the lie claiming a vagabond couldn't hear a command from his Blood and was therefore easy to uncover. So when a vagabond was put to the test, they always passed. It kept them alive."

"Clever!" Richard said.

The first Vagabond grinned.

"So how many of us are there?" Kara asked.

"Ninety eight," Remy answered.

"Is there a way to make more, even if they don't have Grimoires?" Richard asked.

Kara glanced up to her mentor. He eyed her. No one spoke. The room quieted. Not even a chair leg scraped along the floor.

His voice echoed in her head, even though his lips didn't move. "Do you swear never to turn Braeden if I tell you this?"

She nodded. The time for that had come and gone. Braeden knew he would never become a vagabond.

"It's a complicated process, but I'm willing to teach a select few," the first Vagabond said.

Kara pointed toward Richard and Twin. "I think those who can't re-assimilate should be taught how to create vagabonds without the books."

"What do you mean?" Twin asked.

"Gavin knows I turned you. He knows you're a vagabond, and the fact that Richard disappeared at the same time suggests he is, too. Gavin will watch you both at every turn. I don't think you can go back."

Richard frowned. "You have a point."

She nodded. "But you can turn more vagabonds while the rest of us go back to the outside world."

"I'm not sure we should turn more vagabonds," Remy said.

Demnug grimaced. "There's not even a hundred of us. We can use all the help we can get."

Remy shrugged. "I suppose, but every new recruit is a risk our secrets will be leaked to those in power."

The first Vagabond joined in. "Remy has a point. The more you turn, the less control you have over who knows you exist. Anyone you turn should be chosen with utmost care. Not everyone is fit to be a vagabond. The public cannot know your names."

Kara set her elbows on the table. "So it's decided. I'll go to Ayavel and make it clear the vagabonds are not to be trifled with. I'll let them know there are more of us, but not how many. Richard and Twin will continue turning vagabonds while the rest re-assimilate. But that doesn't solve our real problem—making the Bloods listen. Even if they do respect me enough to let me help them end Carden, what happens after? The war will continue. They'll fight each other. We need a way to keep them from killing each other when they run out of common enemies to hate."

"Well put," the first Vagabond said.

"We could make them sign a treaty," one of the Lossians suggested.

Richard shook his head. "Treaties are easy to break. There's no one to enforce it but us, and we would run the risk of becoming yet another common enemy."

Rieve shrugged. "What if we asked them to open their kingdoms to the public? You know, stop hiding the entrances with lichgates and hidden locks?"

Twin nodded. "That would make everyone equally vulnerable. In a way, it would level the playing field."

Kara grinned. Excitement tickled her fingertips. "And on top of that, we could lock up their Sartori blades."

Everyone turned and stared at her.

She pressed her point. "Think about it. The Sartori blades are the only weapons that can kill a Blood. Because of the poison embedded in the sword itself, even a Blood can die from just a scratch. The only antidote must be made from the sword itself, even though I don't know quite how that works. They're the ultimate Blood-killing weapon. And if all of the Bloods put their Sartoris away in a vault—a vault none of them controlled—that would be a powerful sign of goodwill. That, coupled with opening their borders, would effectively make everyone equal. It would force a certain level of trust."

Richard laughed. "It's insane enough to work."

"Could we do it?" Demnug asked.

Kara shook her head and smiled, still pleased with the idea. "It's worth a shot."

"Where would the vault be?" Remy asked.

Stone grinned. "I believe I can be of use."

Kara nodded. "Any ideas?"

"A few. I would need to do some research, but you can leave this to me."

Garrett grimaced. Kara cleared her throat to remind him to play nice, but the muse grumbled under his breath.

Remy knocked once on the table. "We should leave soon."

"Agreed," Demnug said.

Kara leaned back. "Let's have one final dinner together. Tonight. That way, I can explain to everyone what's going to happen. Besides, it'll be fun. We won't get much more of that."

"Richard and I can organize it," Twin said.

Richard caught Kara's eye and frowned. "Are you ready for what you have to do?"

Kara nodded. "More than ever."

⁂

The final dinner sped by too quickly for Kara to fully appreciate it. She spent so long in her training that she never had the chance to truly appreciate her vagabonds. She couldn't even catch all their names before the night ended, but she would never forget those final moments in the village.

She danced with nearly everyone, which left her feet sore and often riddled with bruises thanks to the less skilled dancers. She laughed and joked with anyone who would tell her a story, and she shared a few of her own. Flick blipped into view every now and again, always darting off toward the next bit of bread or fruit anyone would share with him.

Fires blazed in the village center well into the early morning. At one point, Kara stared into the flames and lost herself to thought. She brainstormed about what kind of an entrance would make the Bloods fear her, and the glimmer of an idea began to reveal itself in the back of her mind. It involved fire—a lot of it. And it might not work. But as she began to doubt herself and scratch the idea, someone pulled her up to dance.

A little after two in the morning, Kara slipped into her bedroom and collapsed on the bed. She lay there with a smile on her face, all the while trying not to look at the open traveling sack by her dresser or think about what she should pack before she left.

Crack!

A furry tail brushed her ear, and an even furrier face nuzzled her cheek.

"Hey, Flick," she said.

She sat up and rubbed his head. He purred and leaned into her hand. With a yawn, he trotted to his pillow and curled up in a ball.

Someone knocked softly. She glanced up and waved her hand to open the door. It creaked open at her command, gentle as could be, and her smile widened. She could finally control her magic.

Twin leaned against the door frame and grinned, one hand holding her elbow. "It seems like we don't get to spend time together anymore."

Kara shrugged. "Silly things, wars. They take up so much time."

Twin laughed. "This will all be over soon."

"Hopefully."

"So have you thought about how you're going to make a powerful first impression on the Bloods?"

"A little."

"And?"

"It involves a lot of fire."

The Hillsidian smiled. "Wish I could see it. When do you leave?"

"At sunrise. I won't get much sleep, but I enjoyed myself. This was worth it."

"Are you excited to see Braeden?"

Kara grinned and closed her eyes. "You have no idea."

Twin laughed and sat next to her. She didn't respond, so Kara peeked at her friend. Twin stared at the ceiling, her smile slowly fading. Kara nudged the girl's side, but Twin grimaced.

"What's the matter?" Kara asked.

Twin stretched out on the bed. "I'm scared, Kara. For me. For you. For all of us. The world doesn't want us to exist because we broke the rules. We're free, and I think most yakona hate us out of jealousy. Everyone will fight us tooth and nail because we're different. I'm just...scared."

Kara nodded. "Me, too."

"Really?"

"Of course, Twin. I just try not to show it. I don't feel like I can be honest about that with most people. It's like you said all those months ago—people expect the Vagabond to be a hero. I have to act like one."

"You are a hero."

Kara smiled and nudged her friend. "Thanks, girl."

They lay back on the bed and stared at the ceiling. Kara closed her eyes and listened to the house. It creaked and whispered nonsense as a gust tore by outside. This was home. Ourea was home. And as tired as she was of fighting, she would kill to protect that.

❧CHAPTER TWELVE

REUNION

About two hours after sunrise, Braeden slipped out of his office and shut the door without a sound. The empty hallway stretched out to his left and right. He scratched the stubble growing along his chin, still blinking himself awake. He needed to shave, but he didn't have time.

He'd decided. He would pack what little he owned and leave for Kara's village. His stolen copy of *Conversations with a Drenowith* filled out his pocket, ready to be thrown in a bag. He had enough of the Bloods. He needed their armies to kill his father, but a break from their pettiness would do him well. He could recharge, and perhaps it wouldn't destroy Kara's focus to have him there after all. He would have to restrain himself from stealing her away from her training, but he could manage if she was nearby.

As long as he didn't encounter anyone along the way to his room, he should be able to get out of Ayavel without anyone noticing his absence until it was too late. He might encounter a road block on his way through the main lichgate, but he hadn't found another way to leave Ayavel. He could always lie and say he was going on another mission to the Stele. After all, he wasn't done scouting. No one had to know he was taking an extended detour. It might not be the most responsible choice to make, but even Braeden had limits to what he could endure.

He raced down the hallway and turned into another, his boots barely tapping on the stones as he hurried. He kept to the lesser-used halls, the ones he usually took to avoid maids and guards when he traveled from his room to his office and back.

He turned a corner. Evelyn stormed up the hallway, her gown billowing around her like a cloud. Braeden stopped in his tracks and cursed under his breath. Her eyebrows furrowed when they made eye contact.

"You idiot Heir," she spat.

He forced a laugh. "Now that isn't nice."

"Nice? I should burn you alive for what you did. You are the reason Blood Ithone abandoned us! We just lost the support of an entire race because of you!"

"Aurora deserved to learn to protect herself."

"That's not your call anymore than it's mine. It's her father's decision, and you undermined a Blood. A Blood, Braeden! You're just an Heir, and you made him look like a fool by defying not only a direct order but a cultural law. What did you think would happen?"

"Not this," Braeden admitted.

Evelyn grimaced. "If you can't foresee something like this, why should I trust you to lead the remaining armies into war? You're clearly incapable."

"And I suppose you would do a better job? You know the Stele that well?"

Evelyn tensed. Her lips parted for a second, though Braeden couldn't tell if it was shock or disgust. She reacted almost as if he'd backhanded her.

She tugged on the bodice of her gown and patted down a few stray strands of her hair. "I don't have to take such an attitude from you."

"I suppose not, yet here you are."

"I can't even look at you. I'll deal with you at the next council meeting. We meet in an hour."

"So good of you to invite me."

She sneered and brushed past him, her shoulder missing his arm by an inch. Deep down, she must have wanted to shove him like the child she was. He was amazed she hadn't.

Braeden slipped his hands in his pockets and sulked down

the hallway toward his room. He wouldn't be able to leave now, at least not unnoticed. The guards likely knew about the meeting before he did, just in case he tried to run. He had two choices: endure hours of royal bickering or fight his way out of the golden city. With the number of troops remaining in Ayavel, the latter would only land him in the dungeon again. Gavin would probably enjoy it.

With a groan, Braeden stopped at the door to his room. He leaned his forehead against the wood, wanting to leave but forced to stay. He might as well go practice a few new techniques in the meantime. He would be alone—no one wanted to spar with the city's only Stelian—but at least he could practice a bit and let off some steam.

He turned to leave, but the grate of wood on a hardwood floor stopped him in his tracks. A muffled curse followed from behind his door.

Someone was in his room.

He threw the door open and conjured a gray flame in his palm. He eyed the shadows, tensed for an attack. Only spies would break into his bedroom, and who knew what they wanted. Forget sparring—he could go for some torture. Maybe this would give him a bit more leverage on whichever Blood chose to spy on him.

A blond woman stood at the window, one hand on each of the reams of fabric serving as curtains. She pulled them open. Light poured in, blinding him. He blinked to clear his vision. The musk of lilacs and bark wafted past his nose. His stomach clenched in reflex at the familiar scent of an isen.

"Who—?" he asked.

"You know who it is. I'm not that stealthy," Kara said.

His eyes adjusted. Kara stood by the window, a smile lighting up her beautiful face. A few strands of golden hair fell into her eyes. Her skin was a shade or two darker than he remembered and covered in even more freckles, likely from outdoor training.

Braeden slammed the door behind him and crossed the floor in a few steps. He pulled her into his arms. She laughed and hugged him. He pressed his lips against hers and pushed her into the wall, not caring about welcomes or formalities. Gratitude flooded his gut. He sighed with relief and kissed her again.

She chuckled and ran a hand through his hair. "I missed you, too, Braeden."

He kissed her jaw. "Does anyone know you're here?"

"Nope. Flick and I took the back entrance."

"There's a back entrance?"

Flick squeaked. He stood on the bed, nothing but a walking ball of fur. His ears shot up in what Braeden figured was a welcome, and the little creature trotted toward the pillows. Kara shifted in Braeden's grip, readjusting her satchel.

He cradled her head in his hand. "I'm happy to see you, but what are you doing here? There's no telling what the Bloods will do when they see you."

"I know, but we're re-assimilating. All the vagabonds are going back to their kingdoms. I'm here to talk sense into the Bloods. And you, apparently. What was with the moody entrance? I heard you shuffling down the hallway."

He shook his head and nuzzled her neck. He didn't want to answer.

She leaned back a little. "Braeden, is something wrong?"

"The Bloods are still in charge. Of course something's wrong."

"Don't think like that. We'll work it out, whatever it is. When is the next time you all meet?"

He smiled and held her cheek in his palm. She grinned and ran a finger along his stubble. She was too forgiving. He didn't want a repeat of the last time she trusted these people. He couldn't let them put her in chains again or carve her up with a knife like the now-dead Aislynn did once already. He wouldn't risk it.

He kissed her jaw line and trailed toward her ear. "I'm not letting you back in one of those council meetings."

She laughed. "Be serious, Braeden. I have a lot to tell you before then. When is it?"

He leaned in until their noses touched. Her soft skin brushed his. Desire poured through him.

"Who said I was joking?" he said in a low tone.

Her breath caught in her throat. She grinned, but didn't reply. Her eyes darted toward his lips before she caught his eye again.

"Try to stop me," she said.

He laughed. "You don't think I could do it?"

She kissed his nose. "No."

He grabbed her around the waist and launched them both onto the bed. She squealed in surprise but quickly exploded into laughter. Braeden grabbed her wrists and pinned her to the comforter, but her smile melted away the serious frown he was trying to keep on his face. He couldn't help himself. He grinned and kissed her again.

"I let you do that," she said.

"Sure you did."

"Did so."

He kissed her ear. "Whatever you say."

She laughed. "Fine, you get that one. But I do need you to be serious for a second. Are we going to discuss our game plan, or do you need a demonstration of what I can do?"

"I like the demonstration option."

"Your call, but it would probably tear your bed apart."

Braeden's eyebrows shot upward. He laughed. "I'm game."

"That's not what I meant!" Kara's cheeks burned red.

"What the Bloods did you mean, then?" he asked.

Though he tightened his hold on her wrists, she twisted her shoulder and slipped out of his grip. She bolted upright, and Braeden suppressed a smirk. She apparently learned quite a lot in her training.

Her eyes shot to the floor. "It's just—I—that didn't come out right at all."

"No, but I really don't mind the option. Let's give it a shot."

She laughed again and smacked his shoulder. "I just meant I

don't have very good control. It's something I've been working on. There's a lot of power to manage now."

Braeden's smile faded. "How are you doing?"

"I'm all right. It was pretty bad in the beginning. I lit my desk on fire."

Braeden stifled a laugh. "I'm sorry, Kara."

She shrugged. "Stone fixed it somehow. He loves that desk."

"Where is he?"

"With Twin, Richard, and Garrett."

"I'm glad those two are well. But Garrett's back?"

"Yeah. Long story. He and Stone want to kill each other, so I'm keeping them apart. Stone's going to build—" Kara snapped her mouth closed and caught Braeden's eye.

He frowned. "Build what?"

"I'm not sure you'll like it."

He wrapped his hands around her waist. "Might as well tell me when I'm distracted, then."

She laughed and leaned in. "Tease."

"You like it."

"I do."

Braeden tensed at the words. With a rush of panic, he remembered the stolen journal and the question he'd been dying to ask her. Seeing her flushed every thought from his mind, but this was his chance. He could finally ask her if she would be his forever.

He opened his mouth to push the matter of whatever Stone was building, but the words died on his tongue. He wanted to ask her to be his forever right then, but a small voice in the back of his mind tugged on him to stop. Now wasn't the time. She had other things on her plate. She'd just spent over a month training. She was distracted with the upcoming council. He should wait.

Another, tinier voice mumbled something about the fear she would say no. He silenced it quickly.

"What have you been up to?" she asked.

"Trouble."

She laughed. "Which Blood did you piss off this time?"

"All of them, probably."

She whistled. "That takes skill, my love."

A flurry of nerves rushed through him like a blizzard. He might be a prince with a natural propensity for murder, but he could get used to his new pet name.

"What did you do?" she asked.

He sighed. This would take a while.

※

In the hour before the council meeting, Braeden managed to fill Kara in on most of what happened in her absence. He mentioned Aislynn's death and skimmed over the highlights of his training with Aurora. He explained everything from the princess's progress to his fight with her father's daru, though he left out the bits about wanting to murder the entire Kirelm race. He outlined his basic plans for the attack on the Stele and what he learned while scouting the kingdom's black forests.

Kara, in turn, filled him in on her training and time spent in her grandfather's cottage. She explained the vagabonds' plan and described Garrett's arrival. Braeden hoped he would get a chance to talk to Garrett at some point to find out who helped write his stolen journal.

Flick curled up on one of Braeden's pillows, purring in his sleep while Braeden and Kara settled on the bed. He wrapped his arms around her as he spoke, and she rested her head on his chest. He never wanted to let her go. If he had his way, he wouldn't. Considering Kara's new power, though, he wouldn't get his way much anymore.

Kara snuggled close. "I'm proud of you, you know."

"For what?"

"Helping Aurora. She needed someone to empower her and believe in her. I'm proud of how you forgave her and risked everything to help her even when she didn't deserve that kindness from you."

Braeden smiled. "Thank you."

She hummed into his neck. For a while, neither spoke. Braeden savored the tickle of her breath on his collarbone. Her pulse thumped along, amplified by her proximity. The impulse to flip her over and pin her to the mattress again burned through him like fire, but he restrained himself. He estimated they had about five or ten minutes before the council meeting began. As much as he would love to skip it, he couldn't risk the Bloods discovering Kara if they barged into his room to find out why he missed the meeting.

"What do you plan to say to the Bloods?" he asked.

"You'll see. All I need is a way in."

"There are these great things called doors."

She jabbed his side. He laughed and ran a hand through her hair.

Her finger trailed along his chest as she continued. "I need to make a show of force. Something to get their attention."

"Do I get to know what this show is?"

"It's a surprise. I think you'll like it."

He smiled. "Fine. So how are you getting in?"

"I want to teleport. I just need to know which room you're using."

"It's the row of windows above the throne room. It's hard to miss if you're outside."

Kara hummed again in what he assumed was acknowledgment. Braden glanced down to find her eyes out of focus as she stared across the room.

"I should go," she said.

He held her tighter. "It can wait a few more minutes."

She kissed his cheek. "Hopefully this will go well, and I'll get to stay. Then we can have some quiet time together without interruptions or strategy."

"You're not capable of having a conversation without

strategizing about something."

She laughed and rolled off the other side of the bed but didn't deny it. With a few tugs at her shirt, she straightened her clothes. Flick jumped onto her shoulder and purred.

She winked at Braeden. "See you soon, handsome."

Flick chirped. A loud *crack* broke through the room. Braeden flinched even though he'd expected the noise. When he opened his eyes, Kara was gone.

He sighed and pushed off the bed. He might as well head for the council meeting, too. His feet carried him to the meeting room as his thoughts wandered. This might not be a good idea. This might backfire. He should have probably stopped her and sent her back to the village, but he enjoyed her company too much to try. Besides, he couldn't convince her to go back if her vagabonds had re-assimilated. He cringed. Risky move on their part.

A few stairwells later, he arrived at the assembly room and pushed open the door. A twenty-person table filled the chamber, and windows lined three of the four walls. Evelyn and Gavin sat on opposite sides, with Frine leaning back in a chair a few seats down. No one seemed willing to sit near anyone else.

All three royals glared at him the moment he stepped in. The doors swung shut behind him, and he longed to head back to his room. Instead, he nodded in a forced welcome and took the seat closest to the exit.

Evelyn grimaced. "Where do I even begin?"

"Are you going to chide me like an old woman?" Braeden asked.

The Ayavelian's hands tightened into fists. "Don't be rude. I have every right to be furious. A Blood left our alliance because of your idiocy!"

"Then it wasn't a very strong alliance, was it?"

Gavin slammed a fist on the table. "You had no right!"

"I had every right to train the princess, as did Aurora have the right to learn. She lost a wing, Gavin. She's terrified of—"

"That's not your concern," Frine snapped.

Braeden tensed. "I may be Stelian, but I'm apparently not as heartless as you."

Frine, Evelyn, and Gavin all yelled various obscenities at once. They shouted over each other, none of their words making sense in the din. Braeden could only understand the anger and hatred in their voices. He leaned back and folded his arms against his chest.

These were Ourea's rulers. These idiots. Ridiculous.

A chill swept into the room. Braeden exhaled, and a plume of breath hung in the air. The cacophony of shouts faded, and each Blood eyed his or her breath as well. Evelyn shivered.

Red flames burst to life in a ten-foot high circle around the table. Fire licked the walls. Waves of heat swam through the air, distorting the windows beyond. Here and there, purple sparks leapt through the crackling fire as it reached for the ceiling.

A massive *crack* boomed through the air like thunder. Everyone flinched. Boots landed hard on the table. Kara appeared out of thin air, arms folded as she stared at Evelyn. A floral breeze swept by, laced with the sharp sting of pine leaves. Gavin cursed under his breath.

Flick pinned his ears against his head and bared his teeth from his perch on her shoulder before he scampered down her arm and into the satchel slung over her back. Kara's blond hair swept around her face in the hot breeze radiating off the fires. She glowered, silent and focused on the Ayavelian Blood. Flames darted around her like the seat of a throne.

Braeden leaned back in his chair. Desire burned in his gut and splintered down his legs. Talk about a show of force. She commanded the room. No one spoke. No one moved. All anyone could do was gape at her raw power and beauty. He'd never wanted anyone more in his life.

❧CHAPTER THIRTEEN

RESILIENCE

Kara hated the silence most. At the very least, she expected anger when the Bloods realized she'd come back. Snide remarks. Maybe even laughter. But silence—she suppressed a shudder. It reminded her too much of her first meeting with Blood Lorraine when Kara first discovered Ourea. It reminded her of how the generals had looked behind her, so certain she was nothing more than a clever joke. So certain she couldn't possibly be the all-powerful Vagabond meant to save them from themselves.

She snapped out of the memory and stood a little straighter. The table's surface creaked under her boots as she shifted her weight.

Fire crackled around them. The wall of flames blocked her view of the windows—of escape—but served her purpose well enough. None of the Bloods tried to put it out, at least not yet. Her theory had worked thus far. They didn't know how deep the flames went.

The room settled, as if no one wanted to break the hovering tension by speaking first. Each of the Bloods leaned back in their chairs, though Kara noticed Ithone's absence. Only Frine, Gavin, Braeden, and Evelyn sat at the massive table. Frine's wrinkled forehead became all the more prominent when compared to the young Bloods around him.

Evelyn stood, her chair stopping inches from the wall of flames. A bead of sweat rolled down the queen's temple—probably from the heat of the fire and not from nerves. She frowned and tapped her fingernails on the table.

"Welcome back," Evelyn finally said.

Kara forced a smile. "Why, thank you. I was hoping for a warm greeting."

She hadn't intended to make a pun. Her grin widened.

"We never expected to see you again," Gavin said.

"If things hadn't changed, you never would have," Kara admitted.

"What—?"

Kara let loose the barb in her palm. The purple thorn slid out and curved away from her hand. She examined it, the lingering traces of doubt dissolving in her stomach. Light glinted along the barb's surface.

The Bloods cursed in unison and jumped back. Evelyn pushed away, keeping her hands on the table as she inched toward the far end of the room. Gavin tripped over his chair as he stood, tossing it into the fire in his haste to get away. Smoke billowed upward as the wood burned. Frine sputtered, his chair falling backward as he, too, shot to his feet.

The flames burned brighter with their fear, as if the chaos fueled Kara's strength. She frowned and hoped not. Being feared shouldn't make her strong.

The Bloods cursed as they continue to shift away from her, surprise apparently stripping them of their senses. Only Braeden still sat in his chair, one hand barely hiding a smile as he eyed the melee.

"Quiet!" Kara yelled.

Gavin, Evelyn, and Frine hushed. They hovered along the far edge of the table closest to the door, trapped between her and a wall of fire.

Evelyn's eyes widened. She tensed. The queen barely moved, and it seemed as though she held her breath as well.

Gavin glowered at Kara as if she had betrayed him by being an isen. She wanted to laugh. For a king so fond of manipulating others, he played the part of wounded hero well.

But Frine—Kara paused. He watched her with one eyebrow twisted in a way that suggested curiosity. Maybe even a little awe. A flicker of hope burned in Kara's gut.

She took a deep breath to steady her nerves. This was the plan: make them respect her with a powerful show of force. They had to know the truth of what she could do, even if they didn't know she couldn't completely control it yet.

Kara caught Gavin's eye. "You all fear me. You think I want your power. Well, you're wrong. All I want—all I have ever wanted—is peace. You squabble. You bicker. And for what? You haven't gained anything for it. You aren't safe. Ithone's gone, Aislynn's dead—you're losing allies. You don't trust each other. You can barely get along.

"The yakona people deserve better than that. They are better than that. I've seen it firsthand. The first Vagabond left me Grimoires, tons of them, and I made a vagabond for each one. That's right. There are thousands more of us," she lied, the number inflated.

She plowed on, hoping they wouldn't call her bluff. "But again—I do not want your power. There are now vagabonds from every kingdom, and they help each other. They teach each other. They love their freedom because for the first time, they can fight for what they truly believe in. They can think freely, and they cherish that gift.

"But as I said, I do not want to overturn you. My vagabonds exist to help me bring peace, not to end your reign or take your power. I want your people to know freedom and safety. I want to see the yakona races work together and trust each other like my vagabonds do."

Kara's gaze shifted to Evelyn, and her throat tightened. "Just know that if you betray me—if you kill me or jail me—there will be another vagabond to take my place. And he or she may not have my same restraint. If you instead force me to take one of your bloodlines so you can control me, they will not hesitate to kill me if it means protecting each other."

Evelyn's jaw tensed, and she glared down at the floor. Frine grimaced, and even more wrinkles appeared in his forehead. Gavin rubbed his neck. Braeden watched her, though his eyes crinkled with concern. He knew the plan, but she figured he was worried this had taken it too far.

Kara steeled herself, but never once let her glare waver. This needed to happen. She tried diplomacy. She tried trust. Both failed her. The royals needed to know betraying her again would come at a cost.

She continued. "I don't trust the three of you, nor do I really think you're worthy of help. You're selfish and obsessed with your personal agendas. But I'm not here for you. I don't even like you. I'm here to protect Ourea and its people. You'd be wise to remember that. I'm here to protect your nations, who you have forgotten in your pettiness. I don't owe you anything, nor will I obey any of you.

"If you want my help, my power, and my allies, we must all work as a team. You will listen to me, and you will compromise. Whatever you decide, this is your last and final chance. If you want to defeat Carden, you need my help. But it comes with a price. I will help you end this war if you pledge to make Ourea peaceful afterward. No more bickering. No more wars. Ever."

"And how do you propose we comply?" Frine asked with a smirk.

"That's something we can discuss later," Kara answered.

They weren't ready to hear about giving up their Sartoris. At this point, she knew they wouldn't do it. She had to be careful with how she proposed that idea, and this was not the time.

Doors swung open and slammed against the wall just beyond the flames. Voices thundered through the wall of fire. Kara tensed. Unlike the Bloods, the guards had a better vantage point to estimate how thin the wall of fire really was. They could figure out a way through if she wasn't careful.

Without moving, Kara pushed the flames by the door outward to make her wall of fire thicker. Her knees shook at the sudden drain on her energy, but she steadied herself. She couldn't show weakness, even if the added flames did mean she had less energy to protect herself if the Bloods attacked from within the circle.

With every moment, her bluff grew weaker. She couldn't let the Bloods realize that.

"So are you going to steal our souls, then?" Evelyn asked.

Kara laughed. "I'll never steal a soul. Besides, I'm not sure you have one."

Braeden laughed.

"I don't trust isen," Gavin said.

Kara shrugged. "You don't trust anyone, so that doesn't mean much."

Gavin flinched, and Kara resisted the deep urge to smile.

Frine narrowed his eyes, his frown deepening. "Will you please step off the table and put out the fires? I would like to discuss this further without having to crane my neck, if you don't mind, and the heat is uncomfortable."

A jolt of panic raced through Kara, but she tensed to hide it. This was it—the moment she could lose her last shot at making them work with her. When she let the wall of flames dissolve, she would be vulnerable to whatever guards gathered in the hall. The Bloods could betray her, and betrayal meant she would likely have to choose between killing and being killed.

She eyed Frine without answering and backed toward the table's edge, moving as far away from the door as possible. Her fingers brushed Flick's tiny body through the fabric of her satchel. If the Bloods turned on her, she might be able to get out the same way she came in. Maybe.

The table's edge creaked under her foot, and she stopped to gain her balance. The fire crackled a few feet away. She snapped her fingers, and the wall of flames went out with a *hiss*. A black ring of soot lined the floor where the fires had been moments before. She took a step back and hopped off the table, her boots landing with the barest tap on the tiles.

Sure enough, Ayavelian guards filled the far end of the room, clogging the exit with rows of muscled soldiers. Sunlight glistened off of the iridescent skin not hidden by armor. Metal clinked as they shifted their weight, all of them staring at Kara with eyes that had three pupils. However beautiful Ayavelians were, she had to focus. She tore her gaze away.

She stood straighter, fists tightening. Sweat trickled down her arms.

Evelyn got to her feet and pointed at Kara, the fear apparently gone now that the queen had backup. "You don't get to make demands. Our time of listening to you is over, and—"

Frine sat down and scooted his chair toward the table, the scrape along the floor loud enough to cut Evelyn off.

"I, for one, would very much like to listen," he said.

Kara smiled—a tiny one that lasted only a second. In her peripheral vision, Braeden grinned as well.

"Would you like a seat, Vagabond?" Frine asked, gesturing to an empty chair in front of her at the head of the table.

No, she really didn't. She wanted to be ready to bolt in case anyone tried anything. Sitting would hinder her movement.

"I'd rather stand," she said.

Frine shrugged. "Very well."

"Don't be ridiculous. She should be in chains," Evelyn spat.

"You'll have to go through me first, woman. I want to hear what she has to say," Frine replied.

Evelyn's breath left her in a rush, but she didn't reply. The Ayavelian guards at the far end of the room glanced sideways at each other, apparently confused as to what was going on. Kara wasn't quite sure herself, for that matter, but was grateful for the table between her and those in the room. If the Bloods or soldiers tried anything, the table would hinder them enough that she could escape. Probably.

The queen drummed her fingers on the table yet again. "So, isen, tell us why we should listen to your little plan after you've already turned some of our people against us."

Kara laughed. "Many of the vagabonds found me. They despise the way the war is being handled. They see the way your agendas inhibit progress but had no way to let their voice be heard. I gave them a way."

"You gave yourself more power, you mean. You've made

yourself an army," Evelyn said.

"Hardly. All I did was give them freedom—those who joined me made that choice for themselves. I have no control over them. Don't twist this into something it's not."

"But you could turn all of our people into vagabonds," Frine pointed out.

"I do have that power, but you forgot about my caveat. I won't destroy you if you take care of your subjects and don't try to destroy my vagabonds. It's fairly simple."

Frine gestured toward her. "This new power of yours is dangerous, Kara."

She shrugged. "These are dangerous times."

"We need to focus," Gavin interrupted. "It doesn't matter if she has a few vagabonds. Kara, how do you propose we kill Carden?"

Kara shifted her gaze to the Hillsidian king, but he didn't look up from the table. He tilted his head ever so slightly, though, with his ear turned toward her. He was definitely listening.

"We need to hit Carden with everything we have. That means we have to work together and accept all the help we can get."

Evelyn glared at Braeden. "But we've lost Kirelm."

"I know," Kara said, hoping to draw the attention off of Braeden. He'd meant well. She didn't blame him for helping Aurora. For that matter, neither should the Bloods.

Gavin finally looked at her, and the annoyance in his glare froze her in place. "Vagabond, you seem to have acquired even more power in the time you were away. Why can't we send you in alone?"

The Hillsidian didn't know it, but Kara could. She could do as her grandfather had done all those years before and massacre everyone who crossed her path. She simply didn't want to. She still had so much to learn about control, and the level of power needed to kill Carden meant she would have to take off her wrist guard. She definitely wasn't ready to do that.

She shook her head. "The plan is to accept as many allies as possible. My vagabonds will be at the final attack against the Stele, but you won't know who they are. Meanwhile, I will go to Kirelm and ask Blood Ithone to come back. I also have a powerful isen who will support us in this war, as well as the help of a drenowith, who has opted to help us despite what Aislynn did."

Evelyn smacked the table. "I refuse to be associated with a drenowith!"

Kara narrowed her eyes. "And why is that?"

"You know what those vile creatures did to my aunt! They betrayed her! I would never—"

"Yet you don't care what she did to them. Or me," Kara interrupted.

Evelyn frowned. "Aunt Aislynn was trying to protect her people. Sometimes, safety comes at a cost."

Kara shook her head. "I saw into her memories. She hated muses, and what she did to Adele was her way of punishing them."

"Ladies, please. Focus," Frine said.

"Why would this muse ever fight for us after what we did?" Evelyn demanded.

Kara shrugged. "He isn't."

"What?"

"He isn't fighting for you. He's fighting for Ourea. For yakona. For everything that lives within a lichgate. He's tired of seeing so much blood over these last few millennia. Ourea was great once—all he wants is to see that again. To see peace. So no, he isn't fighting for you. He's fighting for the future generations who may not get a chance at happy lives if you keep on the way you're going."

A soft whistle escaped Frine, and the Lossian Blood tightened his jaw to kill what must have been an involuntary reaction. Braeden nodded, eyes focused on her and slightly narrowed in his concentration. Gavin rubbed his neck again.

Evelyn, still standing, leaned her fists on the table. Hatred radiated from her glare. "We will not work with the muses!"

"*You* will not," Frine said.

Evelyn turned her scowl on him. "What?"

"I corrected you. You said 'we,' but you are mistaken. I have no interest in turning away help, especially a powerful ally like a muse. After what we did, we should be grateful for his cooperation."

"Blood Frine has a point," Braeden said.

"I agree," Gavin added without looking up.

Evelyn sat in her chair, lips parted in what could only be surprise. Kara understood that—the queen had just been outvoted in her own home.

Frine turned to Kara. "For what it's worth, you're ready for this life. I never thought I would see the day when you could handle yourself, but I was wrong. You've become a powerful ally, one I fear we do not deserve."

Kara nodded in thanks, but the compliment didn't mean anything. There had been a time when she ached for him to say she was good enough, when hearing that would have made her proud, but she already knew she could handle this life. She was and would always be the Vagabond. She had sacrificed nearly everything to get here. What others thought of her no longer mattered.

Frine continued. "I'm afraid for my kingdom and for my people. This war needs to end, and I believe you can help us. I vote we allow Kara back into our council and give her full authority as our equal."

Gavin nodded, his voice soft when he spoke. "We need your help."

Braeden grinned. "I'm in."

Kara turned to Evelyn in time to see the queen's expression slide from disgust to disbelief. Just as quickly, her face hardened into something unreadable. She grimaced and shook her head.

"I suppose I have no choice," Evelyn said softly.

Gavin stood. "I need a break."

"Agreed," Frine added.

Braeden stood as well. "Why don't we reconvene after dinner?"

Gavin gestured in what Kara assumed was some sort of agreement before heading for the door. The Ayavelian soldiers parted enough to let the king through, and Frine followed close behind. Braeden stood and stretched.

"May I speak with you alone, Vagabond?" Evelyn asked.

Kara glanced at Braeden, who raised an eyebrow as if you say *are you sure?*

She nodded.

"Very well," he said.

He headed to the door but paused before he reached the crowd of guards. He glanced over his shoulder at Evelyn and nodded toward them. Evelyn groaned. She waved at the soldiers, who bowed in unison and trotted out ahead of Braeden. The prince walked into the hall and, with one final glance to Kara, shut the doors behind him.

Silence settled once more onto the meeting room. Evelyn drummed her nails against the table, the incessant *tap, tap, clack* enough to fray Kara's composure. A minute ticked by without conversation, followed by another and another. Kara bit her tongue, unwilling to break the silence. Whatever Evelyn wanted, she would have to make the first move.

"I don't understand what brought you back," Evelyn finally said.

"I think I've made that fairly clear."

"Hardly. Why are you really here? Revenge for being used as bait? Revenge for the half-wit muse who tried to rescue you? What is it?"

Anger burned in Kara's gut. Tension pulled on her wrist guard, and a body-wide itch smoldered on the top layer of her skin. But with a deep breath, she reeled in her disgust. As much as Kara wanted to break the queen's nose for that insult, she knew better. This was a trap. Evelyn wanted to bait her into a frenzy and make her do something stupid. So she forced a smile instead.

"I want to finish what the first Vagabond set out to do," she said.

"And that's why this muse is helping, too? They don't care about us."

"They care more than you'd think."

"A muse killed my aunt, and you know it. We shouldn't trust them."

"You have no proof of that. It's an assumption that could cost you the war."

"It may be something we can never prove. I know who is trustworthy and who isn't."

"I'm not so sure you do," Kara admitted.

With every second that passed, Evelyn seemed more and more like her treacherous aunt. Dread pooled in Kara's stomach at the similarities, namely the blind hatred for drenowith. Aislynn was only better at hiding her disgust.

Evelyn shook her head and set one hand on her cheek. Still as a stone and apparently lost in thought, she stared at the floor. Kara kept quiet, letting the young queen simmer on the options. Perhaps that was all she really needed to see reason—a quiet room and someone to listen.

"A choice between the lesser of two evils is not a real choice," Evelyn eventually said under her breath.

Kara's intuition flared—if trusting a muse was one choice, what was the other? Alarm spread through her body. The hair on her neck stood on end, and beads of sweat pooled in her palms.

"The muses aren't evil," Kara said.

Evelyn laughed—a bitter, dark laugh that sent a chill down to Kara's toes.

"I'll send a note to Blood Ithone asking for him to allow you into the city," Evelyn said.

With that, the queen stood and headed to the door, their meeting apparently over. But Kara didn't want her to leave, not now. Evelyn had made a choice, and fear twisted in Kara's stomach at the thought that the queen chose wrong.

Evelyn reached for the doorknob but paused and looked over her shoulder. "I would offer you a room, but I figure you'll be staying with Braeden. No use wasting a bedroom if you won't be there at night."

Kara bristled. "I would like my own room, thanks."

"Don't try to be modest." The queen smirked and turned the knob. She slipped into the hall and disappeared with just a few taps of her shoes along the stone floor.

Kara stood in the war room, alone and suddenly afraid that something just shifted for the worse.

❧CHAPTER FOURTEEN

TWO EVILS

Evelyn slammed the door to her bedroom. The walls trembled from the force. Her hands tightened into fists. Anger boiled in her gut, churning until bile burned her cheeks. An ache pulsed in her temple.

She failed. Aunt Aislynn always warned her about how the tides could turn quickly in war and political affairs, but Evelyn never imagined how fast she would lose control of the council. One stupid human girl—worse, an isen—showed a bit of daring, and now Evelyn's opinion meant nothing. Her family's years of goodwill toward the other kingdoms was overturned in one hasty decision.

One *stupid* decision.

Openly trusting a drenowith was as dense as Blood Gavin and Blood Frine could get. The vile muse helping Kara was likely the one who killed Evelyn's aunt, for Bloods' sake. Since the dawn of time, the muses had attempted magic that caused natural disasters and plagues, yet no one held them accountable. Not once. The drenowith certainly didn't care—what eternal creature cared about the fleeting lives of mortals?

This was the Vagabond's fault, all of it. From the moment the girl stepped into Ourea, the drenowith owned her. They must have known how important she would become, or else they would never have wasted their time saving and protecting her. And now, their effort was paying off.

Evelyn grimaced. She leaned against the wall in an effort to calm herself.

In her defense, she only recently realized the drenowith were burrowing their way into the minds of the Bloods. Even she hadn't noticed it at first, but it made perfect sense after she figured it out.

The yakona had caused political strife in Ourea for eons, and the drenowith were probably tired of it. Drenowith always hated the yakona—why else would they do something so petty as lead Aunt Aislynn into a Stelian trap she only barely survived? But when the Vagabond reappeared, the tide turned in the muses' favor. The naïve human girl was easy to control as long as they got to her first. As long as she trusted them. The drenowith had to have known the Vagabond would continue her master's purpose by trying to unite the yakona, and the prospect of luring all the Bloods into a sense of complacency had to be tempting. Those muses had to have known they could weasel their way into the thrones if they played their cards right.

And they did.

Evelyn ran her fingers through her hair. She escaped such a fate, at least. She wasn't a pawn. But the other Bloods—she sighed. A pang of guilt shot through her, followed by frustration. Not long ago she raised her fears to Bloods Ithone, Frine, and Gavin individually. Every one of them dismissed her. None feared the drenowith. Blood Frine even admired them. Idiot.

The other Bloods were beyond saving. They had done this to themselves.

Perhaps there was no way for the muses to have predicted Braeden and Kara would fall in love, but those conniving creatures no doubt played the romance in their favor as well. They controlled Kara and—through his devotion—Braeden. If the muses weren't out to destroy the yakona way of life, Evelyn would admire their cunning.

A breeze snuck through an open window and slid through Evelyn's hair. The wind dried the sweat on her neck. She sighed with relief.

The muses were clever; she could grant them as much. Evelyn only began to understand what was really going on after her aunt's memorial. When Braeden tried to convince her of

Kara's good intentions, something clicked in Evelyn's mind.

The muses helped me more than once, he'd said. *Maybe if you spent some time with one, you'd realize how wrong you are about them.*

She gritted her teeth. Not in a million years. She would never become a tool like him.

Not long ago—just a few days after her aunt's memorial—she finally acknowledged the drenowith plot had gone beyond her intervention. To save yakona from drenowith influence, Evelyn had to disband the council. The Bloods had to simply start over, and she was already well on her way.

Disbanding the Bloods would be difficult, and making it look as though the drenowith planned it would be near-impossible. It would take outside help from someone of influence who was not on the council, which left only Blood Carden.

Evelyn suppressed a shudder. A jolt of fear froze her in place, but she pushed it aside. She made the right choice. Though she never wanted to rely on the evil king, he was the lesser of two evils. What Evelyn wanted most was an escape. She wanted to no longer be alone, for Gavin to name a different heir and join her in Ayavel, forever hers. Better yet, she wanted Aislynn to suddenly appear so her aunt would take the reins once more and free Evelyn of the responsibilities of protecting a nation.

But no one was going to save her. Evelyn was the Blood now, and she always would be. She had to do what was best for her people. And she had to do it alone.

Between Blood Carden and the drenowith, the drenowith were the more imminent threat to Ayavel; she could keep Carden out of her home, but the drenowith already had Kara to spy for them. Thanks to Evelyn's insight and the clarity after her talk with Braeden, Blood Carden was already helping her eliminate the drenowith threat. She spent days on her plan before she contacted him, and now that she'd convinced him to work with her, everything would unfold without the Ayavelian people ever knowing what she'd done. If she was careful, she wouldn't lose even one Ayavelian soldier to the war.

She sat at her desk and dipped the nearest quill in an inkwell. With a deep breath and a muttered curse, she scratched out yet another letter to Carden, updating him on the basics. The quill tip scraped against the parchment, leaving indents of ink in its wake. *Scritch. Scratch. Shuffle.*

As Evelyn's pen traveled along the paper, her mind wandered.

Blood Carden wanted war, and she had already given him his first real taste of it—she'd sent him a map of Kirelm. He would no doubt attack, but Kirelm would survive. When the Bloods caught wind of it, she would plant the seeds of doubt in her fellow royals. She could argue the drenowith had joined Blood Carden once again—as they had when they led her aunt to the Stele's door—to attack the isolated kingdom after Kara filled the Bloods' heads with lies about the drenowith's devotion to peace.

Kara likely wouldn't survive the attack on Kirelm, so the assault would finally rid Evelyn of the human-raised nuisance. She could easily write the girl's death off as the drenowith tying up loose ends.

If the Bloods didn't vote to bar the drenowith from the council after the bloodshed, the fear for their kingdoms would be enough to make each of the Bloods return home. Once the Bloods were finally gone from Ayavel, Evelyn would cut off ties with Blood Carden and refuse to open the lichgates into her kingdom for anyone, thereby retreating from the war and from any chance of retribution from Carden. Ourea would start over in its quest for peace, but it was better than rebuilding from the charred rubble the drenowith would leave behind.

But if this failed—if the Bloods still listened to the drenowith and refused to leave after the attack on Kirelm—she would admit defeat and let Carden end them. If the rulers of nations willingly obeyed creatures as selfish and destructive as the muses, there was no hope for them. Of all the Bloods, Gavin should have seen reason. She wanted to save him, but he just wouldn't listen. Perhaps if she was careful, she could save him from himself before it was too late.

Evelyn would either free the council of their faith in the

drenowith, or she would let Carden destroy them. When the flames dissolved and the world was once more quiet, she would rebuild from whatever was left.

She blinked, her eyes refocusing on the parchment before her. Neat lines of text filled most of the page. A steady pool of ink collected underneath her dripping quill, which hovered near the bottom. She must have lost herself to her thoughts.

The quill clinked against the inkwell as she set the pen aside to read over her letter.

C—

I've been watching Braeden's movements, and he is preparing to take another three-day solo expedition to the Stele tomorrow. Employ the usual decoys for the duration of his stay.

On an annoying note, the Vagabond has returned and is apparently an isen. She will be visiting Kirelm tomorrow to encourage Blood Ithone to rejoin the council. I believe it is in our mutual best interest if she does not survive her trip.

—E

Evelyn rubbed her face and hesitated, her eyes focused on the blot of ink at the bottom, near her signature. After a few seconds of silence, she folded the letter into a neat square.

To her left, at the far corner of her writing desk, lay an Ayavelian heirloom: a small black chest resting on silver claws. The box had existed for as long as the kingdom of Ayavel. She opened its lid to reveal its dark red silk lining and slipped the note inside.

If she closed the top, the note would travel to its brother box—which Carden now possessed. Someday, Evelyn would have to figure out a way to get it back from him. For now, the man she hated but needed nonetheless would use the precious heirloom to kill his son, assassinate the Vagabond, and disband the very council her aunt had created.

Evelyn sighed and reached for the lid. It snapped shut with a *click.*

Carden stared into the fire roaring in his study's hearth, its red flames casting shadows on his charcoal gray skin. He filled the chair, all muscle. His right hand itched, but he didn't indulge the sensation. He didn't want to look at the aftermath of his battle with the long-gone Queen of Hillside, but that wouldn't make the scars disappear. Boils and blisters littered the withered stump of his left hand, and the longest scar ran from his thumb to the crease in his elbow. White bone peered through a tear in the skin on his knuckles.

Disgusted, he leaned back in his chair.

The little black chest on his desk creaked open of its own accord. He glanced at it and hesitated. Evelyn wasn't due to send him any news until after his battle with Kirelm.

He stood and crossed the room in a few strides. A piece of parchment, folded into the familiar perfect square, lay on the box's dark red lining. He snatched the paper with his good hand and ripped it open. It took all of a few seconds to read through her letter, and he couldn't help the sneer that crept across his face afterward.

It seemed as though the young queen's hatred for drenowith surpassed even her aunt's. Carden chuckled and sat in his desk chair. He eyed the lit fireplace, eyes slipping out of focus as he debated how her latest news could benefit him.

The door inched open. A perfume of lilac and pine wafted toward him, the familiar scent of his favorite isen.

"You seem chipper," Deidre said, the door shutting behind her.

The pale brunette sauntered into the room and slid onto a nearby chair, her tight white shirt showing off the curves Carden wished he'd been able to enjoy by now. She tucked her legs to the side like a queen, her red lips twisting into a smile as he examined her. But she teased him—it was her way. He would have her eventually.

"News came from Evelyn," he said.

Deidre frowned. "Replacing me already?"

He laughed. "Hardly. She has her uses, but not your charm."

Deidre's lips twisted into a smirk. "What does the little twit have to say, then?"

"Braeden's on his way back here. Have the builders made any progress on the fake guard towers to the east?"

"Of course. They're nearly done. I assume you'll be shifting troop movements and guard schedules as well."

"Among other things."

She smiled and crossed her legs. A surge of desire flickered through Carden's thighs. He wasn't sure how long he was willing to wait for her to come around to him before he took matters into his own, deformed hands. She tried his patience, but he recently discovered an outlet for that frustration. He could always toy with her by mentioning her fellow isen. She hated them for whatever reason. It never failed to rile her.

He laughed. "That Kara girl is an isen now. Seems like something you should have known and warned me about."

Deidre frowned, the grimace digging lines into the corners of her mouth. "She was turned? When?"

Carden leaned back in his chair, his grin spreading. He wasn't used to knowing things his isen didn't.

He shrugged and ignored her question. "The girl will be in Kirelm when I visit. I can't quite decide if I'll kill her instantly or imprison her long enough to force Braeden to kill her. I prefer the latter, but I can't risk her escaping."

Deidre shifted in her seat. "I suppose you'll have to play it by ear. What do you have in mind for our little Evelyn?"

Carden laughed. The topic change hadn't even been subtle, but he would play along for now. "Like I said, Evelyn has her uses."

"She's already given you Kirelm. What else can she do? She's an infant compared to the rest of the Bloods."

"Perhaps, but I want the Bloods at my mercy. That naïve girl is going to help me achieve that."

Deidre lifted an eyebrow as if to ask, *How?*

He grinned, but didn't indulge the silent question. He owned Evelyn, even if the child didn't see it, and his revenge on the other kingdoms would be sweet. Carden spent his life subservient to the Bloods who ruled the other kingdoms. His people could never expand—any new cities beyond the reach of the Stele were destroyed by the other kingdoms within months. They could never trade or do more than survive in the icy patch of nothing they inherited from a banished race. They deserved better. He deserved better.

Peace was never an option. He planned to rule them all. And Evelyn would help him do it.

Carden studied Deidre, debating whether or not he could tell her the truth. The success of his plan depended on her, but he wasn't convinced she knew it yet. The conniving isen would probably milk him for everything he had if she did.

As per an agreement they made long ago, Deidre would soon lead him to the table his ancestor made—the one Aislynn used to give her niece the bloodline. When Carden owned the table, he would drain each Blood and take their power until every yakona alive answered only to him.

Carden would be the first Blood in recorded history to have every bloodline. He would rule Ourea.

Deidre's lips curved into one of the smiles that unsettled him—her eyes shone as if she knew something he didn't, and that always frayed his nerves. Those smiles of hers left behind the lingering worry that she was up to something.

No matter—she needed him. That was part of their agreement. Only he could kill her master, and she would give him his ancestral table in return. It was their pact, forged years ago. The moment he killed Niccoli, she would give him the table, now that she finally had its location. But until he fulfilled his end of the bargain, she wouldn't leave—she wouldn't risk losing the only man who could kill her master. And thus, she needed him. Carden would keep her dependent upon him as long as he could.

She was useful...and he planned on enjoying her fully before he freed her. For that to happen, he needed more time.

Deidre grimaced. "I don't like it when you're quiet. It means you're plotting."

He grinned. "I suppose you women need your chatter."

Her beautiful face distorted into a scowl that would have withered lesser men. Carden just laughed.

"I doubt you care about my plotting," he said.

"Try me."

"Oh? Have you figured me out already?"

"Perhaps not, but I know that you've begun picking off the Bloods one by one on purpose. This little war of yours is all going according to plan, isn't it? With Blood Lorraine dead, her son Gavin was blinded by a lust for revenge, as you'd hoped. It distracted the boy and made him easy to manipulate even from afar."

Carden raised his eyebrows, impressed. "And?"

"And I know you weren't expecting that son of yours to free the Heirs of Losse and Kirelm after the Gala. You wanted them for something, though I'm not yet sure what."

Her lips twitched. Carden figured that had been a barely-contained lie. She knew damn well what he was doing. His isen was craftier than he imagined, but he didn't know why she would show her hand like that. Perhaps she had a weakness after all—vanity.

Nonetheless, she was right. Carden gritted his teeth at the thought of his escaped prisoners, but he would pay his idiot son back soon enough.

"Why are you killing Bloods but saving Heirs?" she asked.

He examined her in silence, debating. He could tell her. He still owned her. It wasn't as though she would ever get in his way. She didn't care about yakona. Her only desire in life was getting revenge on Niccoli. In that manner—and in only that manner—she was harmless.

So he obliged.

"Young Bloods, when freshly turned, are weaker. Easier to control. Easier to manipulate," Carden said. He would have an easier time of detaining, draining, and killing them than he would their parents.

"What ultimate fate do you have planned for our sweet, naïve Evelyn?" Deidre asked.

"Why so curious?"

Deidre teased him with a glance through her lashes. "Jealousy."

Carden grinned. "It should be fairly easy to leverage her hatred for drenowith even after I control Kirelm. When I have all of the Bloods in my prison, I'm going to reveal her betrayal to them just for fun."

Deidre laughed. "How cruel! I love it."

But Carden wasn't done. He wanted to test the waters of Deidre's supposed jealousy—and that was the only reason he continued. "And once I throw her in a cell, I'll give her a choice: die the same death of her peers or carry my child."

Deidre's smile faded. "What?"

"I still need an heir."

Braeden would die soon enough, thankfully, and Carden wanted a son with all of the Bloodlines. He needed an Heir to every throne, wrapped into one body. Whether Evelyn gave him her blood or had his Heir, the young queen would serve him well.

Deidre frowned and stood, but Carden was faster. He crossed the floor and pushed her back into her seat before she could even step toward the door.

She glared up at him. For a moment, he let himself believe a woman like Deidre could actually feel jealousy. Her past had scarred her too deeply to feel much of anything but hatred, and that was about all he knew of her. She would never want him, not really, but he could toy with her long enough to make her think she did.

His voice came out low, like a growl. "Like I said, the girl has her uses. You have much more."

She smirked, those eyes tinged with the secret knowledge that drove him crazy. She was always up to something, but she needed him. She would never betray him—he would never give her the opportunity.

Without another word, he turned for the hallway and left Deidre in his office. He shut the door behind him and, on his way down the hall, issued silent orders to his generals regarding Braeden's upcoming visit. He hummed all the while.

Carden's days of banishment were nearly over, and he would be the greatest Blood in history. None would rival him. In this finale his son was planning, Carden would finally revel in the blood of those who had exiled his people for so long.

❦CHAPTER FIFTEEN

RESPITE

Braeden stretched out on his bed, waiting. His heart thumped in his chest as he recalled the way Kara took over the council meeting. No hesitation. No fear. She dominated the conversation, and the Bloods obeyed as well as royalty can. She challenged those who had enslaved her with audacity Braeden envied. She spoke about death like she wasn't afraid—and since she met Death once already, perhaps she wasn't scared to see him again. Braeden just wouldn't let her go quite yet.

He took a deep breath to steady his pulse. It didn't work. His heart raced as fast as his thoughts, and he wondered what to say when she came back. He might not say anything, and let his hands speak for him. He wouldn't be able to restrain this desire much longer.

The door opened and shut. Braeden glanced toward the entry to find Kara standing with one hand on the doorknob, staring at the floor. She frowned, eyes out of focus and shifting in their sockets as she lost herself to thought.

The top flap of her satchel lifted to reveal a furry head with massive eyes. Flick's tail curled upward, lifting the lid higher as he examined the room. When the little creature's eyes landed on the bed, he squeaked and, with a *crack*, appeared on a pillow. He circled the plush cotton a few times before curling into a ball.

Kara ran a hand through her hair and cursed under her breath.

"What's wrong?" Braeden asked.

"I'm not sure. That's the problem."

"Was it something Evelyn said?"

Kara nodded. "Something seems off about her, more so than when she and I last spoke. It's like she just made up her mind about...something. I have no idea what, but I have a bad feeling about this."

"Should we talk to her?"

"You really think that will do anything? She seems angry at the world."

Braeden shrugged. "What should we do, then?"

"I don't know." Kara shook her head and sat on the edge of the bed. She rubbed her face and stared at the floor.

Braeden scooted closer and rubbed her shoulders. She leaned back as his thumbs skimmed over her shoulder blades. The muscles along her back barely moved at his touch, strained as they must have been from her training and the stress of Ourean politics.

"You need to relax," he said.

"You weren't there. You wouldn't be able to relax either."

"It's not like she can really do anything. Her aunt exposed Ayavel when she allowed the Bloods inside. She was just outvoted in her own home by guests who are supposed to respect her input, and she's probably upset about it. I don't think you have anything to worry about, Kara. Evelyn is harmless."

Kara twisted to face him. "No Blood is harmless."

He sighed. "Poor choice of words. My point is she's not going to do anything rash. It would hurt her and her people. You're probably exhausted after your meeting. You need to rest up before we go back for round two after dinner. Relax, okay?"

She let out a breath and flopped back on the bed. "I haven't relaxed in ages."

"So I gathered."

She took deep, steady breaths and closed her eyes. Her hair tumbled over her shoulders and framed her head like a halo. Braeden stretched out next to her, smiling from the joy of being near her. When he thought he couldn't adore her more, she did something to make him fall a little more in love.

"I probably won't get to stay long," Kara said, eyes still closed.

Braeden laughed. "You can't even relax for two minutes, woman."

She didn't smile. "Evelyn is going to send a note to Ithone. He'll be curious to see what I want. He'll let me go to the Kirelm capital."

"He'll be more than curious. He'll try to kidnap you."

"The key word is 'try.'"

"I know you're more powerful now, but don't get cocky."

She peeked up at him through a half-closed eyelid. "I'm not. I just know what I can do."

Braeden raised an eyebrow. "Fair enough."

She continued. "Besides, I don't want it to come to that. I want to show him I respect his culture and his position. I won't make the same mistakes I did last time I visited Kirelm. I even brought the presents I got at the gala. I figure wearing the necklace they gave me is a good start."

"A start, maybe. It won't bring him back."

"No, it won't. Hopefully reason will."

Braeden set his cheek on the cool blanket. Silence settled between them, and Kara closed her eyes again. He watched her chest rise and fall with each deep breath. She lost weight in her time at the village. Her cheekbones and jaw had more defined edges. The sharp tip of her nose pointed toward the ceiling. Her eyelids fluttered. She had to be deep in thought, maybe planning what she would say to Ithone.

Braeden poked her side. In a single movement, Kara flinched, curled her knees upward to protect her core, and grabbed his wrist in a vice grip. Her fingers pinched his skin, but he didn't move. He eyed her, impressed and amused all at once. How did she wind herself so tightly?

"What was that for?" she asked.

"Stop thinking."

"That's not something I can just turn off."

He dragged her near and poked her side again.

She laughed and swatted him away. "Stop that!"

Braeden grinned and ran his fingertips up her torso, tickling any surface he could reach. She squirmed, laughing and trying to get away at the same time. He grabbed her waist and tugged her closer, never letting her get more than a foot or two from him. Flick yawned from his pillow and scooted a little farther away to avoid the melee.

Kara grabbed Braeden's arm and wrapped her leg around his. With a twist of her shoulders, she flipped him onto his back. He hesitated, frozen in surprise, but she launched into an attack of her own. She ran her fingertips over his stomach, but he tensed his abs.

Braeden smirked. "I'm not ticklish."

"Unfair!"

"Stelians don't fight fair."

He flipped her onto her back and lay down next to her. She smiled and ran a hand through his hair. She examined his face, though he wasn't sure what she was looking for. He didn't mind. She studied him, smiling all along.

"Thanks," she said.

He nodded. "Someone has to keep you in line."

She tapped his nose with her finger. "There's no one better suited for the task than you."

He swallowed hard, that question bubbling to the surface again: *be mine forever.* Should he ask her now? He didn't even know what to say or what he would do if she said no. Thoughts bounced around in his head. His gut churned. His mouth went dry. He opened his mouth twice to speak, but nothing came out.

"What's wrong?" she asked.

He laughed. "Nothing. Never mind."

"Liar. You look nervous."

"I want to ask you something."

"Go for it."

He caught her eye. She stared at him, blond, wide-eyed, and beautiful. He could do it. He should do it.

He opened his mouth, but the words died on his tongue. Kara was one of the few good things he had in life. If he rushed something as important as a lifelong bond, he could lose her. He could make her uncomfortable. As close as they were, he could push her away if he moved too fast. So instead of asking the question that set his nerves on fire, he sighed and asked the first thing that came to mind. "Will you sleep in here tonight?"

She grinned. "I was denied my own room, so I figure that's the plan. Thanks for reminding me. You'd better behave, mister."

Braeden smiled, but couldn't bring himself to say much more. He may have missed an opportunity. She might have said yes without question.

Though he'd lost his nerve, he would still be able to spend the evening with her. That was enough for now. If Evelyn had denied Kara a room, at least the crazy queen managed to do something right.

His next meeting with the Bloods would begin soon, and he wouldn't leave Kara's side for a moment. The Bloods would ask her to go to Kirelm. She would say yes. They would inevitably demand more from her, and she would have to decide how far to push her luck in the council. Regardless of whatever the two of them faced, Braeden would keep her safe for as long as he could.

And once the meeting ended, they would curl up in his room and sleep. He would wrap an arm around her waist, lean in, and savor whatever time with her he had left.

❧CHAPTER SIXTEEN

JOURNEY

The morning after her return to Ayavel, Kara woke to a hand tightening its grip on her shoulder. It pulled her back a half inch. The force dragged her body along the sheet. For a second, she panicked.

Braeden's hand tensed again as she looked about. His left arm had wrapped around her in the night. It snaked over her waist and across her chest, his hand cupping her right shoulder. He mumbled something and burrowed his cheek into her neck. The man still slept in his Hillsidian form, though everyone knew what he was. Incredible.

Sunlight streamed through the windows along the left side of his bed, the curtains tucked behind a hook on either side of the frame. Clouds sped by on what had to be a windy day. She couldn't see anything but the sky from this angle.

Careful not to wake Braeden, she twisted in his grip to get a better look at him. Strands of his dark hair slipped over his face. The olive tone of his skin lured her in, teasing her to touch him. His eyes fluttered beneath their lids—who knew what he dreamed of. Carden? His old life of killing isen?

Kara's jaw tensed. She wouldn't think about that.

His arm—now around her back—pulled her closer. He smiled in his sleep and mumbled again.

She grinned. "What was that?"

He repeated himself, still mumbling, but followed it up with a louder question. "Well, will you?"

"Will I what?"

Braeden blinked himself awake and glanced around. Darn. She shouldn't have asked so loudly.

"You talk in your sleep," she said with a smile.

He laughed. "What did I say?"

"All I could make out was 'will you.'"

His smile faded. He swallowed hard. "Nothing else?"

Kara narrowed her eyes and grinned wider. "What are you hiding from me?"

Instead of answering, he smirked. His fingers slipped down to her waist, distracting her. Her breath caught at his touch. His dark eyes stole her attention, and he shot her that devilish grin of his. He leaned in, only inches from her face, and—

He tickled her.

A laugh—it sounded more like a hiccup, really—burst through her lips. He laughed along with her but wouldn't surrender. His fingers traveled along her sides, shooting sparks through to her core. She wanted to kiss him and hit him, all at once.

"Nothing else, right?" he pressed.

"Nothing!" she said with a gasp. More laughter escaped.

"Good." He relented and settled back onto the bed.

"Cheater."

"You liked it."

She just shook her head. He kissed her cheek and lay against the pillows, pulling her along with him. His nose tickled the tip of her ear.

"You should stay," he whispered.

"If Ithone refuses to see me, I won't have any other choice."

"He won't. He'll want you close. He'll probably try to kidnap you or trick you into staying."

"That didn't work for Losse. Won't work for him, either."

She tilted her head toward him and caught his eye. A smile tugged at his lips, and he just watched her. She couldn't quite make out the expression on his face—pride?

"You're right," he eventually said.

She ran a hand along his jawline. "Are you going to stay out of trouble while I'm gone?"

He laughed. "I don't know how."

She grinned and inched closer. He became a blur, but she wanted to savor every bit of him—the oaky musk of his cologne, the sparks his warm touch shot through her.

A thrill raced up her thigh. She tensed, her smile widening with a rush of heat through her core. Her pulse quickened. His fingers swept along her back, casual enough that he likely didn't realize his caress set her nerves on fire. Desire shot into her fingers, giving them a will of their own. She wanted to reach under his shirt, to push the boundaries of their relaxed intimacy. He wanted her. She wanted him. It should be simple as that, right?

But this is Ayavel.

Her throat tightened. She couldn't let her guard down, not even for a minute. Evelyn had to have made a life-changing decision back in that war room, one that left Kara sick to her stomach with worry. The tides could turn at any moment. Kara couldn't indulge herself, however much she wanted to. In Ayavel, it just wasn't safe.

Braeden laughed. "I can almost see the smoke coming out of your ears. What are you thinking?"

Heat rushed to Kara's cheeks. "Nothing."

"Lies. You're red as a tomato. A blush usually comes before an embarrassing confession."

She grinned in an effort to be coy and forced back the warmth flooding the pit of her stomach. She didn't know what to say, so she remained silent.

"You're not going to tell me?" he asked.

"Nope."

"Mean."

She laughed. "Well, yeah. I'm terribly cruel. I'm leaving you alone in Ayavel, after all. You'll be utterly defenseless."

He laughed. "All right, I confess. I want you to stay because I'm selfish. I can't focus when you're gone."

She smiled and burrowed her head into his chest. Not fair. Her heart melted. He hugged her closer. At least she'd distracted him from her wanton thoughts about how she would prefer to spend the next hour, but now she wanted to indulge herself even more.

To be honest, she would like nothing more than to stay. To be near him. Her time in the village distracted her enough that she could focus on training or planning, but that changed the moment she saw him. Now that she was with him again, she never wanted to leave. He kept her warm. He made her laugh. His presence cleared her mind. Braeden made her happy.

She took a deep breath of his shirt and caught that oaky cologne again.

"Please," he said.

"You're serious? I have to go. We need Ithone."

Braeden shrugged. "Not really. He's a control freak. He makes everything difficult. It might be easier without him."

"That's a lie, and you know it. We can't lose a fourth of our army and expect to win."

His jaw tensed.

Kara sighed. "I'm not trying to call you out. I just don't want you to lose sight of what's important here. We need Ithone, and you understand that. The problem is you don't want me to go."

"Of course I don't want you to leave. Not when I finally have you again."

She smiled. At least he felt the same way.

"It'll only be for a few days, Braeden. Then I'll come right back, even if he doesn't agree to come with me."

"What can I do to convince you this is a bad idea?"

She smiled. "I'm sure you can get creative."

He lifted her chin until she was inches from his face. His eyes bored into hers as if trying to memorize them. She lost herself in his gaze. He leaned in and kissed her. She didn't want it to end.

She forgot where they were. She forgot why she wanted to leave or where she needed to go. She forgot about her curse and her grandfather and the war she couldn't stop. For a moment, she just enjoyed him. She let herself forget everything else because, really, he mattered most of all.

But no. She couldn't stay.

⚜

Braeden shut the door to his bathroom. He let out a long breath.

He'd told Kara he needed a shower, but he really needed a break. They'd spent nearly an hour talking about everything and nothing—their plans for after the war, old dreams and the places Kara wanted to visit someday. And through every second of it, he'd wanted nothing more than to pin her to the bed and see what happened.

He had to control himself. Ayavel had too many spies to let his guard down. He would convince Kara to stay, to let Ithone come to his senses on his own. And once she promised not to go, maybe the two of them could escape for a while. He wished he could take her to their waterfall in Hillside, but he no longer had access to the kingdom. Maybe one day, Gavin would trust him enough to give him back the key to the city.

Braeden would have other opportunities to give in to his desires. For now, he needed a cold shower.

⚜

Kara settled into the chair at the desk in Braeden's room while he took his shower. Temptation tugged at her to join him, but she had to focus. She already spent an hour enjoying his company and nearly caved three times in the process. Only the fear of Evelyn walking in on them kept her from indulging herself. Considering all she had left to do, even that hour was selfish. But she needed the break. She needed him.

With nothing else to do, she summoned her Grimoire from the blue stone in her clover pendant. Dust spiraled out of it and trailed toward the desk. It formed the shape of a book, the blue dust glowing with its own light. In seconds, the Grimoire appeared from within the glowing grains and rested on the table's surface, waiting for her.

The cover ripped open and flipped ahead several hundred pages. Kara sat back, her grip on the arm rest tightening as she watched the paper fly by. Her stomach tossed with dread, but at least her vagabonds would keep her informed of everything that went on.

The pages settled after a moment, drifting apart to flowing handwriting Kara didn't recognize. She leaned in. At the top was yesterday's date.

Elana, Kingdom of Kirelm

News arrived of the Vagabond's request for an audience. Blood Ithone spent the night in meetings most likely about what to do with Kara when she arrives. I accompany Heir Aurora most of the time, but she was not allowed into Blood Ithone's debates. I believe Remy was invited. He is a famed isen hunter and close to General Gurien, so he is known as a trusted confidant in the royal circle.

Rumors are spreading that Blood Ithone plans to trap Kara in her time here. She must be careful.

Heir Aurora is...irritable. She barks orders constantly. She refuses to see her father, though she will speak to Gurien. That's new. I don't believe she has ever trusted him before, so that confuses me.

Kara rubbed her face. She didn't remember meeting Elana, but only vagabonds could write in the Grimoires. She would have to be better about meeting everyone and learning their names.

She flipped the page to see block letters written in tight, militant rows. Yesterday's date yet again dotted the top of this note.

Remy, Kingdom of Kirelm

I spent six hours in a meeting with Blood Ithone, General

Gurien, and a dozen other military officers. The primary focus was on how to detain and control the Vagabond when she arrives. I offered ideas I knew would not work so no one would suspect me of foul play.

Though I am concerned for Kara's safety, she should still come. I will highlight their plans below and continue to update as they change.

It has been decided she will be captured in the first ten minutes of her meeting with Blood Ithone, chained and controlled with poison spikes until our king can inject her with his bloodline. That will allow him to control her. It has come to my attention Blood Gavin attempted a similar feat using a cursed tiara at the Gala, though I do not believe Blood Ithone knows of this. Blood Ithone believes this will work because it will be forceful and swift. Kara will not have much of an opportunity to resist or escape it if they spike her, nor will I be able to do much to help her.

An approval of her request to visit will be sent to Ayavel soon. Kara must wait to come until it arrives. Otherwise, they will suspect she is being fed information and likely change plans at the last minute.

She will be granted audience, and she must use the time to show her power. All of it, including her blood ties to the infamous Agneon. Without it, Blood Ithone will never listen. If we are to have him as an ally, he must fear her power. He will never respect her otherwise.

When Kara arrives, she will have only a few minutes to fully demonstrate herself. Again, after only ten minutes—long enough for her to drop her guard—soldiers will be sent to restrain her in the court. She should not hesitate to kill them.

Kara groaned. She didn't want to kill. She didn't want anyone to fear her. Only yesterday, she explained her isen nature to the other Bloods without telling them who she really was. *What* she really was. To tell Ithone about her grandfather would mean she had no choice but to tell the other Bloods as well. She could lose their trust over keeping something that important from them.

She might even have to start all over.

"What's the matter?" Braeden asked.

She pivoted in her chair. He stood in the middle of the room, fully dressed. His wet hair hung in his eyes, and she wanted to run her hands through it again.

"Life," she answered.

He clicked his tongue in mock disapproval. "So dramatic."

She glanced back to her Grimoire. If she told Braeden about Ithone's plan, he would press his point that she should stay. He wouldn't care that she had so many Kirelm vagabonds on her side.

"So what are you reading?" he asked.

"Notes. The vagabonds are telling me about the various kingdoms." She could tell him that much, at least.

"Useful. What's going on in Kirelm?"

Kara smiled. "When the call comes from Ithone, I'm not going to stay here. I need to bring him back."

He frowned. "But I said 'please.'"

She laughed and shut the Grimoire. With a mumble, she wished the book away. It dissolved once more into dust and stowed itself in her pendant. The stone in her necklace glowed blue once more, the sign that her Grimoire was safely hidden from the world.

Her satchel sat on the floor by the bed, so she stood to pack for her trip. Braeden stood between her and the bag, his dark eyes following her as she crossed the room. She kissed his cheek as she passed but didn't pause for fear she would lose her resolve and stay. He apparently had other plans. He grabbed her waist and pulled her back. He held her to his body, arms around her.

He kissed her forehead. "I don't want you to go. If you stay here, you'll be safe. You'll be with me."

"I don't need protection anymore, Braeden."

"Doesn't matter. You're still breakable. I'll always want you safe."

"You said you have to go on a few more surveillance trips anyway. It's not like I can just slip out and go with you."

"Sure you can."

"So the Stele is safer than Kirelm?"

He shrugged.

She sighed. "Braeden, come on. This is a war. You are the only one who can plan a successful attack on the Stele. I'm the only one who can bring Ithone back. As much as I never want to leave your side, we can't do those things together."

He pouted—full on *pouted*. A prince. Pouting.

She smiled and kissed his jaw, distracting him enough that she could slip out of his grip. Once more, she headed to her bag. He didn't stop her this time. The satchel's worn fabric reminded her of everywhere she'd taken it: Losse, Kirelm, Hillside, the drenowith Council of elders. She saw more of Ourea than most yakona would in their entire lives, yet she wanted nothing more than to spend as much time as possible in this room.

She reached into the bag and pulled out the silver box Aurora gave her at the Gala. Inside, still on the black silk pillow, was the golden necklace that matched one Aurora had worn that night. A corner of a note stuck out from underneath the pillow, but Kara didn't need to reread it.

Back at the gala when she first opened the box, Kara hated to think she now owned something that would tie her to Kirelm—a nation she believed undermined everything she was trying to do. She was wrong. Too late, Kara realized what the necklace really was—a way for Aurora to share her kingdom's culture. Even the note was just a request for her to respect their differences.

Kara had never given Aurora that respect before. She always thought the Kirelm treatment of women to be wrong. Perhaps that was why she'd never received any respect from Ithone or his people. She couldn't force that; she had to earn it.

She unclasped the necklace, but a muscled hand reached for it. Braeden knelt beside her, one hand open and waiting for the necklace. He didn't say anything—just waited.

She obliged. The chain shifted on her palm and fell into his.

He reached around her—so close she could smell him—and clasped the chain around her neck.

"Come back to me," he said softly.

She smiled. "Likewise."

Someone knocked on the door. A folded note slid underneath and settled on the floor, sealed shut with wax.

Braeden picked it up and broke the seal. He scanned it and frowned.

"Looks like you've been summoned to Kirelm," he said.

Kara just nodded. Time to go.

She grabbed her bag and swung it over her shoulder. Flick yawned and stretched from his place on a pillow on the nightstand. His tail swished, brushing the wall as he blinked himself awake. Kara reached for him from across the room. He chirped. With a loud *crack*, he disappeared and reappeared on her shoulder. She scratched his tiny head.

"Are you going to meet with the Bloods before you leave?" Braeden asked.

"No. They'll just slow me down. I don't need their approval to do something I already promised to do. Will you let them know I left?"

"Yes."

He watched something out the window, but Kara figured he was trying to restrain himself. She didn't want to leave, and he didn't want her to go, either.

She wrapped her arms around him and leaned into his chest. Flick followed suit, nuzzling Braeden's neck and chirping. Braeden hugged her back.

"Three days. No more," he said.

"Three days," she promised.

"Be safe."

"You, too."

He stepped back and smiled. This was it. If Kara waited any longer, she just wouldn't go.

She forced a smile and rubbed Flick's head again, her thoughts focused on the main lichgate that led out to an underwater temple. She could leave through the kingdom's primary lichgate since her dramatic entrance yesterday gave away the fact her pet could teleport. Might as well use it to travel faster. Since Flick couldn't teleport through lichgates, she would have to walk out of the golden temple on her own—but once out, she would simply teleport to the Rose Cliffs. The Bloods kept a close watch on their kingdoms' borders. Even if someone from Kirelm wasn't waiting for her there, they would know she was waiting for them.

With another loud crack, Flick whisked her away. The room disappeared. Braeden disappeared. And even though she knew she would see him in just three days, it broke her heart to leave him.

CHAPTER SEVENTEEN

OLD FOES

Barely ten minutes after Kara left him, Braeden slammed his office door and leaned against his desk. His hands curled into fists. Curse words tumbled out of his mouth faster than he could register them.

He let her go. He let her travel to Kirelm, and she might not return. He let her go without asking her to be his forever. If something happened to him, she would never know how much his life changed since she found him. And if something happened to her, he would raid Kirelm himself. He wouldn't stop until every building burned to its foundation. He wouldn't stop until Ithone was dead and Kara was safely in his arms.

He took a deep breath and closed his eyes. He needed to relax. He couldn't think like that.

With a groan, he walked around the table and sank into his chair. His latest Stelian map covered the desk, rips along the edges from all the times he'd picked at the corners as he sketched. Four new guard towers littered the forests to the north and east, their ink still wet. He'd only just discovered them on his last scouting mission. They couldn't be more than a week old.

Each time Braeden visited the Stele through his secret lichgate, he inched closer to the castle. He had thus far avoided civilians and soldiers alike, keeping as he did to the shadows and forest. Iyra took them through the woods like a ghost, and he could observe in passing. He still hadn't gotten close enough to see Carden's office balcony, nor did he want to. He could sense his father's presence the closer he came to the castle. He didn't want his father to find him out in the same way.

The study door opened. Braeden's head shot up as Gavin walked into the office.

Braeden rolled his eyes. "Do come in."

"You are too kind."

"What do you want, Gavin?"

"Use my title. It's Blood Gavin."

Braeden grimaced. "I'm not in the mood to deal with you. Get out."

"Not until I get answers. You've been holed up in here for a month, feeding us tidbits of a plan while we sit idle. I'm beginning to think you're stalling."

"Think what you like—doesn't make it true."

Gavin sighed and sat in a chair by the bookshelves. "That's not how politics work, Braeden. Perception is more powerful than the truth. You never did understand that."

"I understand it well enough. I simply don't tolerate such thinking."

"The Bloods are losing what little faith they had in you." Gavin set his fingertips together and rested his pointer fingers on his forehead.

"And you're doing what exactly? Giving me a fair warning?"

"I'm reserving judgment until I hear your plan or lack thereof."

"How wise of you."

"Tell me what my patience bought, Braeden."

"My title is Heir Braeden or, if you prefer the more formal option, Heir Drakonin."

Gavin scoffed. "Touché."

Braeden leaned back in his chair. "I've reported on every scouting trip I took, and I should think that's enough to earn your patience while I wrap up my assessment of the Stele's weaknesses. I've outlined my plan, discussed the strengths of each army with you to better—"

"But you haven't shown us a real plan," Gavin snapped.

Braeden frowned. "It's not so easy. Carden adds new guard towers every day, which suggests he's shifting his defensive strategy on a regular basis. His builders are working overtime. Judging from the speed with which the walls and defenses expand, I'd say they don't sleep or break for food. Troop movements don't seem to have a pattern between one visit and the next. If this were easy, we'd have taken the city by now. But it's not. It's near impossible to take this fight to his door in the first place, even without all of these confusing changes. We can't afford a single mistake. I have to know what I'm doing will work before I lead multiple armies to my father's front door."

"Then bring us in on the planning. We need to brainstorm together if this is so hard for you."

Braeden cursed. "You know full well what I meant. This is easiest for me because I know the kingdom better than any of you. If we all collaborate on the attack strategy from the beginning, we'll never get anywhere. Nothing will ever be decided. You all can't even agree on who is in this alliance anymore."

"Yes, thanks to you."

"Don't try to derail me. I have a valid point. Do you really think the four of us can collaborate on attack strategy? Everyone will try to outdo each other in what their armies can handle and who will get the most glory. They won't focus on their actual strengths or weaknesses."

"So you don't trust us to do what's best to win the Stele."

"Of course not. I don't like the fact I need you all to win this. If I could do it without you, I would."

Gavin's jaw tensed. He focused on something through the window, eyes clear but averted. Neither of them spoke. Braeden scanned the map on his desk, wondering what new Stelian landmark would crop up overnight the next time he visited. He wished he could decipher what Carden was trying to do. He more so wished Gavin would get up and leave.

"When are you scouting next?" Gavin asked.

"Tonight."

"I'm coming with you."

Braeden laughed. "Cute. Have you missed spending time with me?"

"It seems like another perspective would help you. I don't see how it would hurt."

"You're the only Hillsidian royal. If you die, your people die. Why would you risk yourself to babysit me?"

Gavin rubbed his face. "You're just being stubborn at this point. I'm offering to help because this shouldn't be a one-man task. I guessed you would be more pleasant and open-minded, considering that Kara's back."

Braeden crossed his arms and turned to look out the window.

"Wait, has she already left?"Gavin asked.

"I figured Evelyn already knew and would tell you first, of all people."

"I miss the days when she did, but we don't speak much anymore outside of council meetings. She won't know I'm going with you on this scouting trip. I will tell only my generals."

"I never said you were going. What's this volunteering of yours really about, Gavin? There's no reason for you to come except to get in my way. Iyra's fast. You won't keep up."

"I have Mother's wolf Mastif with me. We'll likely outrun you."

Braeden smirked and sat back. "Do I hear a challenge?"

"Perhaps." A grin twitched at the corner of Gavin's mouth.

Braeden laughed, and the Hillsidian Blood followed suit. Where had this come from? They hadn't reverted to the brothers they used to be, but it was the second time Gavin had shown him a sign their old friendship could revive itself. Gavin once admitted he still loved Evelyn but couldn't act on it, and Braeden hadn't known what to say. The moment sped by, blipping in and out of existence before he could act on it. But now, he had a chance. A choice. This was Gavin's version of a truce—or, at least, the beginnings of one.

It would help to have an extra pair of eyes to dissect the never-ending changes within the Stele. Though Braeden didn't enjoy the idea of showing Gavin his future kingdom, they wouldn't see enough on this trip to give the Hillsidian Blood an incredible advantage. When the Stele belonged to Braeden, he would lock the forgotten lichgate as a precaution against unwanted visits from Hillside.

Braeden leaned forward and made eye contact. "If I let you come, know I'm willingly showing you my future home. I'll rule there soon, same as you rule Hillside. I've seen your kingdom. You'll see mine. I'm offering this to you, and you're not tricking me into giving this information away. Do you understand?"

Gavin raised an eyebrow. "You lived in Hillside for twelve years. A few days in the Stele isn't an even playing field."

Braeden laughed. "I wasn't offering one."

"So far, I don't hear a cost. You show me the Stele while I follow you around."

"The cost is you finally act like the Blood you are, not the Heir you were. You've experienced more pain and loss than a man should, but you've wallowed in it. It stops now. No more manipulating Kara. No more fighting me. You and I have a mutual enemy—my father. We kill him. We make peace. We move on with our lives."

Braeden held his breath. This could be a wild success or a dismal failure. They hadn't even left yet, and he'd already pushed the boundaries of this unspoken truce. But he had to. No use exposing the Stele to a potential enemy if he didn't have to.

To his credit, Gavin laughed. "Let's see how good those secrets are first."

❧CHAPTER EIGHTEEN

SECOND CHANCES

Thanks to Flick's teleporting ability, it took less than an hour for Kara to reach the Rose Cliffs. She stood on the edge, eyeing the mile-or-more drop to the valley below. The sky tumbled above a beige mountain range on the horizon, darkening with a storm. A hint of lightning flashed in the distance. Behind her, a tangled forest hovered near the cliff edge, leaving a twenty-foot space between its roots and the drop off. Thorns littered the underbrush except for along a dirt path that curved into the trees.

She hesitated, listening for the crunch of boots along the soil. A bird chirped, and something yelped in the woods. Surprisingly, no one waited for her on the cliff.

Perhaps they didn't know how quickly she could travel—not everyone knew what Flick could do. She preferred it that way, but she couldn't waste time pretending she required a mount to get places. With tensions rising between the Bloods and her promise to return to Braeden in three days, she had to make every second count.

She summoned the Grimoire from the stone in her pendant to check for updates from the Kirelm capital. The book solidified and dropped into her hands. The cover popped open. Just as she hoped, its pages opened to another note from Remy, dated for today.

Remy—Kirelm

Kara has arrived on the outskirts of Kirelm. General Gurien has been sent alone to fetch her. She should summon a mount and be ready to leave.

That isen hunter was so controlling.

Kara mumbled under her breath and summoned the Grimoire's griffon—an ancient creature that used to belong to Kirelm. It had taken a liking to the first Vagabond and now lived in the Grimoire, serving those who needed it. Ithone hadn't liked that very much, but she figured a griffon was a more welcome sight than her demonic black dragon.

Silver dust sprang from the book in her hands, twisting into a small tornado. It touched down on the grass beside her and spread, blocking out the forest behind it until the funnel took on the towering shape of her griffon. With a *poof,* the dust dissolved into the white feathers and gold fur of her pet. It tilted its head, black eyes locked on her as it nudged her shoulder in welcome.

She patted its head. "Hey, buddy."

Kara sat back against a tree and gazed into the clear sky while the griffon stared off into the distance. Though the storm still brewed miles away, no clouds dotted the blue sky over the cliff. She closed her eyes and took a deep breath of the late summer air. She didn't even know what day it was—or what month. It didn't really matter anymore.

"Vagabond," a man said.

Flick purred. Kara peeked through one eye to see General Gurien standing about ten feet away. He arched his back, shoulders broad and proud as ever. His white wings framed his body, the glowing feathers reflecting sunlight into Kara's eyes. She squinted. Heavy bags lined his eyes, purple and several layers deep.

Kara frowned. "You look exhausted, General."

He nodded. "It has been a trying time."

"I'm sorry to hear that."

He shrugged. "Blood Ithone and Heir Aurora can't stand each other anymore. Two hot-tempered royals are hard to handle."

She sighed. "This will be fun."

"We should leave. You have a meeting with Blood Ithone this evening."

Kara nodded and stood. The griffon knelt for her to get on, so she swung her leg over without another word. The creature stood, and Gurien took off into the air. Her griffon followed. Flick purred louder in her ear.

She and Gurien traveled in silence, and Kara let her mount follow Gurien's twists and turns. She didn't even pay attention to their path. Last time she tried, they had flown for what seemed like forever. She'd lost all track of time around the same time her body went numb from the windchill.

As the wind whistled past her ear, she took slow breaths to calm her nerves. She would have ten minutes to convince Ithone to forgive Braeden and return to the alliance. Probably more like five minutes, really. She doubted Ithone had become any more patient since he'd come home. He would probably rush the meeting. She doubted he would actually listen, either. Maybe she should try to find him sooner and speak with him alone.

Gurien angled to the right. It would be great to talk to the general and get his advice. Braeden trusted him now, which meant the Kirelm soldier had to be a good person. But she just couldn't trust him with the knowledge that she had vagabonds inside Kirelm. He was, after all, under Ithone's control. He may even still be loyal to his Blood, regardless of that power. She couldn't risk it.

Light glinted off something in the distance. A spire broke through the clouds as they neared. A second followed, as did a third. Within seconds, dozens of silver towers emerged from behind tufts of pink cloud.

Either they took a shortcut this time, or her griffon was much faster than she'd thought. She lost herself to her thoughts, but that couldn't account for how quickly they arrived.

The kingdom hadn't changed from her first visit. A towering wall surrounded the outer edges of the city, a mesh of wires branching from the wall to create a thin dome that arched over the entire kingdom. A gate opened to welcome them, even though they were still about a hundred feet away. A second wall and gate protected the castle and the nicest homes in the city. She could barely make out the dwellings within this inner wall, but the castle spires dominated the floating landscape. A second wire mesh dome encompassed this section as well.

The first gate neared at an alarming rate. Adrenaline shot through Kara's veins in bursts that dried her throat. She held her breath. Gurien dove through the opening, and Kara's griffon followed close on his heels. They tore through the streets, the city's gray buildings a blur in Kara's peripheral vision.

The second gate neared within seconds, its panels swinging open only a moment before Gurien and Kara reached it. The general and the griffon leaned into a turn, following the paved bricks of a road as the street sloped upward toward the castle's main doors.

Gurien slowed and landed on the front steps with practiced ease. The griffon followed suit, its claws scraping the stone road as it touched down. Flick's nails dug a little deeper into Kara's shoulder after the landing, and she almost nodded in agreement. She couldn't quite relax after such a fast-paced entrance, either.

Kara's knees shook from the adrenaline still pumping through her, but she forced herself to dismount. Time was not on her side.

She patted her griffon's neck, wishing it away with a whisper. With another *poof*, the creature dissolved into dust. Though the silver haze settled on the air, she took comfort knowing her pet had actually returned to her Grimoire. She could summon him again any time.

Gurien trotted up the steps, back arched like a king. Ten soldiers lined the steps, one to each stair. Every man saluted the general as he passed and held the salute as she followed him inside.

She and Gurien walked through the castle's hallways at a pace that left her out of breath. She resisted the constant urges to gasp for air and instead forced herself to focus on the path Gurien took. If she needed to escape, she would at least know the way out—whatever good that would do her, considering the guards at the entrance.

"You have two hours until your meeting with Blood Ithone,"

Gurien eventually said.

His voice came out even, as if this was his usual pace. It made Kara want to gasp for breath even more.

He continued. "A change of clothes has been provided, and a hot bath is waiting. Please be ready in an hour. Food will be sent up, then, and you can ask me questions while we wait for the summoning."

Kara nodded. She wouldn't turn down an opportunity to interrogate someone who knew as much as Gurien. She would have to think of a clever way to ask him about the kidnapping without him realizing she knew about it.

Gurien stopped in the hall, feet planted on the carpeted floor. Kara nearly ran into him. She slid a little on the rug but managed to stop in time.

He twisted the handle on a door to his left. It swung inward. Light splintered through the drawn curtains of a window, casting rays of sunlight onto a wooden bed with a white comforter. A matching wooden desk sat by the window, and a similar dresser filled much of the opposite wall. A white bathtub peeked through a partially opened door to the right.

Most notably, a silver dress lay across the bed. The iridescent fabric glittered in a sunbeam from the window.

"Hear me out, Vagabond," Gurien said.

Kara sighed. This again. The last time she visited, they insisted she wear a dress because she was a woman. Aurora warned her that the dress would undermine Kara's power—all Ithone and his generals would see was a little girl with a book, not the powerful Vagabond she was. She had refused to wear it, forcing Gurien to compromise and give her something else. Not wearing that dress had probably been the spark that ruined her reputation in Kirelm and cost her any respect they might have otherwise shown.

She wouldn't make that mistake twice.

"It's fine, Gurien," she said.

"What? Really? You'll wear it?"

She nodded. "I apologize for making a fuss last time. It was rude."

His eyebrows furrowed, and his lips parted in shock. Kara grinned.

"Thank you," he eventually said.

"You're welcome. I should probably get ready."

"Of course. Please leave your old clothes on the bed. A maid will wash them for you so they're clean when you leave."

Kara just nodded again. He knew as well as she did there were no plans to let her leave. Her clothes would probably be burned.

"Thank you so much," he said with a sigh. It came out slow and steady, like a breath of relief.

He left, and the door shut without another moment's hesitation. He probably didn't want to give her a chance to change her mind.

Kara approached the dress to get a better look. Before she could pick it up, though, Flick jumped down onto the bed and curled up on a pillow.

She sighed and headed to the bathroom. She should just get ready. She couldn't afford Ithone hating her, so she had to play nice. Staring at the dress would only make her question her choice.

***

Forty minutes later, Kara sat on the bed with Flick in her lap. He purred as she ran her fingers through his fur. She'd bathed, dressed, and even fiddled with her hair for ten minutes before giving up and letting it flow over her shoulders.

As requested, she left her clothes on the bed before she took her bath. And sure enough, they were gone when she came out. At least they left her satchel, though they probably rifled through it during her bath. It was a painfully obvious way to control her, but she wanted to oblige. Good faith and all.

As much as she hated to admit it, the dress flattered her in every way. Its low neckline plunged a little farther than she would have liked, but it showcased her necklaces nicely. She still wore both pieces: her Grimoire pendant and the necklace Aurora gave her all those weeks ago. The dress caressed her skin like silk, but the fabric stretched and shrank as needed. A slit in the skirt exposed her left leg up to the thigh when she sat, so she might have to stand when Gurien finally came back.

A few men yelled from the grass outside. Their voices blurred together, muffled by the closed window. She shifted Flick into her arms and peeked through the curtains. Kirelms ran by on the road a few stories below. Some shouted orders, others saluted.

Something boomed in the distance. Its shattering echo reminded Kara of thunder—or maybe a bomb.

Heavy footsteps ran through the hallway just outside her door. More Kirelms shouted, their voices louder as they passed her room.

Kara took a deep breath. This couldn't be good.

She set Flick on her shoulder and ran to the door. Another surge of adrenaline pumped through her and pulsed in her fingers. Something had gone wrong, and for once it had nothing to do with her. If it did, they would be surrounding her room, and she would probably already be in chains.

She twisted the handle and flung her door open. Soldiers ran by, racing for a staircase on the far end of the hallway.

"What's going on?" she asked the passing horde.

No one paused to explain. They stared ahead, all of them focused on something else. Their mouths became hard lines on their faces, eyebrows drawn with tension. Many had weapons—drawn swords, bows and arrows—but none of them stopped long enough to answer her.

A shadow passed over the thin light coming through the closed drapes blocking her window. Kara ran to throw the curtains open. Fabric ripped under her fingers. On the horizon, a thin streak of darkness crept toward the castle. She hesitated, trying to make sense of the black mist as it neared. It could be the storm she saw earlier, but that wouldn't explain the call to arms or the flood of soldiers ignoring the guest they were supposed to kidnap.

Within the approaching darkness, the outline of a winged creature bled into view. Its wings pushed against the air, propelling the figure forward. The silhouette grew larger by the second. More figures appeared, one after the other, until the first drew close enough to see.

A black dragon rode at the head of the shadow on the horizon, a man on its back. Steam rolled from the man's arms. He wore no helmet, so Kara could easily make out his charcoal-gray skin. A symbol covered most of his black shirt: a square of silver thorns held together by four swords.

The Stelian coat of arms.

Carden. Carden found them. A cold rush of panic crept clear down to Kara's toes. She would be caught in the middle of a battle between two kings who wanted her in chains. And of all things, she had to wear a dress that limited her movement. How completely useless.

❧CHAPTER NINETEEN

KIRELM

Kara ran barefoot through the halls of Kirelm. Flick held onto her shoulder. She followed the shouting, mostly, and the clink of swords and armor. She had to find Ithone and Gurien. She could help if they would only let her.

"I said no, Aurora!" someone yelled from down a side hall.

Ithone.

Kara skidded along the stone floor and doubled back. Flick's little claws dug into her neck but slipped a bit as he held on tightly.

She raced down the hall, her feet pounding the stone bricks. Two royal blue doors at the far end stood open. Light spilled into her hallway from wherever they led. A cacophony of voices bubbled out of the room, all of it nonsense. Too many men tried to speak at once.

"This is our home, Father! We must fight for it!" Aurora screamed over the din.

The chaos quieted. Even Kara hesitated, though for another reason than a royal debate. If she ran into that room, she would likely be surrounded by soldiers. She would be outnumbered, vulnerable to Ithone's whim. If he saw her, he might even take out his anger on her.

But they needed help. This was as good a chance as any to show them her new power. To prove herself. To make Ithone listen to reason long enough to go back to Ayavel.

Kara took a deep breath and charged through the open doors. The familiar throne room blipped into view, and the memory of her first meeting with Ithone rushed to the surface. She shook her head, trying to focus. Soldiers filled almost every available space along the walls, all of their attention focused on the far end of the room.

On a platform to the left, Ithone stood behind one of the three thrones. Gurien flanked him, sword drawn and wings braced to take off at a moment's notice.

Aurora leaned on the armrest of another throne, keeping it between her and her father. Her one wing stretched into the air. The stump of her other wing—the one Carden sliced clean off when he tortured her—twitched as the remaining one moved.

Gurien seemed to look everywhere but at the princess. "We'll cover you as you leave, Blood Ithone. Several units will mount a counter attack while the rest guard your escape."

Ithone nodded.

The general turned to his troops. "Head out!"

The troops around Kara stood at attention and turned in unison. Kara darted to the wall seconds before they trotted out the main doors, line after line.

Aurora cursed. "Father, we must fight for our home! I don't understand why you would run away like a coward!"

Ithone frowned. "This is not a debate, Aurora. The Stelians have somehow found our city. It isn't safe here. The citizens are already evacuating. We must leave as well, or they are all in peril. If you and I die, our entire race will die with us. You know this!"

"The Stelians are circling the city. We couldn't leave anyway! If we set up defenses along the outer walls, we can take them out one row at a time. They are exposed. Our walls can't be broken, but if they manage to break down the gates, we will lose an incredible advantage!"

Kara nodded. That was a good idea.

But Ithone's frown deepened. "Come with me now, or I will force you to obey me. I do not want to control you, child, but I will."

"That is all you have ever done, Father!" Aurora spat.

The princess ran down the steps toward the soldiers as they left. Ithone reached for her, his glare focused on the back of her neck. He was no doubt about to take over her, to force her to turn around like Carden had so often forced Braeden to do what he didn't want to do.

Gurien set a hand on the king's arm. "I'll bring her back, Blood Ithone. Please, get to safety. She and I will join you soon."

Without waiting for an answer, Gurien jumped off the platform and raced after Aurora. Ithone huffed, but lowered his hand. His gaze followed his general until the man ran outside. The giant doors slammed shut behind Gurien, and Ithone's eyes landed on Kara. She froze.

"Vagabond," the king said.

She nodded, tensed and ready to bolt if necessary. "How can I help?"

His hands balled into fists. He hesitated, watching her for a moment, still as a stone. He had to be debating with himself as to whether or not to carry out his original plan to kidnap her. They didn't exactly have time. She would put up a fight; he must have known that much. To waste time on her might mean he would lose his opportunity to evacuate.

His jaw tensed, but he offered her a hand. "Would you be so kind as to join us? You can't stay here."

She expected a rude remark or maybe sarcasm, but not courtesy. He must have been trying to lull her into a false sense of security.

"Aurora's plan might work. May I ask why you aren't fighting?" she prodded.

His fists tightened further. "If they found the kingdom, we've already lost. Are you coming, or would you prefer to be Blood Carden's prisoner instead of mine?"

She flinched. He must have already lost patience with her.

"I would rather not be a prisoner at all, Blood Ithone. I want to help. Just tell me what I can do."

"You can stop wasting time and come with me. Remy, help

the Vagabond up the steps."

Kara twisted around in time to see Remy nod to the king and begin toward her. With his back to Ithone, Remy mouthed, *Run.*

She backed away. Every inch of her wanted to beg for Ithone to see reason, to protect his home. She wanted to fight for his people. She would kill the invading Stelian army to keep them safe if it meant proving herself to him. She wanted to make things right between Ithone and the alliance, but he wouldn't give her the chance. He didn't want help. He wanted a weapon.

Ithone shot one final glare at the massive entry before he turned toward the wall behind his thrones. A hidden door slid aside as he neared and closed once he passed through it.

Flick cooed from his place on Kara's shoulder. She rubbed his back, mind racing. They had to get out of there, but she didn't know if it was safe to teleport back to the Rose Cliffs. Kara didn't know much about lichgates, and it was possible there could be one in the air between the kingdom and safety. Since Flick couldn't teleport through a lichgate, Kara didn't want to appear mid-air and have a sudden surprise fall to the ground.

Instead of focusing on her room or the cliffs, she imagined the front steps just beyond the throne room. Aurora would likely be there, no doubt trying to convince her people to fight. And if Kara teleported from the throne room, Remy would have no idea where she'd gone. He wouldn't try too hard to find her, either.

Crack!

"...so who's with me?" a woman asked.

Kara opened her eyes. Flick purred on her shoulder. She stood at the base of a set of stone steps that led into a grassy courtyard. Aurora stood on the entry. Gurien stood to her left, arms folded as he stared at the ground. Just behind Kara, hundreds of soldiers filled the lawn in militant rows. The soldiers glanced at one another, but none of them answered their princess's question.

Aurora's fist tightened. She took a deep breath and opened her mouth to continue, but Gurien set a hand on her shoulder.

She turned toward him, her brows furrowed. Tears clung to

the edges of her eyes, and Kara recognized that fear. Aurora was close to giving up. She couldn't protect her home by herself, and she probably figured Gurien was there to drag her back to her father. Kara reasoned as much, at least.

Gurien arched his back and turned to the soldiers. "Unit one, follow Blood Ithone into the tunnels and protect him with your lives. Go!"

A block of about fifty soldiers broke off and ran around the castle. Kara had no idea tunnels existed beneath the castle, but it didn't surprise her. Kirelm likely had many such secrets.

Gurien continued. "The rest of you, to your wall posts! This is home, and we will fight for it. You are Kirelms, and you obey your crown. If the Heir ever again gives you an order, you will not question her or hesitate. Do you understand?"

"Sir!" the soldiers shouted in unison.

Block by block, they took to the sky. Some slipped into doors within the inner wall; others raced through the secondary gate to the main streets beyond the castle. Hundreds more swarmed the sky within the wire mesh domes, until the flutter of wings drowned out the gusting wind. Kara figured the soldiers who had assembled in the courtyard were likely elite soldiers or squad leaders. In all likelihood, they had probably gone back to their troops to report Gurien's orders.

Within moments, the courtyard was empty. Relief flooded Kara's gut. At least someone in this kingdom could think clearly. Aurora studied the general, her eyebrows twisted in confusion.

"You're helping me?" she asked Gurien.

He nodded. "You're right, Aurora. To abandon home is a cowardly thing. I don't think Blood Ithone ever expected his city would be found, much less attacked. He panicked. I can't reason with panic. I can, however, reason with you. I lied to him—told him I would fetch you and bring you back—but I didn't want him to control you. Blood Ithone can take care of himself, and I will suffer the consequences for my actions, whatever they may be. But we will save our home."

Gurien slipped a hand around Aurora's waist and pulled her

around to face him. Kara blushed and looked away, but it wasn't like she had anywhere else to go. She still hadn't been acknowledged, and she didn't yet know how to help.

The general sighed. "I know we don't have much time right now, Aurora, but I have to tell you something, and I don't know if I'll ever have another chance to say it. I have loved you since the day I met you at your seventeenth birthday ball. I couldn't take my eyes off you the whole night. From that moment on, I knew I would do anything for you. The only reason I climbed the ranks as quickly as I did was to get to you. Your father had to respect me, and it was the only way you would even know I existed. But I respect if you don't want me. I do. I would still gladly die to defend my kingdom and my Heir."

Kara peeked at the young woman in time to see Aurora smile—a real, rich smile. She set her hands on Gurien's cheeks. The princess opened her mouth to speak, but she never got the chance.

Aurora arched her back. Her spine curved too far for it to be natural. She screamed and collapsed on the steps, her body shaking. Something snapped in the princess's leg.

Gurien knelt and lifted Aurora in his arms. She whimpered.

Kara raced over. "What the hell just happened?"

Grief shattered Gurien's face. His knees shook as he held the trembling princess.

"Aurora, it's okay," he whispered.

"Father, he—"the princess choked. Sweat pooled on her temple.

"Gurien, please tell me how I can help," Kara said.

He pulled Aurora closer to him. "You can't, Vagabond. Blood Ithone must be dead. Aurora was just awoken as our Blood, and that means the Stelians are in the castle. They found Blood Ithone. If he's dead, it's more likely Blood Carden found and killed him."

"How?" Kara pressed.

"They must have found the tunnels." Gurien cursed under his

breath.

Gurien lifted Aurora into his arms and stood. Her body convulsed, tremors tearing through her limbs. Gurien gripped her tighter.

He ran back into the castle. Kara kept close behind him, Flick still on her shoulder. They tore through the now-empty throne room and back down the hallway Kara took to find it. Gurien stopped at a sconce halfway along.

He tapped his elbow on one of the stones. "Push that!"

Kara obliged. The stone slipped back into the wall at her touch. The wall groaned. A section of the stones split apart from the rest with a hiss. This hidden door pulled backward about three feet—barely wide enough to slip behind.

Gurien raced in, and Kara followed. As soon as she slipped through, the door hissed again and inched shut.

More sconces lined a curving stairwell with no windows. Gurien trotted down the steps, Aurora still whimpering in his arms. Kara hadn't realized how painful being made Blood could be for an Heir. It reminded her of her own awakening as an isen, of the paralysis that froze her body as Stone drowned her in the hotel bath tub.

She shuddered. Never mind. She didn't want to remember.

A doorframe appeared beyond a curve in the stairwell. Gurien darted in. Kara followed. As she entered, yet another door slid from the stone walls behind her to seal off the room in which they now stood.

Yet more sconces lined the walls. Fire raged within them, giving the room more than enough light. A red couch lay not far off, a square table on either end of it. Aside from that, the small room had no other furniture. Not even portraits or artwork.

Gurien set Aurora on the couch and brushed the hair out of her face. She sobbed. Sweat poured down her face and drenched the edges of her gown.

The general turned to Kara. "You're a force to be reckoned with, Kara Magari. It is for that reason alone I must ask you protect Aurora. You are the last defense between Blood Carden and the last remaining royal of Kirelm. Please keep her safe."

Kara nodded. "Where are you going?"

Gurien stood up straighter. "To protect my home and my love, like I promised."

He stormed off toward the section of wall where the door appeared earlier. Yet again, it slid aside for him.

When the entry sealed behind him, Kara was left in a secret room below the one kingdom that hated her most, yet was now the most vulnerable. But for the sake of Ourea and ending this war, she wouldn't let the Kirelm people down.

❧CHAPTER TWENTY

MISTAKEN

The midday sun beat on Braeden's neck through breaks in the forest canopy. A bead of sweat ran down his back. He sucked in a breath, wishing for a breeze. The humid air clung to him. Not even the forest's shade could shield him from the heat. His clothes stuck to his skin, but he pressed on toward the hidden lichgate he'd used on every scouting mission thus far.

Iyra bolted through the underbrush with Braeden on her back. Gavin followed closely behind, his giant wolf Mastif grunting with every footfall. Once he'd found Iyra and prepped her to leave for their trip, Braeden shared Gavin's taunt about how she wouldn't be able to keep up with his wolf. She made a point of proving him wrong.

It took roughly two hours and six lichgates to arrive at the stone arch that would take them to the Stele. The two statues framed the lichgate, mouths still frozen in silent screams. Braeden sighed with relief, itching to be through the portal and in the cool mountain air of what would soon be his home.

Braeden urged Iyra through. As they passed, a flash of blue light broke across his peripheral vision. His stomach churned. Once he was through, he smiled. This kingdom belonged to him.

Iyra stopped. Her feet dug into the earth, kicking up dust. Braeden tensed and tilted forward, sliding in his seat, but she hunched her shoulders in an effort to keep him on her back.

He looked over his shoulder. Gavin sat on his wolf's back, eyes narrowed as he eyed the lake. He squared his shoulders and sat up straight, fists tight around his mount's reins.

"Is there a problem?" Braeden asked.

Gavin cleared his throat, but didn't speak. Mastif took a step back. A growl tumbled from the beast's mouth.

"We're definitely in the Stele," Gavin finally said.

A muscle twitched in Braeden's jaw. "What makes you say so?"

Gavin shook his head. "Never mind. Lead on."

Annoyance bubbled in Braeden's gut. He opened his mouth to press Gavin, but Iyra growled. He set a hand on her neck to see if she had any input.

Focus, Braeden.

He rolled his eyes. *Don't scold me.*

You have enough to deal with as it is. Don't start bickering with him when you're in Carden's kingdom. You can't be distracted here.

He sighed. As usual, she was right.

She laughed, the husky growls grating on the air. Mastif shuddered behind them.

Braeden nodded to the forest. "Come on."

He charged into the woods without a backward glance. He assumed Gavin followed, though he couldn't hear the Blood's mount as they tore through the trees. He would have preferred Gavin sneak back to Ayavel.

After a few minutes, the black spires of the Stele appeared through the canopy. The towers loomed in the distance, visible only because he was still so high up in the mountains, but Braeden shivered nonetheless. A dozen cliffs and a hundred acres of forest separated him from the castle, but a steady buzz began in his ear. His father wasn't here, or the unease would be stronger. Still, Braeden swallowed hard, and Iyra slowed without being asked.

A few yards to his right, the ground broke away into a steep cliff. Rocks jutted through the underbrush. A dead trunk toppled over the edge, half of its decayed branches hanging in the air beyond the forest.

"Why are we slowing down?" Gavin asked in a whisper.

"You wanted to see the Stele. That's the castle."

Gavin pulled up beside him. "How close are we going to get?"

"Close enough to see into windows. I hope you haven't lost your edge sitting in all those council meetings."

Gavin smirked. "I've always been a better tracker than you. That doesn't disappear after a few stuffy meetings."

Braeden laughed. "You've always had a bigger ego, you mean."

Iyra snorted and stomped her foot. Her silver claws dug into the dirt.

Gavin nodded toward the castle. "What's our focus while we're here?"

"We need to see if any more towers go up, and if so, we need to figure out why. Track troop movements. Look for routines. So far, they change every time I visit."

"That doesn't worry you?" Gavin asked.

Braeden grimaced. "Of course it worries me. He's planning something, and I can't determine what it is."

Gavin opened his mouth to speak, but shut it with an audible click.

"What were you going to say?" Braeden asked.

"Nothing. Let's get going before someone spots us."

Braeden frowned, but nudged Iyra forward. Gavin had a point, and they couldn't sit around talking all day. He wanted to examine the most recent towers and search for clues as to why they existed at all.

Carden's absence tugged on Braeden's mind, distracting him. Instinct warned Braeden to run, as it always did when he visited the Stele. But Braeden didn't run anymore. The Stele belonged to him, and his father belonged in the next life. Braeden would end the man himself—and soon.

※

Four hours later, Braeden inched toward a newly constructed

guard tower. He slunk behind a bush on his forearms, keeping low as he crept closer to the half-built pile of gray bricks and mortar. Dozens of Stelians bustled around the construction site, carrying stones and buckets to and from the clearing. Some wore rags around their heads to keep their black hair from their eyes. Sweat dripped down their gray arms as they toiled. Not one man looked away from his work.

One Stelian lifted a charcoal brick the size of his head and wobbled on his feet. He stood for a moment, eyes on the ground as if waiting for a dizzy spell to pass. Eventually, he hoisted the block up to his shoulders and set it on the tower's growing framework.

"They're exhausted," Braeden said under his breath.

Gavin nodded. "Whatever Carden's doing, he's doing it in a hurry."

Braeden gestured backward and retreated. Gavin followed suit. They snaked away from the tower and stole the fifty yards to where they left Iyra and Mastif near a dense patch of thorns. They ran without so much as crunching a leaf thanks to their childhoods of Hillsidian stealth training.

Once they returned to the thicket, Iyra raised her head in welcome. She and Mastif lay curled near the thorns, mostly out of sight. Though Iyra's black hide blended in with the thick underbrush, Mastif's gray fur clashed with the vines.

Braeden crossed his arms and stopped in his tracks. "This is the twelfth tower I've seen since I started these surveillance trips. They're everywhere, circling the outskirts of the castle. I don't think I ever ventured this far before."

Gavin shrugged. "He's setting up a perimeter."

"The Stele has a perimeter already, farther out. There are towers or guards by every lichgate and at every corner of these woods, except for in the impassible mountains. Not even Stelian guards can survive up there for very long, and nothing can survive a trip over the mountain except for drenowith. Every known entrance is well guarded, and as soon as Carden finds the lichgate I've been using, he'll guard that as well. But these towers he's building don't serve a purpose."

Gavin frowned. "Unless..."

"Unless what?"

The Blood grimaced and shrugged. "Never mind."

"This is the second time today you've almost said something. Get it out of your system."

"Fine. If none of this makes sense, that's probably for a good reason. He might be throwing you off. What if he knows you're here?"

Braeden laughed. "There's no way he can know I'm here. And if he did, why wouldn't he use the knowledge as an opportunity to kill me? He has no idea what I'm planning."

"Are you sure?"

Braeden tensed and mulled over the question. He hadn't been seen. He spent twelve years in Hillside with the finest trackers and hunters in Ourea. He learned from the best. He used to track isen for weeks without his prey knowing. He even managed to get three royal prisoners out of Carden's dungeon. If Braeden didn't want to be seen, no one could see him.

"It's not possible," he finally said. But even as the words left his mouth, doubt tugged at the corners of his mind. The Stele obeyed its Blood. Even if Carden hadn't seen him, it was possible the forest had betrayed him.

The hair Braeden's neck stood on end. He took a deep breath to calm himself, but panic shot through his nerves like a bolt of lightning. He took a deep breath and pushed his worry to the back of his mind. He needed to focus.

Braeden nodded toward Iyra. "Let's see what else my father has waiting for us."

❧CHAPTER TWENTY ONE

DEFIANCE

Kara leaned against the stone wall of a secret room beneath Kirelm's castle. Aurora lay on the red couch not ten feet away, still muttering under her breath. An occasional sob escaped the princess—well, she was the Blood, now—but the pain seemed to have subsided. She shivered less, and Kara took that as a good sign.

Every five minutes or so, explosions rocked the castle. Tremors would shoot through the walls. The sconces lighting the room would rattle, their light flickering with the echo. Kara tightened her fists with each boom, but forced herself to take deep breaths. She didn't know what else to do.

Flick paced at her feet, wearing circles into the carpet. Now and again, Kara debated using the little creature's gifts to teleport Aurora away to Ayavel. She ultimately scratched the idea—Flick couldn't teleport through lichgates, and Kara couldn't carry Aurora through the portals once they reached them. She would end up dragging the already ill royal through the dirt and might even get caught in the process. She couldn't risk being that exposed.

She cursed. There had to be something she could do.

Ten minutes passed. Twenty. Thirty. Still, the world above shuddered and shook. Kara couldn't tell who was winning.

"Vagabond," a small voice said.

Kara's head snapped toward the couch. Aurora lifted her chin enough to peek over the armrest without moving. Her neck strained. A vein pulsed near her jawbone.

"Please," Aurora said. It came out like a moan.

Kara walked to the Kirelm and knelt. She slipped her hand into Aurora's. Sweat slid over the woman's fingers, and she didn't squeeze back.

"What can I do to help?" Kara asked.

"Save them," Aurora said.

"I'm supposed to protect you. Gurien can handle them." Even as she said it, Kara wasn't sure she believed herself.

Aurora shook her head. "I can feel them. They're losing."

"How do you know?"

"I don't...I have no idea," Aurora said.

"Where are they? Can you tell where Carden is?"

"Throne room."

Aurora leaned her head back against the armrest. Her chest rose and fell with exaggerated breaths, enough to make Kara's lungs starve for air as well.

"Please," Aurora said again.

"But you—"

"A Blood is useless without her people," she said, her voice almost too low to hear. Aurora's eyes fluttered closed. Her breathing slowed, and the color drained from her cheeks.

Kara rubbed her own face in frustration. Staying meant waiting for a horde of Stelians and who-knows-what-else to tear down the door. Leaving meant abandoning the already vulnerable Aurora. Either way, this story ended with the enemy kicking in the door. If she stayed, her finale would be a final, hopeless battle in close quarters. Kara might as well take the fight to them.

Aurora's fingers tightened around Kara's hand, but the new queen didn't open her eyes. Only her chest moved in its labored breaths.

"I'll do my best," Kara said.

She picked Flick up off the floor and set him in a small gap between Aurora's head and the back of the sofa. He stared up at her with his wide eyes, and she forced a smile. She scratched his ear.

Kara didn't stand a chance against an army. Not really, not even after all of her training. If the army found her—if Carden found her—she would have to take off the wrist guard that kept her power at bay to even stand a chance of survival. She didn't want to do that, but she didn't want Flick to be caught in the crossfire if it happened.

"If anyone but me comes in, teleport her somewhere else. I don't care where. I'll find you," she said.

He whimpered and pushed his head into her hand. She swallowed hard and forced herself to her feet. In a few strides, she crossed the room and set her hand on the wall.

The hidden door slid open at her touch to reveal the empty spiral staircase. Stone stairs disappeared into the darkness on either side of her. Sconces still lit the stairwell, but the lights hung too far apart to provide steady relief from the shadows.

If Aurora's hunch was right, Kara had to get to the throne room. What she would do when she got there, however, was another matter entirely.

She inched up the stairs, ears twitching at every half-imagined whisper. The explosions settled. No more booms rattled the sconces. No one screamed.

The stairs leveled off into a narrow hallway. Kara stopped, certain the door to the castle had to be in the wall. She pressed her ear to the stone, listening for a voice on the other side. For footsteps. Anything.

A distant scream shot through the rock. Kara shuddered. She took a deep breath to steady herself and listened once again. On occasion, a mumble drifted through the cracks. No loud voices passed by on the other side.

Now or never.

Kara ran her hands along the stones, pushing each of them in an effort to find the one that opened the hidden door. One after another, the solid rocks resisted her touch. She moved down the wall, pressing stone after stone after stone.

A minute passed. Two. Five. She cursed. Finally, one gave way under her touch. As it sank into the wall, Kara sighed with relief.

A gentle hiss escaped from the bricks to her right. The stones groaned. A section of the wall inched backward into the hidden stairwell.

Kara peeked out before it stopped moving. The empty hallway stretched off on either side of her. It took a moment to get her bearings. On her left, the hall split away into a labyrinth of rooms and corridors. On her right, the blue throne room doors stood ajar.

A scream broke the silence. Definitely a man. Someone spoke, the voice too fast and low to make out. The man screamed again, but it died off with a gurgle.

Kara took a deep breath and stepped into the hallway, her back sliding along the wall as she moved. The door creaked shut behind her until it once more looked like just a wall. She took a mental note of its location: between the ninth and tenth sconce. Hopefully she would be able to open it again.

A chorus of men's laughter bubbled through the crack in the doors. A woman whimpered. More laughter.

Kara inched closer, her bare feet registering the cold stones beneath her with each step. Her dress swished along her legs, the slit revealing too much of her thigh. The frayed ends tickled her shins.

She peeked through the door and forced back the reflexive curse that shot into her mouth.

Stelians filled the throne room. Thousands of them. Many grinned. Others chuckled. But all of them watched the front of the room—the platform on which Ithone, Gurien, and Aurora had argued barely an hour earlier.

Kara shifted until she could see the platform through the crack in the main doors.

Carden stood in front of the center throne. He sneered at a Kirelm curled at his feet. Silver wings drooped to the floor, twitching. Off to the side of the platform, four Stelians held Gurien at bay: two held his arms, and two held his wings. He fought against them, but their grip dragged him backward with each attempt to escape.

"She's only a girl! Let her go!" Gurien shouted.

Carden's grin widened. Without looking down, he kicked the Kirelm at his feet. Something snapped. The Kirelm screamed, her voice breaking.

The Stelian Blood eyed his victim, a smile still on his face. "I can make the pain stop, Elana. Just tell me where Aurora is, and we'll be done."

Elana—that name struck a chord in the back of Kara's mind. Why?

She scanned through her thoughts, palms sweating, until it clicked. Elana left a note in the Grimoire warning Kara of Ithone's intention to kidnap her. Elana was Aurora's lady in waiting and—more importantly—a vagabond.

Hatred burned through Kara's gut. The skin on her neck prickled. No one touched her vagabonds.

Her hands tightened into fists. Her core tensed. Her elbows shook from the sudden strain. The hallway dissolved from her peripheral vision as Carden kicked Elana once more.

Kara's eyes narrowed. The world around her faded until the Stelian Blood's laughter shoved aside the last of her rational thought. Elana's screams faded. Gurien's shouts dissolved until it seemed as though he moved his lips without making a sound.

A green glow raced along her arm. It spiked and faded as quickly as it had come. Another trail of light pulsed beneath the skirt of her gown. It raced across the slit in her dress. Its brilliance left a white streak on her vision.

A dull ache throbbed in her wrist. She glanced at the band Stone forced her to wear for her own good. It gave her the modicum of control she had over her power. It limited the flow of magic through her body, even though that was exactly what she had been designed for: power.

If she walked into that room with the wrist guard on, she didn't stand a chance. If she took it off, she could kill them all; just like her grandfather, she would leave nothing but corpses.

Hopefully her allies would simply get out of the way.

Time slowed. She tugged at the leather strap. It unwound itself. Tension in her arm eased as the restraints fell away. Her pulse raced. She sucked in breath after breath as her stomach churned with excitement. She slipped her fingertips between her skin and the leather, prying the band away from her body.

Small spikes in the band lifted away from her body. Shivers of delight raced through her. The air settled against the sweat-soaked arms.

A spark slithered through her veins. It traveled from her wrist clear down to her heels. Another appeared within her, and another, until electricity coursed through her core.

Her fear became glee.

The glow returned, brighter now. It flickered and raced over her skin, reflecting off the door like the northern lights. Something clicked in the back of her mind—this same green glow preceded a murder in each of her grandfather's memories.

Good.

A smile spread across Kara's lips. She could take on the whole room. She would kill them all.

She clutched the wrist guard in one hand and walked through the doors. The room hushed. Everyone turned and stared. Gurien stopped fighting his captors. His lips parted in shock—horror, maybe—but he must have been terrified Kara left Aurora alone. That didn't matter.

Carden frowned. "Kill her."

Kara's grin widened. Power burned within her, igniting the last traces of her self control. This would be *fun*.

❧CHAPTER TWENTY TWO

DESTRUCTION

Kara never took her eyes off of Carden. He stood on the platform beside the Kirelm thrones, one of her vagabonds curled at his feet. Elana whimpered from what had to be lingering pain after Carden's abuse.

Green light pulsed over Kara's skin, casting a glow across the ash-gray faces surrounding her. Thousands of Stelians shifted in the audience around her, most likely wondering what made her glow and whether or not they should run.

Carden glared at his army. "What are you waiting for? Kill her!"

The wrist guard hung limp in Kara's hand. Carden could probably smell her, so he probably knew she was an isen, but he couldn't know of her ties to Agneon. He didn't know that taking off her cuff meant sacrificing her self-control. He didn't know she was about to kill everything that came between her and ripping off his head.

And nothing could stop her.

Ten of the nearest Stelians inched closer. They drew swords, but it didn't matter what they held. They would die.

Her eyes shifted to them. The one in front froze. His hands tightened around the padded hilt of a sword. Kara's ear twitched at the creak of skin on leather. He licked his lips, eyes darting to his neighbors as if uncertain what to make of this girl he was supposed to kill.

Kara smiled.

Sparks danced along her arms. The glow raced again across

her body, stronger now. A string of light broke away like a lasso aimed for the Stelian's head. He screamed. The light thickened, casting its aim at more of the soldiers. When the light touched them, they dissolved into ash that fell to the floor. Steam radiated from their remains.

Kara hadn't even moved.

Voices boiled over the crowd. Panic. Fear. Kara's grin widened. Joy and madness ripped through her like the light had ripped through her attackers. It ignited something within her—something dark. Beautiful. Terrifying. A voice echoed through her head—it sounded like her but came unbidden.

Fear me.

Carden's smirk faded. He hesitated on the platform, apparently surprised. Without another thought, Kara sprinted toward him.

Her dress pulled on her legs, the slit widening with each step as the fabric ripped from the strain. Her bare feet slapped along the floor—*pit pat, pit pat.* Loose strands of her hair floated about her as she ran. Air soared through her lungs when she should have been breathless from the exertion. Too much power tore through her. Too much adrenaline. She couldn't stop.

Any Stelians between her and the invading Blood gasped and shifted out of her way. The smile never left her face.

Carden frowned and stepped over Elana's now-still body. He walked toward Kara, his body growing with every step. His shoulders stretched. His arms thickened. His eyes burned red. His charcoal-gray skin darkened until he became like a shadow.

All Stelians within a hundred feet buckled and fell to their knees as Carden sucked the energy out of them to dawn his daru—the most powerful form a royal yakona could assume. And according to Braeden, the Stelian daru could even feed off of fear. Kara had never fought a royal's daru before, though she had seen one—Braeden lost control of himself when she refused to make him a vagabond all those months ago. Back then, she was terrified of his sudden surge of power and hatred. But not now.

With the power-limiting bracelet gone, Kara didn't fear

anything.

Her mind buzzed. She disconnected from the world, from everything. She saw only the evil man walking toward her. Lights faded. Time slowed. Only the patter of her feet on the floor reached her ears, marred of course by the occasional rip in her dress as she pushed the boundaries of what it could endure. Sweat trickled down her neck.

Nearly to Carden, Kara dropped her wrist guard.

"You're mine," she said to the king.

"We'll see," Carden answered. His voice came out as a growl.

A black mist shot from Carden's fingers. It sailed toward Kara. She didn't think. She didn't slow. She didn't even react. Instead, a flare of green light hurled away from her on its own, tearing into the smoke. The fog burned away in a green blaze. Dust hung in the air.

Carden ambled toward her, apparently in no rush. Another bolt of smoke shot from his hands. And another. And another. Each met the same fate as the first.

In seconds, she reached him. Her hands moved on their own. Red sparks burst to life in her palms. The flickers hummed, jumping back and forth in arcs that formed bridges between her fingers.

Carden lunged for her neck, his red eyes blazing. He didn't make it.

She grabbed his wrists. The red sparks burned through him, racing along his arms. He yelled. With an alien strength she didn't understand, Kara twisted her body and flung him toward the front doors at the far end of the throne room. He sailed through the air like a disc and crashed into the kneeling throng of his people.

The Stelians came to watch their king torture Kirelms. They would get a different show.

Carden pushed himself to his feet, but Kara reached him before he stood. She moved like fire across paper, or water through a brook. She didn't understand it. She didn't really care, either.

His eyes widened in surprise a split second before Kara kicked him in the gut. He sailed backward once more, victim to a strength Kara didn't know she possessed.

Again and again, she knocked him backward. More and more Stelians bent over as he passed, but it didn't matter how much energy he stole from them. It wouldn't be enough.

Kara paused. He had to be drawing every last drop of energy from his subjects. Idiot. Sending them after her in one mob would have been smarter. She would have still killed them, sure, but it would have been a more effective means for him to escape. He probably still didn't realize retreat was the only way he would make it out of this alive.

Arrogant bastard.

A fresh wave of glee burned through her. He wouldn't make it out of this alive.

She shot a bolt of green light into his gut, expecting it to tear him to pieces like it did the other Stelians. It somehow didn't. She frowned. Instead, the attack shot Carden back through the main doors and onto the courtyard where Aurora had become the Blood of her people not much earlier.

Kara expected sympathy to tear through her at the thought of the princess's pain. Worry, perhaps. At a minimum, she expected anger for Carden's rampage. But only the burning joy of murder kept her company.

She shrugged the thought away.

Carden hunched. His knees shook, despite the raging power that must have come from his daru. Kara stopped barely two feet away.

"What are you?" he asked, his red eyes wide.

"Efficient," Kara answered.

She shot another bolt of green into his face. He sailed backward through the air and hit the stone wall opposite the castle. It crumbled beneath him. Boulders flew in every direction. Though he broke through the stones, the wire mesh of the great dome above them caught the king and stopped him from flying over the edge. The second dome lay just beyond.

Dense clouds appeared past that, shielding a sheer drop to the valley below.

Through a gap in the white fluff, a forest appeared. Sunlight glinted off of silver roofs. A road twisted away, far below. Funny—Kara hadn't thought there would be a village so close to the kingdom, much less in plain view.

She and Carden had apparently come to the edge of the floating city on which he had declared war. He was inches from freedom, yet he would never be able to tear through the wire dome protecting the city from invaders. How beautifully ironic.

Carden slumped against the cage, his fingers twitching. Smoke radiated from his clothes. Bulges and small domes appeared in his skin, slithering just beneath the surface—likely bones popping back into place.

Time to end this.

Rays of green light blossomed over Kara's body like solar flares. Another whip of energy attacked the slumping king. It hit him. He yelled in agony. The force shot him backward yet again into the mesh. Black blood coursed down his arms from fresh cuts in his neck, yet the blow still didn't break him.

Kara knew what would.

She set the heels of her palms together and steadied them against her chest. Without effort, she redirected the green light humming along her skin into her hands. It leaked away and congealed into a hot ore of energy. It pulsed. It burned. It slithered over itself, flares shooting off in every direction.

And with every second, the ball of light in her hands grew. It grew from the size of a baseball to a volleyball. A basketball. It grew bigger and bigger and bigger until Kara knew it would finally be enough to kill Carden. With one attack, she would end him forever.

She should have thought of Braeden. She should have wondered how he would react to becoming Blood. She should have worried about what he would become when the power was his. But she didn't. Only murder mattered.

She focused on Carden's twitching body. A cloud passed by.

Rooftops from the village below came into view once more. Carden lifted his eyes to watch her, but evidentially couldn't move. Perhaps he chose not to.

She aimed.

Fire.

But the light continued to grow. It wouldn't obey.

Kara couldn't move. She couldn't release the energy. It pulsed in her fingers, sucking the life out of her.

A pang of dread sank to her toes. The power merely used her as a vessel; she couldn't control it. Sparks broke out over the ball of light. It sizzled. Smoke drifted into the sky. Something hummed.

Panic sent her pulse racing. The orb of light grew ever larger, blocking out everything else. Flares broke away so quickly she could no longer see the true edge of the glowing ball.

She cursed.

With a jolt, the energy left.

A kick to her chest shot Kara backward. She flew, or perhaps she hovered in the air. She couldn't really tell.

Her head cracked against a stone wall. Her vision blurred. She gasped.

The world dipped in and out of focus. Numbness ate away at limbs, inching toward her core. She tried to move her fingers or blink her eyes, maybe, but her body didn't respond.

Someone screamed. Someone else joined in. In fact, several people joined them. The voices pushed against Kara's mind, tearing it to bits. She longed to cover her ears, but she still couldn't move. She whimpered instead.

Pain tore through her right wrist. She flinched. Hands grabbed her, and she pushed against them. They wouldn't leave. A strap tightened. Sharp spikes dug into her arm.

Her mind cleared.

The world rushed back. A cold wind tore through her hair. She shivered. Her wrist throbbed. She couldn't see straight. White and silver and dark gray blobs streaked across her vision.

Guilt burned through her without her understanding why. Shame.

A silver blur leaned in. White blurs blocked out the world behind it. She blinked until her eyes could focus on it.

Gurien.

He stared at her, mouth a tight line. His wings blocked everything behind him, almost like he had encased her within them. Like a cocoon.

The ground moved beneath her. No—she moved. Her body swung back and forth, as if someone held her.

Bit by bit, the world pieced itself together. Gurien cradled her in his arms. Sconces whizzed by. The stone walls passed too quickly for her to focus on any side passage or doorframe.

"What—?"she asked.

"Not yet," he said.

Kara closed her eyes. Something hissed. Stone scraped against stone. Fire flickered in a dark hall. Boots slapped against rock. Another door groaned as it opened.

"Is she alive?" a woman asked.

"Barely," Gurien answered.

A warm cushion pressed into Kara's neck. She smiled and hummed with pleasure. Something furry brushed her cheek. It purred. The last of Kara's energy faded away. Her neck relaxed into the soft pillow beneath her, and she slept.

❧CHAPTER TWENTY THREE

DISCOVERED

After two days of nothing but Stelians building more guard towers, Braeden raced through the Stelian forests on Iyra's back, Gavin and his wolf Mastif in tow. Branches whipped by, their dead twigs nothing but gray blurs in Braeden's peripheral vision. The sun glittered through gaps in the canopy, the occasional beam casting a spotlight on the trail as he led their small party back to Ayavel.

He couldn't wait to leave. Gavin's offhanded comment burned in the back of his mind, but Carden couldn't know about Braeden's plans. It wasn't possible. He always kept to the fringes of the kingdom, observing with stealth he acquired from the best Hillsidian trackers. That sort of silence couldn't be noticed. He'd put so much care and effort into remaining hidden—Carden could never have suspected his presence.

The trail curved to the left. A hundred yards off, the forest ended along the banks of a lake. Sunlight glinted off the water. Mountain tops huddled in the distance, marking the kingdom's edges with a frame of impassable barriers. The forgotten lichgate Braeden found still lay hidden in a dense patch of bushes beside the lake, far enough from the water for a horde of soldiers to easily access. It would serve his still-developing attack plan well as long as Carden didn't know it existed.

Without warning, the light dimmed. Braeden blinked to clear his vision, but the forest darkened further. His jaw tensed as the light faded away. A tendril of white smoke curled before him. Fog rolled through the trees.

Gavin gagged. "Braeden, what—?"

"I don't know. Hurry!"

Iyra grunted and charged forward. Braeden clung to her back, head low to avoid the thickening smog. It had no scent, and though Gavin choked on it, Braeden could still easily breathe. He didn't know what was going on, but he needed to get out of there.

The smoke condensed. It swirled and churned before him, no end in sight. He couldn't see the ground or his own feet. He couldn't even see Iyra, though her quickening breath pushed against his legs as he tensed on her back. Iyra skidded to a halt. Leaves crunched and slid beneath her paws, but Braeden couldn't see anything.

Gavin cursed somewhere nearby, suggesting he had stopped as well. "I can't see!"

"Be quiet," Braeden snapped.

Something rammed into Iyra. They fell. She screamed, the roar like a knife scraping across iron. Ice shot through Braeden's body. Iyra fell on his leg, trapping him beneath her. Her weight snapped bones in his knee and ankle. He stifled a yell of his own.

He reached for his sword but never made it to the hilt. A fist connected with his cheek. Another shot into his neck. A third hit his chest, and a fourth knocked his head into a rock on the ground. He cursed and examined the thick mist. It hid everything from view, and the fists only appeared seconds before they hit him.

The barrage stopped. A moment of silence set his nerves on fire. A sudden bolt of lightning coursed through the fog, casting exaggerated shadows of his attackers. A stream of energy crashed into his midsection. He curled around himself. Another shocked his back. His skin burned. Smoke hovered along his pores. His body couldn't heal fast enough.

Iyra still wouldn't move. She didn't even breathe. Panic and fear ripped through Braeden's core. He couldn't lose her, but he couldn't let himself die, either. He slid a hand beneath her and lifted in an effort to slide his leg free. She didn't budge. Another bolt of lightning hit his neck. Agony splintered down his back. He stifled a scream and fell against Iyra's torso. His body shook. Yet again, he tried to slide free.

The rush of fabric pulling against metal drifted through the fog. A man screamed, but Braeden didn't recognize the voice. Whimpering followed. A heavy step landed by his head. Braeden twisted, trying to get a solid view of his attacker, but smoke distorted everything.

Braeden conjured a gray flame and shot it toward the footsteps. He summoned another, and another, until a volley of fireballs sailed away from him in every direction.

A green blade cut through the smoke. It sliced Braeden across the chest, the wound only an inch or two deep. Pain blistered from the cut. Black blood coursed down his shirt, boiling as it touched the air. Pressure sank into Braeden's chest. He couldn't breathe. For whatever reason, his body wouldn't heal the wound. With each passing second, the pain worsened. It was as if the wound were getting bigger.

A wave of adrenaline fueled every muscle in Braeden's body. He pulled on his leg with everything he had. It gave an inch. He sucked in as much of a breath as he could muster and pulled again. This time, his leg slipped free of Iyra's still body.

He pushed himself to his feet, but agony cracked through his chest. He fell to his knees, reaching for his sword, but he couldn't even find the hilt. The world spun around him. His breath caught in his throat. More blood poured down his shirt. Small drops of the black liquid fell off into the mist as it thickened.

A gust ripped through the fog. The mist thinned. Shapes came into focus: trees, men, underbrush. The haze dissolved. Gavin stood five feet away. Green stains lined rips in his shirt. He furrowed his brows, focused on whatever he was doing. He'd probably created the gust blowing away the dense smoke.

Five Stelians stood around them in a circle, blocking both the exit and the way they'd come. The soldiers wore black pants and shirts, and each had a black cloth wrapped around his head so that only his eyes and hands showed through the layers of fabric. Black eyes stared at Braeden. Fists tightened. And though

Braeden tried to stand, the gaping wound in his chest suffocated him whenever he tried to move. He remained on his knees.

A flash of green caught his eye. His head snapped around. A sixth Stelian crouched nearby, breathing through his teeth in sharp bursts. He lifted a sword into the air, eyes locked on Braeden.

Braeden's gaze shifted to the sword in the soldier's hand. The green hilt struck a chord in Braeden's memory, but it wasn't until the blade swung down toward his head that he recognized the Hillsidian Sartori.

He didn't have time to question why the soldier had the sword Carden stole from Gavin's mother after he killed her. With what little energy he had left, Braeden pulled the air toward him. Tension burned along his arms. His fingers twitched. The air by his face compressed into the tip of an arrow. He aimed and released the attack. His body shifted, ducking the blade on impulse. The arrowhead sailed toward the soldier and sank into his forehead.

The assassin collapsed in a heap. The Hillsidian Sartori dug into the dirt where Braeden had been an instant earlier.

Pain splintered through Braeden's chest. He screamed and stretched out on the ground, too exhausted to move. Every breath sent a fresh wave of agony rippling through him. He froze, trying to regain his composure, but even thinking hurt.

A boot crunched nearby leaves. Braeden opened his eyes and tensed. Gavin picked up his Sartori, staring at the green blade. A smirk crept over his face. He swung the sword, testing the weight in his hands, and stepped over Iyra's body as he returned to the circle of soldiers.

Braeden's vision blurred. Through the haze of his unfocused eyes, he managed to make out two corpses, apparently victims to Gavin's years of fighting experience. The remaining three attacked at once, each employing a different technique as they rushed the king. White smoke, lightning, and fire blazed toward the Hillsidian, but he didn't break his stride. Another gust broke through the trail, likely on Gavin's command, and he swung the

Sartori without hesitation.

Braeden took a deep breath, but pain splintered through his torso. He examined his chest. A two-foot wound split him open at a diagonal from his shoulder to hip. His muscles tensed. He lay back and set his hands on his wound, conjuring what few healing techniques he knew. He'd never had to heal himself before. He didn't know if anything could heal a Sartori wound, but he had to try.

His palms glowed white as he focused on the blood seeping from him. He channeled what little energy remained into healing himself. The energy slipped from his fingers, but the wound continued to grow. The skin around the edges of the cut dissolved away as though burned by acid. Panic bubbled through him. Another surge of adrenaline rocked him to the core, but he couldn't move. He couldn't breathe. He couldn't even heal himself—something he had never failed to do.

Iyra twitched beside him. She whimpered and curled around herself, her silver claws glinting in the murky sunlight pouring in from above. Her body shook as she woke. Her head hung low as she blinked, eyes unfocused.

"Iyra," Braeden called. His cry for help came out like a gasp.

Her head snapped around. Her eyes slipped into focus. She shot to her feet, only to wobble and sink to her knees. She slid the final few feet between them and nudged his neck with her nose.

Why aren't you healing? she asked.

He licked his lips, trying to muster the energy to respond, but nothing came out. Even his thoughts were too fuzzy to control. His mind wandered over the smoke and the soldier's attack. He hoped she would make sense of his loose thoughts.

She growled at the image of the assassin.

We have to get you out of here, Braeden.

He nodded and sank back against the ground.

Boots crunched again along the forest floor. Braeden glanced around, trying to see who was walking closer. Gavin's tattered shirt came into view, followed by the Blood's face. Black blood stained his jaw, evidence of the soldiers he must have killed.

The Sartori glinted from its place at Gavin's side. The Blood still wielded his newfound weapon. He stared at Braeden with the subtlest of smirks. His fist tightened around the Sartori's hilt.

Gavin nodded to Braeden's chest. "I could let you die, you know."

Braeden didn't respond.

Gavin continued. "I could finally be done with you and your wretched race. They knew you were here, Braeden. All along. These soldiers are unlike any I've ever fought or seen. They were elite. Your father sent them to kill you. Why do you want anything to do with this world? I would be doing you and Ourea a favor if I let you die."

Iyra growled and shifted her weight. Her legs buckled as she fought to stand.

"I have no problem killing your pet either, Braeden," Gavin snapped.

"Iyra, stop," Braeden said. She couldn't protect them. She needed to reserve her strength in case she had to escape to save herself.

She whimpered again, frozen in place, but eventually slid back down beside him. She nudged his shoulder and let out a low growl.

"Kara would kill you," Braeden said.

"She would try."

Braeden laughed and closed his eyes. "Tell her I'll wait for her, then."

Gavin hesitated. "Just like that? You give up?"

"I enjoy life, but I'm out of options. You're too blinded by hatred to see reason anymore."

Warmth pooled near Braeden's side even as ice sank deeper into his core from the wound. It couldn't end like this. Not here. Not on some nameless trail in the middle of the Stele. Especially not at Gavin's mercy. Braeden couldn't die this way, but he had no other options. His body stiffened.

"If I heal you, what will you do?" Gavin asked.

Braeden couldn't open his eyes anymore. His voice came out in a whisper. "Punch you in the face for waiting this long."

Gavin laughed. "You're making this difficult, Braeden. I need to trust you."

"You don't. You never will."

A breeze rushed through the canopy. The clapping of leaves drowned out all other sound. The last of Braeden's warmth left him. Pebbles in the dirt trail dug into his back, all the more painful because he couldn't move to brush them away. Braeden sucked in a breath, but it barely filled his lungs.

"Please, Gavin," he said.

Cloth rustled beside him. Someone sighed. A blade cut into skin, though Braeden couldn't tell if it was his or not. He couldn't feel his body anymore. Liquid trickled over steel. Drops of something fell into the grass. Iyra sighed—in happiness or resignation, Braeden couldn't tell.

Relief flooded through Braeden's gut. Gratitude and a hint of warmth followed, melting his icy core. Someone lifted him. He settled against something solid, and the last of his energy faded. He resigned himself to the peace of the moment. He had no say anymore.

If he survived, he would never again let Kara out of his sight. If he didn't, he would wait for her with Death until she followed him. He should have never let her leave.

❧CHAPTER TWENTY FOUR

CONSEQUENCES

Gray mist enveloped Kara. She glanced around, but the world had a white sheen to it. She tried to make sense of where she was, or why she was there, or perhaps the time, but nothing made sense. She shuddered and rubbed her arms, even though she hadn't felt a chill.

A hot breath rolled down her neck. Someone approached her from behind.

She spun. A tall man stood perfectly still not two feet away. She gasped and covered her mouth with a hand. His features blurred and sharpened, as if she stared at him through a camera that wouldn't focus. Olive skin. Black hair. A charming smile.

Braeden.

She hugged him. He wrapped his arms around her and held her close.

"I think I did something terrible," she whispered into his chest.

He didn't answer. His chest didn't move—was he holding his breath?

Panic raced through Kara. Her fingers went numb. "I remember cornering Carden against that wire dome. He couldn't move. He looked broken—I was going to kill him, Braeden, and I was happy about it. But something went wrong. I lost control and...and I really think I did something horrible."

A hand cupped the back of her head, but he still didn't say anything. He still didn't breathe. Kara leaned back so that she could see his face. He smiled.

She took a step back. Her body shook with fear, anger, and a remorse she didn't understand. "I lost control, Braeden! What if you'd come with me after all? What if you'd gotten in the way? What if an innocent person had gotten in my way back there? I'm afraid—I'm terrified that I would have killed anyone I came across, even you! I'm scared to even have that much power!"

Instead of saying something helpful, he leaned in and kissed her nose.

Kara gasped herself awake.

Awake—that had been a dream? She glanced around, trying to make sense of her surroundings. Red sofa arm. Pillow under her head. Blanket up to her shoulders. Big ball of blurry fur blocking her view of about everything else.

Flick licked her nose in the same spot Braeden had kissed her in her dream. She leaned back, pressing her head into the sofa until her pet came into view. He purred and blinked those massive eyes of his.

Someone let out a deep sigh of relief. "Bloods, thank goodness. You're all right."

Kara rose to lean on her arm and get a better look at the room. Gurien sat in a chair by the stone wall, his hands on his thighs, elbows out. His wings blocked a fair bit of the wall behind him. He took another deep breath. Shadows played along his face because of the low light, but the bags under his eyes had a darker tint than before the attack. He probably hadn't slept this whole time.

The aromas of sweet bread and the salty sting of jerky drifted by. Kara's stomach rumbled. A plate of rolls, cheese, and dried meat lay on a small table in front of her. She grabbed a roll and took a bite, relief coursing through her.

"Thank you for the food," she mumbled between bites.

Gurien just nodded.

Kara's head throbbed with every movement, so she tried to remain still as she canvassed the rest of the room. Light flickered from only a few candles along the wall. Most of the room lay in a dark shadow, but from the sofa and layout, Kara guessed she was in the same place where she'd left Aurora earlier. Her wrist guard once more clung to her.

"Did you put this back on me?" she asked.

Gurien nodded. "I noticed you holding it before you attacked Carden. It seemed important."

"It is. What happened?" Kara's eyes stung. She rubbed them.

"That's a question Aurora should answer, not me," Gurien said.

Kara hesitated. Either Gurien didn't know what happened, or he refused to tell her. Bad sign.

She pushed herself upright. "Okay, then. How long was I out?"

"Two days."

"Two—seriously?" She cursed under her breath. She had a day left before she needed to meet Braeden back at Ayavel.

"I'd begun to fear you weren't going to make it. You used an obscene amount of energy in that last attack and hit your head against a stone wall. We didn't know which hurt you more."

Kara's head throbbed again. She rubbed the ache only to find a bandage wrapped from her neck to her forehead. She ran her fingers along the linen, thankful they hadn't used something itchy. She hadn't even realized she wore a bandage at all.

"Is Aurora okay?" she asked.

A broad smile broke over the exhausted General's face. "Quite. Thanks to you."

"I left her alone even though you told me to protect her. I figured you would be furious."

He shook his head. "You chased off Carden when I failed to protect our home. If he had stayed, he would have eventually found her."

Gurien had a point. Kara had succeeded where Gurien had failed. She should be brimming with pride and joy that it was over, but regret swam in her gut instead. Her stomach churned, and her appetite dissolved.

"If I did something great, why do I feel so terrible?" she

asked.

Gurien's smile fell. "How much do you remember?"

Kara stared at the floor and tried her best to recall everything. Flick jumped into her lap and curled into a purring ball. She ran a hand over his back.

"Last thing I remember is losing control of my final attack. Well, and then you carrying me someplace. Here, I guess."

He nodded. "I was afraid of that."

"Why can't you tell me what happened?"

"It's Aurora's duty, not mine. Can you walk? I'll take you to her."

Kara set one bare foot on the floor. Flick jumped out of her lap. The long rip in her dress gave her free movement. The soft fabric soothed her skin. With one hand on the sofa's arm, she slowly pushed herself to her feet. Her arm shook. Blood rushed from her head. She swayed.

Gurien shot to his feet and grabbed her elbows. Kara steadied.

"Thanks," she said.

He nodded and let go. After a few tentative steps, Kara regained her sense of balance. She gestured toward a wall, hoping it was the one with the hidden door.

"Lead the way, General."

�֍

With Flick on her shoulder, Kara followed Gurien through twisting hallways until they stepped out of the castle. Aurora stood by a granite wall. A sizeable chunk of the bricks had been blown to bits. Several of the stones lay in the grass nearby.

The wire dome protecting the palace had a hole twice the size of Kara. The impenetrable metal strands curled outward into the sky, but most of it had simply gone missing. Ditto for the wire in the second dome.

Kara couldn't speak as she neared the new Blood. She simply stared at the hole, keeping her distance from the edge. Clouds tumbled by. A sheer cliff of gray rock lay just below the wall. A hundred feet down, a thin road curled around the cliff on a ledge. A few buildings separated the road from the second dome's wire mesh.

Something caught in Kara's throat—that familiar guilt.

She opened her mouth to ask a burning question just as the clouds separated to reveal the village below. Half the rooftops lay in rubble. A charred circle covered most of the village visible through the clouds. Kara's question died in her throat.

"You missed," Aurora said.

Kara covered her mouth with her hand. She choked on a sob. Flick jumped off her shoulder and stared out of the hole, shaking with his ears pinned back against his head. Kara, on the other hand, couldn't move.

Oh God, no.

Aurora sighed. "Your attack blew a hole through a material we believed could not be destroyed. Carden and many of his troops escaped through it. The rest escaped through an abandoned lichgate in the tunnels below the castle. Only Kirelm royals knew the portal exists, and it has always been locked. While I don't understand how he could have found it, much less used it, I suppose we became arrogant. I don't know the last time its locks were changed, and it's possible one of his allies learned of its location. Regardless, I have since changed the locks on that lichgate, and only Gurien and I have access to it now. That portal is how Carden and most of his army got into the city, while a small portion of his troops distracted us by attacking the front gates. His dual attack crippled us."

Tears welled in Kara's eyes. She sobbed again. Regret snaked through her body like lead, weighing her down. Her knees shook.

Aurora continued to stare through the hole. "This morning, the village's final tally of the dead and missing was ten thousand four hundred seven. As their Blood, I could feel each one."

Kara dropped to her knees and wept into her hands. Her shoulders trembled. The tears would not stop.

A warm hand rubbed her back. Someone knelt beside her.

Boots crunched along the rubble and grass, suggesting someone else had walked away.

"I'm not angry," Aurora said, her voice soft.

Surprise slowed the tears. Kara glanced through her fingers. "What?"

"Lives are irreplaceable. I feel the guilt, same as you. But if you hadn't intervened, Carden may have claimed the palace. He would have captured me and killed Gurien. And then those in the village below would have died anyway. More than ten thousand for sure."

"But I killed—" Kara couldn't finish the sentence.

"Yes."

The young queen looked again at the hole in the wall. Her eyebrows bent with the same grief that tore through Kara. Something had changed in the Kirelm royal—Kara couldn't quite name it. She seemed older, somehow. Tired.

Aurora set her hands in her lap. "Only four Kirelms witnessed your final attack, and I have ordered them to never breathe a word of it to anyone. No one else in Kirelm knows what happened, nor will they ever. When I spoke to the kingdom, I told them Carden attacked the village out of spite after he threw you against the wall."

The guilt tunneled deeper into Kara's core. "You can't lie to cover for me."

"I already did, and it cannot be undone. The Kirelms are wounded, Kara. To hear the Vagabond killed their people...they would never recover. They would demand I kill you as retribution, but that would undo everything we've achieved thus far. It would ostracize us from the other kingdoms and throw our world deeper into war. Regardless, I could never hurt you. Not after what you sacrificed to save us when we needed you most. But I cannot change the will of an entire people, and thus, I lied to protect them from themselves. You must live that lie with me."

Kara rubbed her face. Every bit of her trembled. Still kneeling, she curled against herself in the vain hope it would help her steady her shaking limbs. It didn't work.

This can't be happening.

Aurora continued. "For what it's worth, you have Kirelm's loyalty. You have my loyalty. We will follow you wherever we are needed."

Kara nodded. It was all she could think to do. She couldn't speak, so it would have to suffice.

Aurora stood. "We should return to Ayavel soon, but not until I make sure Kirelm is safe in my absence. The village's survivors are already evacuating. For the last couple of days, I have been scouring our old texts for ways to move our floating city, and I believe I've found one. We're not safe here anymore and need to find a new location. The move will take a great deal of energy, but I should be ready to leave with half our army in four days."

"I need to go back sooner than that," Kara said. Her voice came out so much softer than she intended.

"That's fine. I will meet you in Ayavel when I can."

Kara nodded again.

"You missed my father's memorial," Aurora added.

Kara looked at her. The newly appointed Blood stared at the ground, her shoulders hunched. A loose curl hung over her long neck.

"I'm sorry," Kara whispered.

A tear slid down Aurora's cheek, but she wiped it away. "He and I fought so often. I didn't think I would miss him this much."

"Losing family always hurts," Kara said.

"I suppose so."

Kara stared through the gap in the wires, her eyes going in and out of focus as clouds passed by. She didn't want to move or talk or think. If anything, she just wanted to curl into a ball.

"You don't look well. Please rest," Aurora said after a while.

The young Blood stood and offered her hand. Kara forced a thin smile and accepted, whistling for Flick to join them. He ran to her, and she picked him up before following Aurora into the castle without looking back at the disaster she created. Her eyes remained on the floor as she walked.

At some point, Aurora's shoes disappeared. A maid's slippered feet took the queen's place. Kara didn't really take note of who it was, when it happened, or where they were going. Her ears buzzed as her feet moved on their own. Step after step, stair after stair, Kara lost herself to her thoughts.

When she came to, she stood in the bedroom where she'd prepared to talk some sense into Ithone. Everything was exactly as she left it, except that her now-clean traveling clothes lay across the bed alongside a white nightgown and a blood red dress that reminded her of her Gala gown.

Kara drifted through the motions of getting ready for bed and barely registered the world around her. She bathed and slipped on the nightgown before folding the other clothes and setting them on the floor.

She crawled onto the mattress, and the plush comforter dipped under her weight. She slipped under the blanket. Flick curled under her chin. His warm fur pressed against her neck, and she set a hand on his small back. He vibrated as he purred.

A cold hand rested on her shoulder. Even through the comforter, her skin chilled like she'd been touched by ice. She didn't have to turn around to know it was the first Vagabond, Cedric. She wanted to confess to the thousands of murders, but he already knew everything.

"Why didn't you stop me?" she whispered.

"I tried, but I couldn't get through to you. The sheer amount of power you harnessed trapped me inside the Grimoire. I couldn't move the entire time. I could only watch. I even tried to stop you from taking off the wrist guard, but you silenced me. I don't think you even realized you did it. It was like something else controlled you the entire time."

The cool comforter soothed the burning ache in her body, but tears pooled in her eyes. She wanted to apologize for letting him, Stone, and her long-dead grandfather down, but it wouldn't be enough. Nothing could undo what she'd done.

Her mentor sighed. "You didn't disappoint me, Kara. You did what had to be done. I see it clearly now. You had no choice. For what it's worth, I'm in this with you. Aurora is with you. Braeden will be, too, if you choose to tell him. You're not alone."

A ball formed in her throat. Braeden—what would he think of her if she told him how many innocent people she killed?

"Get some sleep. I'll be here if you need me," the first Vagabond said.

She didn't say anything. The cold hand disappeared. She wished she could go back to Ayavel right then, but her resolve crashed around her. She cried into Flick's fur. Taking off the wrist guard cost ten thousand people their lives. People she never met dissolved into dust the moment her attack touched them. Children. Mothers. Families. Pets. Despite whatever good it may have done for Aurora and Gurien and even the Kirelm people overall, Kara had ignored every warning her grandfather left for her when she took off the leather cuff. She wasn't ready for that kind of power.

An icy wave of fear raced through her. It didn't matter if she was ever ready. She would never, ever take off the bracelet again. Nothing—and no one—was worth losing control of herself. She was already a mass-murderer. She wouldn't repeat that mistake.

❧CHAPTER TWENTY FIVE

LOST

Braeden's skin burned. He itched, as if a thousand spiders bit him at once and wouldn't let go. An ache seeped through every muscle. He tried to scream, but his voice caught in his throat. Bones cracked. Pressure weighed on his chest, seeping through every pore in his body. He tried to move, but his fingers wouldn't twitch. He couldn't even open his eyes.

He slowly lost all sense of his limbs. The sensation in his fingers faded away. The pain in the soles of his feet dissolved. Numbness wound its way up his legs and arms, seeping toward the gaping wound in his chest. He craved the apathy. He wished it would hurry and dull the pain. Flickers of agony pricked at his gut like hundreds of needles stabbing him again and again.

A chill pooled in the wound. He took a deep breath, but still couldn't open his eyes. Relief washed through him. The numbness stopped. A cool wave rippled through his veins, washing out the pain. He sighed and smiled—or tried to, anyway.

Voices filtered through his dulled senses. Men. A few cursed. Others spoke his name, though he couldn't understand anything else. One voice called to him, familiar and louder than the rest. It had a name, this voice, but he couldn't remember it.

Hot water dribbled down his neck. Steam pooled in his ear. He shuddered. Cold linen pressed against his forehead. He sighed again.

A searing pain cracked against his temple and splintered through his neck. He screamed. His muscles tensed. The pain worsened. His entire body roasted. Every vein boiled. He screamed until he couldn't hear himself anymore. He thrashed, trying to shake whatever attacked him, but every movement amplified the pain.

Tears rolled down his face. He couldn't take this. It was worse than anything Carden subjected him to in life. It broke him, right to his core.

Darkness pulled at him. It tugged him under, down toward the agony breaking his body. He couldn't think. He couldn't shake the pain. And eventually, he couldn't move. The agony wrapped around his limbs, binding him to whatever attacked.

He searched for the white light—the one that saved him from Carden's torture the last time he visited the Stele's infamous prisons. Kara would be there, waiting for him. She would shield him from the pain until the worst passed. He could survive if he found her.

His mind sifted through his shifting thoughts, searching for the white light. Nothing came to him. No one stepped in. His searching became panic. His memories faded. And right before he lost himself to the searing pain, he screamed her name.

❧CHAPTER TWENTY SIX

THE HERO

A steady pulse beat in Kara's ear.

Da-thump. Da-thump. Da-thump.

Something warm pushed against her chin. Blades of fur tickled her neck. She smiled, half-awake, as a wet nose burrowed against her jaw. She laughed and pulled away, her eyes snapping open. Flick batted her face with his tail and chirped.

Kara glanced around the room. It took a moment to remember where she was, but the realization crushed her.

Kirelm.

Her smile faded. She curled her head back into the pillow and pulled the blanket up to her neck. She didn't want to think about the guilt or murders or her conversation with Aurora. She just wanted to go back to sleep.

A wispy figure bled into view by the window, the trails of his cloak turning solid as she watched. The ancient ghost of the first Vagabond stared into the bright sky outside, a hood over his head, his arms crossed.

Kara's heart skipped a beat. She didn't know what to say.

He turned. "Are you all right?"

She hesitated but ultimately shook her head.

He nodded. "It's understandable. The situation is hardly fair. Though I'm heartbroken at how many were killed, Aurora is right. If the truth got out, you would never again have a chance of establishing peace in Ourea. You would be hated, despite however much you were trying to help."

Kara burrowed her face into her pillow.

"Are you going to lie in bed all day?" he asked.

"Sounds tempting, actually."

"You can't hide from this. Guilt or not, you have to accept what you've done and find a way to move on."

She rolled her eyes. "I know, Vagabond. I'm just trying to process it."

The wispy ghost sat on the edge of her bed. "You're right to do so. Grief is part of life, and you can't deny it. The modest acknowledge their mistakes. The wise both confess to their failures and vow to never repeat them. But it takes a strong warrior to forgive herself as well."

She hugged her knees and nodded. She didn't figure she fit in any of those categories at the moment.

He smiled. "You're all three. Just give yourself time."

"Thanks." She forced a smile.

"It's the truth, or I wouldn't say it."

Her grin became real, and she rubbed the Grimoire pendant around her neck out of habit. The smile faded ever so slightly.

"I guess I should find out what I missed while I was asleep," she said.

He nodded. "I'm sure there are dozens of messages waiting for you."

"I can't even tell them the truth, can I? The other vagabonds?" she asked.

The first Vagabond hesitated and turned to look out the window again. After a few silent moments, he shook his head. "I'm afraid not. If any of them defected and told the public, your reputation would be ruined. This burden is yours alone. Well, ours."

Kara leaned back against the headboard and closed her eyes. She forced herself to swallow the ball in her throat. Crying wouldn't do any good.

She summoned the Grimoire, its blue dust leaving a glow on

her skin as it took its solid form. She set it on her knees and left it closed. The words to her confession were already forming in her mind, but she would never be able to release it. She wanted to tell the unfiltered truth—all of it. Everything. The guilt. The loss. The terrifying glee that came with knowing she could kill. The desire to end a life. The loss of all sanity in her moments of absolute power. But most of all, she wanted written evidence of her vow to never again succumb to power she couldn't control.

She took a deep breath, suppressed the desire to absolve herself, and opened the cover. The pages sprang apart, flipping to the messages her vagabonds left her overnight. With no way to vent the guilt churning in the pit of her stomach, she settled in to read.

※

An hour later, Kara stared at the open Grimoire. She still couldn't quite process what her vagabonds had told her.

Overnight, Kara had become a hero. The kingdom of Kirelm apparently already had a life-sized marble statue underway. It would go up in an empty patch of grass in one of the public parks for all to see.

Aurora sent out a notice the day after the attack explaining the assault and subsequent rescue to the other kingdoms. At first, the notice had been met with silent shock—only Bloods had ever survived a battle with another Blood. Yet here was the Vagabond, a girl not even raised in Ourea, nearly killing one of the most powerful kings to ever rule the Stele.

According to her vagabonds, the Bloods of each kingdom learned about the attacks in a council meeting with a few advisers present. Gavin laughed. Frine smiled. But Evelyn stood without a word and left. No one saw her reaction.

Details of Kara's battle with Carden spread like wildfire. According to a Hillsidian vagabond, drinking songs had already emerged in her honor in the farthest cities from the capital. In Losse, tapestries of the battle had already been ordered to cover walls in wealthy homes. Ayavelians prepared a banquet to honor her return. And in Kirelm, maids vied for any excuse to visit her room and see the now-famous fighter.

Kara's stomach churned with disgust. She didn't deserve any of this.

Her ghostly mentor had disappeared sometime while she was reading, most likely to give her privacy. She toyed with asking him about his heyday as the Vagabond—had the yakona ever fawned over him? Legend remembered him as a hero. Perhaps he would know how to handle the attention.

Someone knocked on the door.

Kara pulled the covers tighter around her waist and wished away the Grimoire. It dissolved once more into blue dust and drifted into her pendant.

"Come in," she said.

The door opened to reveal a thin Kirelm woman with a black braid that fell down her back. Her left arm hung in a sling, and her right balanced a silver tray with a cover on it. The Kirelm smiled as she made eye contact.

A twang of recognition shot through Kara. This was Elana, Aurora's lady in waiting and a vagabond to boot. The last time Kara saw Elana, the girl was curled at Carden's feet, bloody and broken from his torture.

With small flourishes of her free hand, Elana set the tray on the desk and shut the door. The moment the door clicked shut, the Kirelm raced to the bed and slipped her right arm around Kara in a tight hug.

Elana sobbed. "You saved my life. Thank you. Thank you so much."

"I protect my own." Kara grinned at her fellow vagabond.

"You protected us all! Everyone is dying to meet you. I was amazed Blood Aurora let me in to see you."

Blood Aurora. The title fit her.

Elana continued. "After the Stelians attacked, one of them somehow discovered I was close to Blood Aurora. When I wouldn't tell them anything, they dragged me into the throne room. I nearly fainted when I saw Blood Carden waiting for me. I knew I would die. I simply knew it. Legend is no one but royalty can survive his torture. By the time you arrived, I had already resigned myself to death. And then you appeared, my saving grace. I couldn't believe it."

Kara tensed. "How—well, what did I look like?"

Elana's smile fell. "Let's just say I'm glad you're on our side."

"Please. You can tell me."

The Kirelm sat on the edge of the bed, her wings flowing over the comforter. "Green sparks shot along your body. You had this look of...I don't even know how to describe it. Calm? But you weren't calm. You looked wild. And when you sneered..."

The girl cleared her throat and wouldn't lift her gaze from the floor.

Kara leaned in. "Please, Elana."

Elana took a deep breath. "When you sneered, I saw evil in your eyes. It was clear you could kill anything in that moment. Your hair almost floated around you—it was incredible. With your bare feet and ripped dress, I thought you had perhaps gone insane. I mean, you had to be unhinged to take on Carden. Or so I thought. No one expected you to win."

Kara sighed and rested her head against the headboard. Evil? She hadn't expected that. A hand on her knee pulled her attention back to her fellow vagabond.

Elana smiled again. "I know you aren't evil. And like I said, it's a blessing you're on our side and not his."

Kara laughed. "I guess so."

"Blood Aurora said she will be up shortly to check on you. But if you need anything, please let me know. I'll stay nearby. Blood Aurora asked me to care for you while you're here."

"Thank you. I won't be here much longer, though. I need to go back to Ayavel."

Elana frowned. "So soon?"

"Afraid so."

"May I ask why? The Kirelms want you to stay. We're

preparing a celebration to last for weeks!"

"The war didn't stop, Elana. Carden will want revenge, and he won't wait for us to finish our party first."

Elana stared again at the floor, the fingers of her free hand toying with her sling.

"I guess I hoped we could relax for awhile. Take a break," she admitted.

Kara rubbed her neck. "We'll celebrate when Carden is dead. For now, we can't afford to lose focus."

"I suppose so."

Elana stood and brushed off her skirt, avoiding eye contact the whole time. She retrieved the platter from the desk—Kara had forgotten about it—and set it on the bed.

Kara sighed. "I don't mean we can't enjoy life, Elana. I just don't want him to catch us off guard again."

"No, you're right. I simply got caught up in the moment. I understand. But know this—celebration or not, you're my hero. You always will be."

Kara's chest tightened. She wasn't sure how to reply. A thank you wouldn't quite suffice, but she didn't deserve that kindness, either.

Before Kara could react, Elana bowed and ducked out of the room. The door shut with a *click*. That familiar guilt settled into Kara's stomach, killing her appetite. She nudged the silver plate away with her toe as silence settled over the room.

CHAPTER TWENTY SEVEN

RETURN

After a bath and a clean change of clothes, Kara's hunger returned with a vengeance. It took all of ten minutes to empty the silver plate of fruits and cheeses Elana had brought in—a thankful thing, considering someone knocked on the door not two minutes after she finished.

Kara crossed to the entry and opened it, only to find Aurora standing in the hallway. The young queen waited on the threshold with her hands behind her back and a thin smile on her face.

"May I come in?" the queen asked.

Kara stepped aside. "Of course."

"Elana tells me you need to leave as soon as possible. Is the rumor true?"

"Yes."

Aurora nodded. "Fair enough. It might take longer to join you than I originally thought. Moving the city is taking more energy than anticipated."

Kara sighed. "Will the Kirelms be upset if I leave now? I heard they were planning a celebration and—"

Aurora laughed. "If you never stop a Kirelm's celebration, it will last for years. Don't feel obligated to stay. My people can celebrate even without the guest of honor."

Kara chuckled. "I'll keep that in mind."

The queen turned to gaze out the window, and her eyes went out of focus. For a moment, the conversation died while Kara examined the Blood before her. In the past, the kings and queens of Ourea had sacrificed peace treaties and even their soldiers to keep Kara in their homes. They always wanted to keep her power close, especially when they didn't yet know what she could do. She had been kidnapped, held hostage, and nearly killed.

But the tides had finally turned. The yakona people actually liked her—for now. She could protect herself for the first time in her tenure as the Vagabond. Where she would have once feared what Aurora might say next, Kara figured she could probably handle whatever came her way.

Movement in her peripheral vision broke Kara's reverie.

Aurora smiled. "You've always been so obstinate. I never fully understood why."

Kara shrugged. "I didn't want to be swept aside, I guess. I wanted to be heard."

"I understand. I already see you changing, though. I almost didn't believe it when I saw you wearing the necklace I gave you at the Gala."

The queen nodded to Kara's chest, and Kara reached for the pendant. She toyed with the golden wires, still not sure what the symbol meant. Part of her didn't care—Aurora gave it to her as a sign of peace. She could respect that.

"I guess I grew up a bit," Kara said.

"We both have, I suppose. I never thought I would say this, but we might even be friends someday."

Kara grinned. "Stranger things have happened."

Aurora cleared her throat. "So will you need an escort to take you back to Ayavel?"

"I should be fine on my own as long as there isn't a lichgate between here and the Rose Cliffs."

Aurora laughed. "No such thing exists."

"I should start packing, then."

"If you would like to leave, then by all means you are free to go. I won't be far behind, and I promise to meet you in Ayavel soon. For now, please take care of yourself. And Vagabond"—

Aurora set a hand on Kara's shoulder—"you are the hero everyone claims you to be. Please know it. You did the right thing."

Kara tensed, regret barring her from believing the compliment. "Thank you."

The queen smiled and left without another word, much like Elana.

Kara sat on the bed with a sigh. No matter what Aurora said, she couldn't bring herself to believe she was a hero. Heroes didn't murder thousands of people and lie about it. Cowards did that.

She cleared her throat in a failed attempt to get rid of the urge to cry. Leaving would make all the difference. As soon as she got out of Kirelm, she wouldn't have the constant reminder of her miserable failure. That was the hope, at least.

꙰

After one hour, eight teleportations, and a hearty welcome from the Ayavelians, Kara sat in the same war room she'd set on fire. She twiddled her thumbs in the empty chamber as she waited for Evelyn. Apparently, the Blood wanted to speak to Kara. Alone.

Kara shuddered involuntarily.

Flick purred from his place in her lap. She scratched his ear, and he twitched in his sleep. The little beast could sleep anywhere. She envied that.

Her packed bag sat in the chair next to her. A guard had offered to take it to an empty room, but it held the necklace Aurora had given her. She didn't want to risk the necklace sprouting legs and walking off. She had also packed the red dress Aurora left for her, though she doubted she would ever wear it. Most of the social gatherings in her near future would involve killing someone.

The door creaked open.

Kara turned in time to see Evelyn slip in. Sunlight glinted off of the queen's iridescent skin, casting rainbows of color along the table's surface. The young woman smiled, but her eyes narrowed.

A forced smile. Great.

"Welcome back," Evelyn said.

"Thank you. I've missed Ayavel," Kara lied.

"How was your trip?"

"Besides the Stelian attack on Kirelm? Lovely."

Evelyn grimaced. "Yes, tell me about that."

"Blood Aurora already sent a notice about it." Kara was careful to use Aurora's full title. She needed to get used to it.

"Those notices never contain everything. Tell me what really happened."

"I would, but I have nothing to add." Kara smiled. She'd gotten good at lying.

"If Blood Carden was truly as near-death as the letter claimed, he would never have had the energy to destroy so much of the city below. Something is missing from the story."

Kara's hand tensed in her lap. Flick batted her wrist, and the movement distracted her from the panic shooting through her chest. She took a slow breath, hoping with all her heart that she could keep a straight face.

"He wounded me—shot me back into the castle wall. I hit my head and blacked out. I believe Gurien saw him attack the village, so perhaps you should ask the general instead."

For a second, Evelyn sneered. The expression slipped through what had to be a carefully sewn mask, because the queen relaxed her face an instant later. It happened so quickly that Kara almost didn't believe she'd seen the ugly snicker in the first place. Almost.

"At least the Kirelms are safe now," Kara said, trying to change the subject.

Evelyn set her fingers together and leaned back. She stared out the window without answering.

Kara leaned closer. "You know, you almost seem disappointed."

The queen laughed. "How so?"

"You don't hide your expressions as well as you seem to think. If I had to guess, I'd say you're disappointed I'm back."

Evelyn caught Kara's eye, and the queen's body stilled until she seemed like a statue. Her beautiful face froze, the eyes hardening until Kara had to do everything in her power to suppress a shudder from running down to her toes. She met Evelyn's gaze. The Ayavelian couldn't intimidate her. Not anymore.

Someone knocked on the door. A muffled voice drifted through the wood. Before either Kara or Evelyn could get up, the visitor knocked again. And again.

"What is it?" Evelyn snapped.

The door swung open, probably from some silent command of Evelyn's. Kara flinched as it slammed against the wall.

An Ayavelian man stood in the hall, his hand frozen as if about to knock on the door again. He cleared his throat and set his hands behind his back, but he tensed. His eyes darted to Kara, and however often he returned his gaze to the queen to address her, he still peeked back.

Wait a minute.

He was one of her vagabonds. Zimmermann. He'd sat in on her final meeting in the village, the same day she managed to keep Garrett from killing Stone. She groaned inwardly. Time flew by too fast. That all seemed like ages ago.

"Speak, soldier," Evelyn commanded with another grimace.

"I'm afraid Heir Braeden has been hurt. He's not well. I thought you and the Vagabond would want to see to him, my Blood."

Panic shot straight to Kara's core. A chill swept through her. For a moment, she couldn't even breathe.

Kara held Flick tighter. "What happened?"

"He and Blood Gavin were ambushed on their way back to

Ayavel from a reconnaissance mission to the Stele."

"Is Blood Gavin well?" Evelyn asked.

"Yes. He wasn't harmed."

The queen let out the tiniest of sighs and relaxed ever so slightly. Kara wanted to hurl a ball of fire at her.

Kara shot to her feet. "Please take me to him."

Zimmermann nodded. "Of c—"

"We're not done, Vagabond," Evelyn said.

Kara didn't bother hiding her own sneer of disgust. "We are now."

She grabbed her bag, set Flick on her shoulder, and nodded to Zimmermann. The soldier hesitated, but ultimately turned down the hall and led her away.

A flicker of doubt burned in her gut, but she didn't falter. Evelyn would have kept her there, using Braeden's health to unsettle her as the queen continued her interrogation. It didn't seem like there was much compassion left in the girl at all.

When Kara first returned to Ayavel after her time in the village, she sensed something off about Evelyn. Something had changed for the worse. That same concern flooded through her as she stormed after Zimmermann as fast as she could, but soon even that couldn't hold a candle to her dread.

Braeden healed instantly. The only thing powerful enough to seriously wound him was a Sartori—and that was a death sentence.

Somewhere in the distance, Braeden screamed. Kara's heart jumped into her throat. His yell echoed along the walls of the Ayavelian palace. Zimmermann flinched, pausing at the cry.

Before Kara could blink, a loud *crack* tore through the hallway. The world around her shifted, and she appeared in Braeden's room. Flick must have felt her panic, too. He cooed from his place on her shoulder and nuzzled her cheek.

Braeden lay on the bed, yelling. Sweat covered his brow and

soaked through his clothes. Four Hillsidian soldiers held him to the mattress, one to each of his limbs, but they couldn't keep him from writhing out of their grips.

White sparks shot along his body. Gray flame burst from his skin here and there, torching the threads of the soldiers' clothes. A guard's beard caught on fire and went up in smoke.

"What are you doing? Let him go!" Kara threw her bag against the wall, ready to pry the soldiers off if she had to.

"They can't, Kara," someone said from behind her.

Gavin sat in a desk chair she hadn't noticed before, though only splinters remained of the desk it belonged to. The center sank inward, cleaved in half as if someone had been thrown onto it.

"Braeden did that," Gavin said with a nod to the table.

"Don't even get me started on you—"

Gavin raised his hands in a gentle surrender. "They're protecting him, Kara. I promise. He might throw himself out the window by accident. He threw himself into the desk here, and that's why we tried to get him on the bed. He can't control himself right now."

"Tell me what happened!"

"A Stelian ran a suicide attack on him with my Sartori. Braeden was cut. I gave him the antidote."

"Then why is he still in pain?"

Gavin sighed. "I don't know. This started a minute ago. He was quiet after the antidote, so I brought him back. But this—this has to be something else. I did everything right."

Braeden screamed again.

"Gavin!" Kara pleaded.

"There's nothing else I can do."

"How do I know you even gave him the antidote?"

"I—"

Braeden suddenly quieted. The guards pushed his limbs into the bed, probably getting ready for another round, but Braeden didn't move.

Kara shooed one of the guards away so she could kneel beside the Stelian prince she'd grown to love. His brows creased in pain. His breathing slowed. She reached for his wrist to check for a pulse. Steady. A little too fast, but evening out.

A long line traced up his torso from his left hip to his right shoulder. Dark green goo stuck to the skin, hiding everything beneath it. She'd never seen anything like it before. All things considered, it was probably the antidote.

Gavin was probably telling the truth, but Kara couldn't quite bring herself to trust him with something as important as Braeden's life.

"You can leave," Gavin said to the guards.

The soldiers backed away from the bed. Within seconds, the door opened and shut. The room settled into the sound of Braeden breathing.

After a moment, Gavin knelt beside her. "He was attacked over twenty minutes ago. I truly gave him the antidote, Kara. He would be dead by now if I hadn't."

Kara checked again for Braeden's pulse. Steady. She let out a shaky sigh of relief. Still, she needed to be sure. She needed to know. Perhaps she could summon the Grimoire, ask it what the antidote looked like, or—

Braeden's fingers tightened around her hand.

She examined his face. His eyes flickered open—though not together. He couldn't seem to get them to work. He fought for a second until his lids cooperated.

Braeden caught her attention through half-raised slits and smiled. "Missed you."

She laughed and leaned closer. "Missed you, too."

He closed his eyes. Flick chirped and jumped onto the bed, trotting up to the prince's pillow. The little creature curled up right by Braeden's head and nuzzled his hair.

Gavin leaned his elbows on the bed, still kneeling. "I think he'll be fine, but we can take shifts watching him."

"You can come and go if you want. I'm not leaving until he wakes up."

"We still don't know what happened. He shouldn't have had the second episode of...whatever it was."

"That's not typical?"

"Not to my knowledge."

"Did you give him the antidote in time?"

The young king didn't answer.

"Gavin!"

"Bloods, Kara, will you ever use my title?"

"Does that really matter right now? Did you give the antidote to him in time or not?"

Gavin sighed. "I think so. I don't honestly know."

"Did you not have access to the Sartori in time? How did you even get it back?"

"Blood Carden gave my Sartori to one of his elite guards so the soldier could kill Braeden. They seemed to know he's been visiting, but I think they expected him to be alone. If I hadn't been there, he would have died."

"But you had the sword back. You could have healed him instantly, right?"

Gavin rubbed his face. "Not everyone is as altruistic as you, apparently."

Kara tightened her grip on Braeden's hand to keep from doing something rash, like punching Gavin in his stupid face. She really wanted to do that. She gritted her teeth to restrain herself.

Gavin shook his head. "I almost let him die. I did. I'm not proud of my hesitation now. It was a mistake. But when all you can think of is revenge, you don't think straight. I haven't for a long time. I've plotted and manipulated and stolen to get what I want, and it's cost me everything. When I lost my mother, I lost a bit of myself to the hatred. It clouded my judgment. I couldn't think straight anymore, and I lost both my father and brother because of it. I lost the love of my life. I lost the respect of my fellow Bloods. I lost control over you. By using deception to get my revenge, I lost everything, Kara. I lost everything that ever used to matter to me.

"And today, I had Braeden at my mercy. Without the antidote, he would have died an agonizing death. Part of me wanted to see it. I've hated Stelians for so long, it seemed just. I thought of a world without them in it, without Carden, and it felt right. But to think of a world without Braeden—I was surprised to feel sadness. Remorse. Loneliness, even. I never expected to feel such emotions for him. I didn't understand it...not until I remembered sparring with him as a child. Wrestling. He would let me win sometimes, and I always got so mad. I was the Heir. He was supposed to lose because I was better, not because he wanted to."

Gavin laughed and continued. "But he's always been the better man. He's always been my brother. I was too much of an idiot to see the truth until I nearly killed him."

Kara watched the Hillsidian Blood out of the corner of her eye, hope flaring within her. Apparently, even monsters could change.

"I'm sorry for the pain I've caused you, Kara," the king added.

She shrugged. The shock from his confession strangled her voice.

Gavin pushed himself to his feet. "I'll leave you be. I can come back later. There will be guards outside. If he worsens, please send one of them for me right away. I'll drop what I'm doing."

"Thank you," she managed.

He nodded. "It looks like he's fallen asleep. Please let me know when he wakes."

"I will."

He stared at the floor, hands in his pockets, as if he had something else to say. Kara waited, not sure what to expect, but fear slithered through her. She figured what he wanted to ask: what if Braeden didn't wake up?

But instead of asking that dreaded question, Gavin cleared his throat and bowed. With a few quick steps, he was out the door. It swung shut behind him and clicked.

Kara kissed Braeden's hand and slipped her fingers free of his grip. He mumbled in his sleep. She reached for the desk chair and dragged it until its back faced Braeden. She sat on it the wrong way, staring at him as he rested. She would sit there until he woke up. She wanted him to know he'd never been alone.

An icy hand rested on her shoulder. She shivered.

"Hey, Vagabond," she said.

"I hate to ask you this again so soon, but are you all right?"

The adrenaline of walking in on a screaming Braeden kept the rush of emotion at bay, but her defenses were failing now that Gavin had left. Panic tore through her again. Fear. Anger. Loss. Helplessness. She shook her head and bit her lip.

What if he doesn't wake up? What will I do?

Two cold arms wrapped her in a frigid hug. Another shiver raced through her body. When she didn't return the hug, her mentor sighed and pulled away.

"Kara, there are those who have received the antidote and still died. It's possible Gavin wasn't fast enough. Will you be able to finish this if Braeden doesn't make it?"

She set her arms on the back of the chair and burrowed her face into them. She didn't want to think about it.

"My girl—"

"He's going to make it."

"But what if he doesn't? You have to—"

"He *has* to make it."

The first Vagabond didn't respond. It was better he didn't, since Kara didn't have any other answer for him.

❧CHAPTER TWENTY EIGHT

REBORN

A dull ache throbbed in Braeden's temple. He groaned and rubbed his head. What the hell happened? His mind meandered through fragmented memories. Iyra, trapped on top of him. A broken leg. Fog. The Hillsidian Sartori. Blood.

Braeden's body ignored his attempts to move. He opened his eyes. Light blinded him. Pain shot through to the back of his neck. He blinked a few times. Streaks of brown and beige settled into odd shapes, which eventually became furniture. He lay on a bed underneath a white comforter. The splintered remains of a desk piled against the wall to the right. Windows and gold curtains lined the wall to the left. Clouds passed by, casting shadows into the room.

A hand wound around his torso. He flinched and rolled to the side, trying to get a look at his attacker. Kara lay next to him on top of the covers, eyes pressed closed. She frowned in her sleep and tightened her hold on his waist.

"She never left your side," a familiar voice said.

Braeden whipped his head around. The walls spun from the effort. He groaned and sank back into the pillow until the dizziness passed. When the room settled, he turned his head enough to see the man sitting beside his bed.

Gavin stared at the floor, his legs straddling the chair as he rested his arms along its back. He leaned his chin against his hands.

"I still get to punch you in the face," Braeden said.

Gavin laughed.

"I'm serious. You were going to let me die."

The Blood's smile faded. He nodded.

"Why didn't you?"

The king looked at Kara, his eyes resting on her for a fleeting moment. He stared at the floorboards again. Instead of answering, he pulled a key out of his shirt pocket. Light glinted off the emerald set in the handle.

Gavin placed the key on the bed and stood without another word. His boots brushed along the floor with barely a whisper, and he shut the door without looking back.

Braeden stared at the familiar trinket, unable to fully grasp whatever just happened. It was a key to Hillside, the only means of returning to the kingdom's capital. Braeden lost his when Gavin realized he was the Heir to the Stele, and now he had it back. But he still couldn't quite understand why.

He reached and pulled it closer, too weak to pick it up. He examined the ornate golden curves of the handle as he brushed his thumb along the polished base. This was a truce. This was forgiveness. After losing his brother for so long, Braeden could finally go home.

Only, Hillside wasn't his home. Not anymore. The Stele belonged to him, and all he had to do was kill his father to get it back. Still, he couldn't ignore such a powerful truce. He was welcome in Hillside, free to come and go as he pleased. He never believed he would have such an honor after all of Ourea discovered what he really was. He took a deep breath and leaned into the pillow, happy with this development.

A little gasp jarred him. He peered down at Kara, only to find her gray eyes wide open. A smile broke across her face. He grinned back, but she launched toward him and kissed him. Her hands cradled his head, her lips brushing against his until his mouth went numb.

He cradled her head with one hand and held her near. He nearly lost this. He would savor every second he had with her.

She ran a hand through his hair. "I'm never letting you out of my sight again."

"Good idea. I just get in trouble when you're not around."

She laughed and kissed him again. Her kisses trailed to his jaw and down his neck. After a while, she rested her cheek on his shoulder and sighed. Her arms wrapped around him, and he pulled her in as close as she could go. He relaxed and enjoyed the silence. Kara's body pushed against his each time she breathed. Her pulse beat in his ear, amplified by her proximity. He didn't want to move. He would be content to lie like this forever.

"How are you doing?" Kara asked.

He shrugged. "I still can't feel much of anything."

"What happened?"

He hesitated. "Carden knew I was there. He sent some of his elite soldiers with Gavin's Sartori to kill me. I guess they weren't expecting Gavin to be there."

"He nearly let you die?"

Braeden nodded and kissed the top of her head.

"I would have killed him," she said.

"I know."

Her grip around his chest tightened. Braeden flinched.

She gasped. "Did that hurt you? I'm sorry."

"It's all right. Hopefully I'll heal soon. I can barely move."

"You need to eat. Let me get you food."

He tightened his hold on her so she couldn't get up. "I'm fine."

She laughed. "Liar."

"I'll be fine as long as you stay with me."

She nuzzled his neck. "Then I'll stay with you forever."

His heart skipped a beat. "Forever?"

"Of course."

The fear of rejection dissolved. If he asked her to be his and bond with him, she would say yes. He couldn't tell what shifted in his mind, but he no longer feared the question would rush her or push her away. He didn't even have to ask, but he wanted to. He wanted to make the moment as special as possible, so he wouldn't ask now. He would pull her away from Ayavel and the

Bloods for a short escape, and he would ask her to be his. For now, he would savor every second of her company.

"How was Kirelm?" he asked.

She tensed. Her entire body froze, and she even held her breath.

He lifted her chin with his finger. "That bad?"

She craned her neck toward him. Tears pooled in her eyes. Her eyebrows pinched her face, and worry lines marred her forehead.

A jolt of panic shot through him. "What's wrong?"

"Carden attacked Kirelm while I was there. I had no choice, Braeden. I took off my wrist guard. I won, but..."

"Wait, you fought my father?"

She nodded.

He wrapped her in a hug and pulled her on top of him. He didn't let go, even as she started crying into his shoulder.

"I tried to kill him, Braeden, I promise. But I missed."

He released her and stared into her eyes. Another tear streaked down her face. He wiped it away with his thumb.

"What do you mean, you missed?" he asked.

"My attack hit a village below Kirelm. I killed...I..."

Dawning realization crashed into him. She slaughtered innocent people.

He cradled her face in his hands. "You'll feel better if you say it."

She stared at the bedspread. She wrung her hands. A golden curl fell over her shoulder and covered part of her face.

Her voice trickled out as a whisper. "I killed over ten thousand people with just one attack, Braeden."

His jaw tensed. He didn't know what to say or how to respond.

She sobbed. "Ithone's dead. Aurora is Blood now, and she forced whomever saw my attack into silence. The people think Carden did it, and that I'm some hero. I feel disgusting, Braeden.

I'm a liar, a murderer, a—"

"A hero," he said.

She looked up, eyes bloodshot from crying. A blush seeped along her cheeks, but he doubted it was from embarrassment. She stared at him for a few seconds, mouth slightly agape.

"But I killed people," she said.

"You did. Taking off the wrist guard was a risky move. I'm not sure what the best choice was, but war has casualties, Kara. People die, even when they're not part of the battle. I can only assume Aurora has a perfectly good reason to lie. I know you didn't hurt those Kirelms intentionally. My father's damn near unstoppable. You had no choice but to take off that wrist guard, and that means you gave up your self control. I understand what it's like."

Braeden's daru gave him unimaginable power, but he lost all sense of sympathy when he used his hidden energy. He could only imagine Kara faced something similar with her newfound abilities.

She swallowed hard. "Thank you."

He smiled and wiped away the last of her tears. A smile twitched along the corners of her mouth, but she didn't seem able to fully grin. He wished he could take away the pain, but it was a guilt she would live with forever. At least he could share her burden.

"I thought you would think less of me," she admitted.

He laughed. "I'm a Stelian Heir who asked you to murder my entire race by making me a vagabond. It was a selfish, stupid request, and I see it now. But I have no room to judge."

She laughed. "I'd forgotten about that."

"I was afraid so. I have to remind you of what a horrible man I am."

"Hardly. There's more good in you than bad."

He smiled. "Not before you, there wasn't."

She grinned and ran a hand over his mouth. "There was always kindness in you, even if you tried to hide it. I wish you would realize that."

He pulled her into his chest and took a deep breath. Her isen scent of lilac and pine crashed into him, but the natural perfume of her race no longer triggered a jolt of panic. It was part of her now she'd been awoken as a creature of Ourea, and he would forever respect it. His woman was an isen, and it didn't matter one bit. He was the luckiest man alive.

A week after Braeden awoke in Ayavel with Kara at his side, he reclined against the wall of a cave in Hillside. He'd stolen Kara away, as he planned. She sat beside him, head on his shoulder. He took her to the waterfall in Hillside where the two of them often trained when she first arrived in Ourea. It became their spot, back then, so he hoped it would be the perfect place to ask her to be his forever.

Their cave sat in the cliff directly behind the waterfall. Afternoon sunlight burned through the thin veil of water. Fragments of red and green light danced along the mists hovering above the stream. A river broke away from the falls and ambled through the forests below. Blurred outlines of the green trees on either bank swayed through the shifting water.

"You're awfully quiet," Kara said.

"I'm enjoying your company."

She laughed. "Oh, you little heartthrob."

He grinned. "You know it."

She ran a hand over his chest. Her fingers caught on the scar from the Sartori's blade—the only scar on his body.

"How do you feel?" she asked.

"Incredible."

"Be serious."

"I am. Every day, I feel stronger. I can see better, move faster. I'm more clearheaded than ever. I mean, maybe I'm readapting to life after a near-death experience, but I can't really ask anyone if this is normal. Not many survive a Sartori attack."

"You're lucky."

He kissed her forehead. "Yes, I am."

She laughed and leaned into his shoulder. Sunlight cast a warm glow on her face. She closed her eyes and hummed with pleasure. He couldn't have picked a better moment if he'd orchestrated it.

"Kara, you said you would stay with me forever, right?"

She grinned, eyes still closed. "Yep."

"Did you mean it?"

"Of course. Why?"

"I—uh, this book—"

Panic flared in his gut. The words died in his mouth. He cleared his throat, but a few seconds of silence followed. He should have rehearsed this. Now he would just have to wing it, and he would probably mess everything up.

He plowed ahead. "I read a book about Ourean history. Apparently humans, isen, and yakona all share a common ancestor."

She smirked. "Cool. I'll have to read that."

"It got me thinking about how humans and isen are compatible. Seems like yakona and isen would be as well."

"Compatible? What do you mean?"

He grumbled. "I'm not doing a good job of it, am I?"

"Of what, exactly?"

She shifted and opened her eyes, tilting her head until her beautiful face focused on him. He tensed. He'd completely destroyed the moment.

"You keep twitching. Are you nervous?" she asked.

He laughed. Twitching? How attractive. Forget it. He'd already ruined the proposal, but there was no way out now. He had to go for it.

"Kara Magari, will you try bonding with me? And if it doesn't work, will you still be mine forever?"

She sat up straight, a half-smile on her lips. Her eyes never left his face, but she didn't speak. Several seconds passed. Uncertainty crept into his gut. Was this a no? Should he assume the smile meant yes? Or did all girls do this to mess with their men?

He forced a laugh. "I should've bought a ring or something. I didn't think this through. You were raised human and all. I can buy something. Try again, maybe, or—"

She reached for his face and pulled him into a kiss. He sighed with relief. Their noses brushed together, and her fingers ran through his hair. The fear in his chest melted, even though she still hadn't said anything.

He held her an inch from his face in an effort to tease her. "An answer would be nice, woman."

She laughed. "You're the only one I want, Braeden Drakonin."

He grinned and brushed his lips against hers. His attempt at romance must have been the worst proposal in history, but at least it worked. His fingers glided down her back and inched along her waist. She smiled and leaned in closer. At least in their hidden cave, no royals would disturb them.

Water rushed overhead, splashing into the river below as he held her. They would likely spend the night in the cave, listening to the forest preen and croak around them. It would be their last moment of peace before he brought the war to Carden's gates, and he would savor every moment he was given. In just a few weeks, Ourea would forever change. He merely hoped it would change for the better.

❧CHAPTER TWENTY NINE

SOLACE

Kara ran her fingers through Braeden's hair. He smiled and closed his eyes. Relief shot through her once again—she'd almost lost him.

She reclined against the cave wall and stared through the curtain of water pouring over the entrance. The setting sun slipped through cracks in the waterfall, burning through the sheet in a kaleidoscope of color that danced along the floor.

Her right hand slid through his hair again, and she couldn't help but catch sight of the wrist guard. She grimaced. That thing. She'd become used to the ache of the spikes in her body, and in a way, she was also grateful it kept her power at least somewhat at bay. But it served as a constant reminder of what she truly was and what she could do.

She might be able to control the flood of energy over time, but she still had so much to learn—and no time left. It wouldn't be long before Braeden led the final siege against the Stele. And then what?

Doubt tugged at her mind. Killing Carden didn't guarantee the war would end. She needed that trump card—the Sartori vault. There was no telling if Stone had finished it yet, since she hadn't heard from him in ages. It was possible the isen had changed his mind or simply gotten bored.

She grumbled under her breath and sighed deeply. Braeden reached for her hand, but he kept his eyes closed. He might even be asleep. She smiled, but it lasted only a second. With Carden dead, Braeden would become the Blood of the Stele. In the past, he admitted he feared what the change would do to him; that power had nearly ruined Gavin, after all. But for all Braeden's doubt, Kara knew he wouldn't become like Carden. He fought too hard against his father's cruelty to succumb to it.

He nuzzled against her head and smiled again, his eyes flitting behind his eyelids, lost in some dream. She brushed his cheek. He wouldn't forget who he was. He was too strong for that.

Kara settled back against the cave wall, trying her best to relax. She couldn't sleep. Even her quiet moments these days were tense. She had no peace anymore—she wouldn't, not for a while. Perhaps she could relax when the war ended, or perhaps the stress would last longer. She didn't know. She didn't want to think about it, but she couldn't help herself. She discovered a family secret that would haunt her and any children she had, if that ever happened. She had to live with a curse she might never control. And since she arrived in Ourea, three Bloods had died. Families had been torn apart. Friends turned on each other. And it wasn't over yet. Despite everything she and Braeden already endured, life would probably get worse before it got better.

The sun dipped below the horizon, scorching the sky in its wake. Darkness crept into the world as it left, and a handful of the most brilliant stars glimmered in the growing haze.

Kara smiled. It didn't matter how bad things got as long as she remembered all the good in her new life. Braeden. Flick. Twin. Richard. Her vagabonds. Her village. Cedric. Stone. She finally knew what happened to her mother and maternal grandparents. She could learn from their mistakes. And now, Kara had a new family of her own.

During her tenure in Ourea, Kara had become used to fear and uncertainty. Yet, despite all the suffering, at least a little good had come from all the pain.

❦EPILOGUE

REVENGE

Back before Braeden awoke in Ayavel, even before Kara took her seat in Evelyn's war room on her return from Kirelm, a maid lit a fire in Blood Carden's study. Servants went about their business, always listening for orders from their king.

In a corridor on the fourth floor, a guard raced to Blood Carden's office with news of the Vagabond's movements. In a different hallway two floors below, yet another guard received orders to deliver the news of Braeden's escape from the failed Sartori attack. Neither guard realized his respective superior didn't like him very much, nor did they realize the Blood of the Stele quite often killed the messenger.

❦

Deidre lounged on a sofa by the fire in Carden's study. A wooden chair whizzed by her head and smashed against the stone wall, shattering into splinters from the force. Deidre just sighed.

Men.

Carden hurled another chair from its place along the wall. It met the same fate as its brother.

"How does the boy do it?" Carden screamed.

Deidre didn't answer. The question was no doubt rhetorical.

Carden returned from Kirelm as nothing but a broken mess, all thanks to the little Magari girl's brutal beating. In his tantrum, he'd sent out an elite force to kill Braeden without pausing to think of the implications or risks. Such rash thinking. He would've been lucky to have even a modicum of Deidre's patience—she'd planned her revenge for centuries.

Apparently out of things to throw, Carden punched the wall. Cracks splintered through the stones like a spider web beneath his knuckles. "How does Braeden escape everything I throw at him? He's an insect compared to me, yet he seems to anticipate my every move!"

Carden leaned against his now-empty desk, shoulders heaving as he caught his breath. He tightened his hands into fists. His gray skin bleached from the tension.

The Blood spat on the floor. "He's supposed to be dead. No one can survive a Sartori attack without the antidote, yet his corpse wasn't rotting next to my soldiers! He's still out there. I can feel it. Why won't he die?"

Deidre stifled a groan. Prima donna. Then again, this was the same man who had been pummeled to death's door by a girl raised in the human world. Even as a descendant of a legendary isen, Kara should never have had the power to overcome Carden. Not yet, at least. Not unless she'd received highly specialized training. Deidre doubted the girl had those kind of isen connections.

Carden's loss to the Vagabond was all the proof Deidre needed. He'd become irrelevant. Too weak to be of much use any longer. She would be rid of him soon, but she needed one more favor. She had to get him to focus.

She changed the subject. "At least you'll have the lost table of Ethos, soon. Then Braeden won't even matter."

He grimaced. "Right. Our agreement."

She forced a smile. Carden swore to kill Niccoli in exchange for the location of the lost table of Ethos. She didn't care why he wanted the old artifact. She only wanted her master dead.

Deidre shrugged in an effort to feign indifference. "All you have to do is kill Niccoli. It shouldn't be a challenge for you."

"It won't be, nor will it be difficult for me to ensure you uphold your end of the bargain."

Deidre suppressed an eye roll. "I wouldn't dream of doing otherwise. I'm a woman of my word. He and I are meeting tonight. Will you be there or not?"

Carden took a deep breath. "Fine. Tonight. I suppose killing something would help me let off steam."

Deidre's heart leapt into her throat. He'd finally taken the bait. It took all of her control not to grin with pleasure. Instead, she merely nodded to the door.

"Shall we?"

⚚

Twenty minutes later, Deidre leaned against a tree in one of the Stele's dark forests, consumed in the moment.

Her body tensed more with every creak of the branches. Every leaf scraping along the ground sent a shiver up her spine. She bit her lip. Spots crept along the corners of her vision on occasion, a result of the tumultuous give and take between her excitement and her anxiety.

Almost three hundred years of planning had come down to this night. Even Deidre, of all people, trembled. She couldn't fail. She didn't want to think about what she would do if her evening didn't go as planned.

Carden lay stretched on the ground at her feet, feigning unconsciousness. His chest rose and fell with steady breaths marred by the occasional sharp intake. Under different circumstances, she would have known the Blood was faking. She hoped Niccoli would be too arrogant to notice the occasional irregular breath.

In less than sixty-four seconds, Niccoli would arrive as scheduled. Though sometimes early, he was never late. He would think Deidre had done it, that she had brought him a Blood's soul on a platter for him to steal. He would rehash some version of the lie she told him: that absorbing Carden's power would finally give him enough of an edge to get revenge on the muse for killing Aislynn. He would smirk and say yet again she had done well.

As he praised her, she would force a smile. She didn't want his praise. All she wanted was his heart in her hands, still beating. And tonight, she would have it. Her previous two attempts to kill her master had failed, though he only learned about one of them. But this time, Carden would kill Niccoli for her.

"You continue to amaze me," someone said from the darkness.

Deidre's eyes snapped toward the voice, though the rest of her remained rooted in place. She couldn't move. Too much of a thrill boiled within her.

"I live but to serve you," she lied. Deidre only served herself.

Niccoli emerged from the forest's shadows, his pale skin a sharp contrast to his dark hair and thin beard. The isen strolled forward, his black eyes trained on the Blood at Deidre's feet.

She nodded to Carden. "He'll be easier to take while unconscious. I can't guarantee how much longer he'll be out."

Niccoli rested his hand on her shoulder. She stiffened. It would give her no greater pleasure than to light him on fire, but she had to bide her time. She had to be patient.

Her master had only walked toward her trap; he still needed to take the bait.

He smiled. "I owe you dearly, my girl."

She forced a smile.

Niccoli circled Carden, eyeing the Blood from head to toe. He might have been checking for a trap—Deidre couldn't be sure. As her master examined his prey, she slipped backward into the forest step by tiny step until she was out of range.

Her master knelt. His hand reached for Carden's neck. Deidre tensed. What was that idiot of a Blood waiting for?

In the blink of an eye, Carden jumped to his feet, drew his Sartori, and swung the blade at the isen master's neck. Niccoli flinched and ducked. The sword whistled past, missing him by a hair.

Deidre frowned.

Niccoli lunged. Carden swung. The blade missed, but Carden followed through with a fist to Niccoli's nose. *Crack.* Red blood rolled down the isen's face, and he spat some of it to the ground.

He spun, his heel aimed for Carden's neck. It made contact with a *thud*.

The king dropped to one knee from the force, black blood gushing from a fresh tear in his jaw. He pushed himself up almost as quickly as he fell. The broken skin on Carden's face stitched itself together as he healed.

Deidre wished she could steal a Blood's healing ability. How useful.

The men lashed at each other, grunting and cursing as they fought. Deidre leaned against the tree, watching every movement with a hunger she couldn't describe. Hundreds of years rode on the outcome of this battle, as did her future and freedom. She paid for this moment with every sacrifice and cashed-in favor she had at her disposal. She could not fail.

She let her mind wander into the unthinkable: defeat. True, she wouldn't suffer, regardless of the winner—neither Niccoli nor Carden knew the truth. Neither knew her plan. If Niccoli somehow won, she would just have to begin again. And with every year she waited for her revenge, Niccoli's suffering would double. She would see to it personally.

Carden's breath came in short bursts. Black blood trickled from wounds on his neck. They weren't healing for some reason. Deidre's jaw tensed. How could Niccoli possibly know how to keep a yakona Blood from healing?

Niccoli ducked and spun again, probably to land another kick on Carden's face. Carden grunted and met the kick with one of his own. Bones cracked in both men's feet. Niccoli screamed and fell to his knees. Carden's ankle twisted too far to the right, but he landed on his broken foot anyway. He grimaced and grinned at the same time.

He'd won.

Carden shoved his Sartori into Niccoli's gut. The isen choked. His hands inched toward the wound, his fingers twitching. He stared down at his stomach, his mouth trying to form words that wouldn't come.

Deidre laughed and ran to them. She fell to her knees,

skidding a few inches along the blood-drenched grass. The fabric of her pants stuck to the ground as she inched toward Niccoli, but she didn't care.

Her master caught her eye. His eyes widened, twitching even as he focused on her. His vacant stare cleared for a moment. He choked on a breath.

"You're smiling—?" he asked.

Deidre laughed again. "I am. I've waited to see you on your knees for hundreds of years, and now I have finally seen everything."

She ran her thumb along his bleeding jaw, his coarse stubble grating against her skin. He sputtered. Blood trickled out the side of his mouth. She smiled. She would savor this.

"But you've always helped me," he said.

She frowned. "You idiot. I had no choice but to help you. You're my master. You control me. I learned as much the first time I tried to kill you—a servant can never kill her master, but she can get someone else to do it. She can break the world around him until he succumbs to the weight of his own weaknesses. She can wait, ever patient, until she finds someone who can kill him.

"I unraveled you, Niccoli. Everything you lost in the last hundred years was my doing. Your precious Agneon? I poisoned his wife's mind by telling her your plans for their daughter. I told her provoking Agneon would guilt him into letting the child leave, even though I knew he would lose control. I knew her death would destroy him, and his death would destroy you. I didn't care what happened to the girl. But you thought you could replace him with Kara, so I let her get away from us in Scotland. I didn't even put up a fight—me, of all your isen! You should have known better, but you have always underestimated me.

"And speaking of your isen, master, they will disband soon. Without you to lead them—to control them—they will squabble and bicker and fight until the isen Guild you spent centuries building crumbles from within. You were too arrogant to choose a successor, and they will fight for power until there's nothing left to take. Everything you built in life will mean nothing in just a few months."

Deidre grabbed his hand and brought it to the hilt of the Sartori. She wrapped his fingers around the handle. The blade's defenses burned his skin. He choked back a scream. Smoke barreled from his palms. With his hand blocking hers from the blade's poisonous touch, she twisted the sword and shoved it deeper into his stomach. He screamed.

She leaned in until her lips brushed his ear. "And as for your lover? I tortured Aislynn until I was sure her death would be as miserable as yours. You certainly saw the aftermath, but it wasn't enough. I wanted to end you, too. I wanted to see you die. So I convinced you a muse killed her. I knew your arrogance would lead you to believe me when I said you could absorb a Blood. You failed, fool. I've owned you for years."

"Why?" he spat.

His neck tensed. She could barely hear him. The Sartori's poison worked its way through his system faster than she'd anticipated. He wouldn't survive much longer, so she had to make her next words count.

Deidre caught his eye. "I did all this because I hate you for killing Michael. You deserve this, all of it. I wanted to watch you suffer before I watched you die, and I have. Michael was the only light in my miserable human life, and you took him away so I would have nothing left but to become an isen and obey you. Why did you think I would ever forgive such a thing?"

He sputtered and coughed. Deidre leaned back in time to avoid a spray of blood. Niccoli gurgled, his body convulsing. His head tilted to the side. A stream of red liquid tumbled out like drool.

"It wasn't me," he whispered. His lips brushed grass as he repeated himself again and again. After a moment, the words slowed. It didn't take long for them to stop entirely.

Deidre grimaced. Why would a man let his last words be a lie?

Niccoli's foot twitched. His breath escaped through his

broken nose, whistling as it left, and he didn't take another. Lie or not, his last words didn't matter.

She was free. Deidre laughed. She'd done it. After centuries of misery, she'd gotten her revenge. She spun around in a circle and reached for the moon. A giggle raced up her throat, and she laughed into the sky.

"I'm free!" she screamed to the clouds.

A man chuckled. Deidre snapped her head toward the sound, only to find Carden sitting on a log. A trail of blood ran down his arm, and several more rivers trickled from his nose and a tear on his cheek. He watched her through two swollen eyes, his white teeth gleaming in the moonlight as he grinned.

Deidre smirked. Right. The useless royal. He could still serve her if she played her cards right. Though this time, he couldn't see it coming. She would have to trick him into letting her get close. Considering how often he leered at her, seduction would work best.

Now for part two of Deidre's plan.

"Why aren't you healing?" she asked.

Carden held up his right arm to reveal a white handprint across his forearm. "He cursed me with some technique I've never seen before. It slowed my healing but didn't stop it. I'll be fine in about an hour."

Deidre smiled and sat on his lap. She wrapped her arms around his neck and leaned in, careful to run her fingers along his pulse. His heartbeat sped up at her touch. Good—he did want her after all.

He rested his hands on her hips. She suppressed a sigh. The man was just too easy to control. At this point, the only way to turn him off would be to lean on a wound. She would have to be careful to avoid them.

Deidre brushed her lips against his ear. "However can I repay you for freeing me?"

"I have several ideas," he muttered. His voice came out as a rumble, as if the tension of said thoughts was too much to bear.

No thanks.

She reached her hand around him, positioning it closer to his neck. The barb in her palm itched as it neared his spine.

Part two of her plan still worried her. If she did this—if she went for Carden's soul—there would be no room for error in a scheme riddled with unknowns. If she succeeded, she might control the Stelian bloodline, or she might not; she had no idea. Alternatively, Carden might be strong enough to escape. Worse, he might even take over her body. Thus, why he had to be at his absolute weakest.

If he overpowered her now, she would never finish her work. She had a final task to see to before she joined Michael in the next life—one she needed the Stelian Blood's influence to accomplish.

Her fingers tensed on his neck. "We have some time to kill. Why don't we explore some of those ideas of yours?"

He laughed. "You'll have to wait a little while, princess. I can barely move."

She kissed his ear. "Good."

The barb in her palm dug into the base of his neck.

He screamed and pushed her away, but it was too late. She wrapped her free arm around his head and her legs around his waist. He fell to his knees.

An image flashed across her vision: a Stelian woman with a slender face and warm eyes. The forest returned just as quickly. Who—?

Wife. Dead. Carden's voice echoed in her mind, obeying her request for information. She smiled. The Stelian Blood would belong to her soon enough.

Emotions and flickers of thought raced through her mind. Hatred. Resentment. Arousal. Greed. He intended to drain the Bloods and take their power. He would run Braeden through with the Stelian Sartori next chance he had. He would happily do the same to Kara if he could get Braeden to watch—anything to wound the boy further.

An image of the little gray teleporting creature he kept with him flashed in Deidre's mind. The creature sighed, nothing more than Carden's prize from a deal he made with a snow demon years ago—Carden transferred his ability to feel heat to the demon in exchange for the animal and its abilities. The thing had no name, nor did the Stelian Blood plan to give it one; it was his servant and could teleport him through lichgates. Only its function mattered.

His emotions blurred by again. Fear. Panic. Betrayal. Devotion. He had always wanted Deidre. He always wanted her love. Craved her attention. He tested the boundaries of their relationship, waiting for the day he could shove her up against a wall and—

She reeled back from the thought. Disgusting.

Wave after wave of Carden's thoughts flowed over her. The high of stealing a soul built in her navel and reached through her chest toward the base of her neck. A familiar chill shot through her, followed by the growing warmth she loved. When she could finally leave this retched world, the only thing she would miss was this high.

Her world shook.

White fuzz spread over the memories like developing mold. The images blurred into a mess of color. Reds faded to brown. Brown to black. Deidre's mind reeled. An ache crept through her temples. Something had gone wrong.

Pressure wrapped around her neck, almost like fingers around her throat. The ache worsened. The white fuzz continued to grow, consuming everything. She couldn't think. She couldn't react. She couldn't fathom what was going on.

You conniving little slave! Carden's voice rang through her head.

Oh, no.

I gave you everything, he continued. *I gave you everything, and I wanted to give you so much more. I would have killed a dozen more like Niccoli for you. I would have given you any head you wanted on a silver platter, but you betrayed me.*

Deidre tried to gasp through the blur of Carden's emotions and corroding memories. An icy wave of fear melted in her gut.

His voice thundered on, deeper with every word. *I gave you your revenge, as you wanted. How was it not enough? How was I never enough? You may have killed my body, but I would sooner take you to the next life with me than let you trap my soul in the wretched carcass of your mind!*

With a jolt, the fear in Deidre's gut condensed into a knot. Carden wanted to kill her and drag her soul with him into the next life. She wasn't done yet. She couldn't let him overtake her.

Adrenaline spiked through her body. The white fuzz receded. Her mind cleared. In the black recesses of her mind, Carden appeared in front of her, his hands around her neck. The grip around her throat tightened.

She grabbed one of his hands and bent it back. Bones splintered in her grip. Carden screamed. His hold on her neck loosened.

Her mind, her rules. Even though they were two lone souls fighting for dominance, she would ensure he experienced every ounce of pain his body would have endured.

On her command, electricity burned through her. A bolt of light struck him in the chest. He flew backward. Deidre gestured to the empty space behind him, and a rock wall appeared from the darkness. Carden hit it with a *whack*. His head bounced against granite, and he crumpled into a pile.

He struggled to his feet, ankle still broken from his earlier fight with Niccoli. Deidre threw all of her energy into an uppercut to his gut. He groaned and dropped again. She elbowed the base of his neck, right where she'd pricked him with the barb in her palm. He cried out in pain and fell on his face.

She flipped him onto his back and set a knee on his stomach to keep him from moving. He groaned and reached to slap her, but she easily ducked out of the way.

This would be over soon.

Before he could swing again, she touched her pointer finger to the space between his eyes. He froze, his stare glossing over. A lustrous sheen spread from under her touch, coating his body as it traveled over him. After only a few seconds, he lay still and polished as a wax statue.

Deidre blew him a kiss. "I'll see you later, dear."

With a deep breath, she pulled herself back to the present. Her cheek lay against something solid. A sharp pain shot through her arm. Her neck ached.

She blinked herself awake, only to find her hands around her own neck. She grimaced and pried them away, careful to stretch her fingers until the tension began to dissolve. She cursed Carden's murderous strength and ran a finger along her sore throat. The trauma would leave a mark.

The moon had shifted above her and now sat along the edge of the forest's dark canopy. A howl echoed in the distance. A strong wind rushed through the foliage until the clap of leaves drowned out the distant creature's wail.

Carden's corpse lay beneath her, his eyes frozen open in shock. Deidre laughed and flicked his ear. Black dust drifted to the ground, leaving behind black piles of sand instead of blood. She loved the way yakona began to dissolve into dust so quickly after death, even if she never understood why it happened.

Another pain shot up her arm. Red blood trickled from a gash in her bicep. She frowned, her muscles tensing on instinct. Though she hated pain, this would be a perfect chance to test Carden's healing ability.

She sorted through his memories for an answer as to how he controlled the gift, but found nothing useful. This talent wasn't something he could manipulate. It merely happened.

Her frown deepened. She usually absorbed all of her victims' gifts, but absorbing a Blood was new territory. To her knowledge, it had never been done. Considering the power of the yakona bloodlines, there was no telling what gifts she'd retained and which she'd lost.

It didn't really matter. She'd won. All she needed from Carden was his face.

Deidre stretched and smiled up to the night sky, pondering

this little change in plans. She now faced an interesting dilemma: if she couldn't heal instantly, she probably also couldn't control the Stelians—which likely meant Braeden had become Blood after all. She shrugged. No matter, since he probably didn't know. Last she'd heard, he was on his way to Ayavel, unconscious from wounds he might not even survive.

Even if Braeden did survive, he would fail like his father. The young king would give her the final revenge she craved. The world hated Carden, and Braeden would lead whole armies right to the Stele to end him—and unknowingly end her.

Only, Deidre had other plans for Braeden's soldiers, and she would see to the new Stelian Blood herself. She didn't expect to survive the coming battle. She didn't want to. Before the war ended, she would meet Death once more—and leave the world burning in her wake.

A NOTE TO READERS

I hope you enjoyed *Heritage.* If you have a moment, please leave a review on Amazon, Goodreads, Barnes & Noble, your blog, or any combination thereof. If not, that's cool. You're still amazing.

I love hearing from my readers. If you want to reach out and say hi, feel free to tweet me (@thesmboyce) or send me an email by heading over to my contact page (smboyce.com/contact-boyce).

Like free stuff? Me, too. Well, I like giving it away. For chances to win prizes four times a year, join my Street Team (check out the footer on smboyce.com for the link). It's really a lot of fun, so head over when you can.

You can also get signed eBooks and sign up to get ARCs of my future novels. To learn more, check out the "Awesome Extras" section of the footer on smboyce.com.

If you want more Grimoire goodies, take a look at The Grimoire Online (GrimoireSaga.com). It's your lichgate into Ourea and has a host of bonus material—including free chapters and free access to an online encyclopedia of the world.

The biggest Grimoire geeks can also check out my store (store.smboyce.com), which has tons of fun extras that bring the magic of the Grimoire Saga to life. You can even find real-life Grimoire pendants and blank journals that let you write a Grimoire of your own.

Thanks again, and stay awesome.

—S. M. Boyce

ACKNOWLEDGEMENTS

This novel would be wordier if not for my charming and talented editor, Chase Nottingham.

My amazing beta readers helped shape this novel, so special thanks to: Nikki Jefford, Thomas Winship, Wynne Channing, Christie Rich, and Raye Wagner.

And of course, my content editor/husband is an epic badass who helped make this story even better than I ever imagined. Thank you, Geoff.

ABOUT THE AUTHOR

International Amazon Bestseller. Fantasy Author. Twitter addict. Book Blogger. Geek. Sarcastic. Gooey. Odd. Author of the action-packed Grimoire Saga.

S.M. Boyce is a fiction novelist who loves ghosts, magic, and spooky things. She prefers loose-leaf tea, reads far too many books, and is always cold. She's married to her soul mate and couldn't be happier. Her B.A. in Creative Writing qualifies her to serve you french fries.

Boyce likes to update her blog a few times each week so that you have something to wake you up in the morning.

To learn more about Boyce, visit her website.

smboyce.com

BONUS AUTHOR

Hey there! It's Boyce. I want to share one of my new favorite authors with you—Morgan Wylie. She has an incredible epic fantasy voice for fans of the genre, and her stories are both complex and vivid. I hope you take a moment to check out her debut, *Silent Orchids*. Happy reading!

6821357R00174

Printed in Great Britain
by Amazon.co.uk, Ltd.,
Marston Gate.